I0769342

Last on the List

BARTHOLOMEW SERIES
BOOK FOUR

LANEY HATCHER

Copyright

Developmental Edits: Nicole McCurdy, Emerald Edits
Editing: Jenny Sims, Editing4Indies
Cover Illustration: Blythe Russo
Proofreading: Judy's Proofreading

Author's Content Note

This story features an on-page pregnancy and a brief (non-graphic) labor and delivery scene. If you are sensitive to topics surrounding pregnancy, fertility, conception, and childbirth, I advise you to read with care and proceed with caution.

I always want to handle your reader heart with respect and kindness, so if you need to pass on this one, I completely understand.

One

MARY

December, 1863

Carriage rides to the country provided entirely too much time for one's intrusive thoughts. Especially when being conveyed alone.

I glanced around the empty cabin as my vehicle trundled roughly over the road to Hampshire. It wouldn't be long until I arrived at Laurel Park—my final destination and the country estate of the Marquess and Marchioness Northcutt. I was to be their guest for the next fortnight and the prospect had me equal parts weary and pleased.

A quick glimpse beyond the windowpane showed the deteriorating conditions. A generous layer of white clung to the rolling landscape while more snow fell from moody gray skies. The flakes were big and heavy and seemed to descend with purpose.

I'd always been the sort of person to enjoy a snowy day. Tucked up in front of a fire with warm tea and a good book, I didn't mind foul weather. However, when the aforementioned snow made travel treacherous and worrisome, I found I wasn't quite so agreeable.

The weather had worsened the farther we'd traveled. I could tell the coachman had slowed the conveyance gradually over the past several hours in an attempt to traverse the increasingly icy and muddy route. I knew we were getting close, and I was eager to warm myself by a roaring fire.

The marchioness's annual house party took place in December and was a festive Yuletide celebration for her four children, their families, and close friends. I only wished the weather wasn't mucking things up this year.

I'd been journeying to Hampshire for several years. My best friend in the world—Patricia Henney, the Duchess of Cawthorn and the eldest daughter to Lord and Lady Northcutt—had an estate neighboring her parents at Laurel Park. Patty's sister, Emery, possessed a residence nearby as well. I'd been happily embroiled with the Bartholomews and former Bartholomews for over a decade, and I'd enjoyed many a holiday in the country as a result.

My friendship with Patty had been born out of shared suffering. We'd survived Mayfair events through snarky commentary, and I'd found a kindred spirit who appreciated my brazen behavior and forthright demeanor. And over time, I'd been pulled into her family's loving orbit and accepted there as well.

Now for the upcoming celebration, the majority of the Bartholomew brood were settled safely in Hampshire, having arrived days ago and avoiding this snowy mess entirely.

I thought of my friends enjoying their time together with families and children and nieces and nephews running amok. A twinge of something selfish and unwelcome made this journey a touch more reluctant and complicated. I had time to wrangle these wayward thoughts, however. By the time I arrived on the grand Laurel Park drive, I'd be everyone's favorite friend—the outspoken, entertaining, and reliably affable Mary Lovelace.

Perhaps I should practice smiling just to ensure my maudlin mood hadn't impeded my ability to appear winsome. As soon as that thought materialized, the carriage jolted roughly. The momentum caused the cab to rock briefly before jerking forward and then moving no more.

I peered closer to the window, but I couldn't see what was happening with the horses or the coachman from this angle.

Moments passed before the door to the carriage was pulled open, and Marshall stood outside, hat in hand. A gust of frigid air heralded his arrival and swept within. "My lady, I'm afraid we're well stuck." My mouth formed a surprised "o." "But we're not far from Laurel Park. I think it best if you remain here. I'll take the horses and fetch some footmen to help dig us out. Then we'll be back on our way, good as new."

I frowned in concern. "Are you sure you'll be all right?" A layer of white covered the young coachman's shoulders already. The brown of his great coat was hardly visible as the snow continued to fall.

"Yes, m'lady. The horses shouldn't have any trouble. It's just the carriage wheels are stuck down in the muddy tracks of this wet snow. I won't be long. I assure you." Marshall's brown eyes were earnest. I didn't want to make him stand out in the cold and delay his journey any longer simply to reassure me.

"Very well," I returned. "If you think that is best. I'll remain here."

Marshall smiled. "Good, m'lady. You cover up and stay warm. I'll bring help. You have nothing to worry about."

I swallowed around my unease and nodded. "Take care, Marshall. I'll see you shortly."

The handsome driver, a few years younger than my own two and thirty, flashed me a wide grin before bowing his head and closing the door.

Sounds of him unhitching the horses reached my ears as I sat in the chilly interior of the cabin. I pulled out a thick blanket from the hamper by my feet.

It was quiet without the constant motion and noise from the rattling carriage. The snow beyond the window seemed to make it quieter still. If I listened closely, I could imagine hearing the flakes striking the frozen ground.

Normally, I wouldn't be making this journey unaccompanied. My parents—the Earl and Countess of Thisby—typically joined me for the marchioness's yearly event. She and my mother were friendly, and our families had been guests of each other many times over the years.

However, my mother was currently visiting her sister in Dorset. Aunt Maude had written weeks ago saying she was recovering from a fall and desired my mother's company during her convalescence. My father hadn't wished to join the house party in the countryside, so he'd remained in London while I traveled to Hampshire on my own. It wasn't too terribly scandalous. I was well into my spinsterhood and didn't keep a lady's maid fully employed.

So here I was, alone on the road awaiting rescue and bored out of my mind. I should have just taken one of the horses and ridden along with Marshall. I wasn't an expert rider, but surely, I could have made it the short distance to Laurel Park while riding bareback . . . in the snow.

Or perhaps not.

Reaching over, I opened my valise. Ignoring my embroidery, I pulled out a leather-bound notebook. I removed my gloves and thumbed through the blank paper until the pages separated around a folded note tucked carefully between the sheets.

On a deep, bracing breath, I unfolded the list—no longer hidden away in an unused journal. My eyes scanned the twenty-two names written neatly by my own hand. Once again, the lunacy of my plan struck me and I resisted the urge to rip up the paper into tiny bits and scatter them out among the snow.

But this list—these names—were perhaps my very last attempt to have something of my own. For as long as I could remember, I'd wanted to be a mother. Perhaps it had begun with a strong sense of nurturing as a young girl. As I'd grown in my family's household surrounded by my parents' unhappy marriage, the desire to create a loving family—something counter to what my mother and father shared—had taken root. From there, it had transformed into the expectations of womanhood and the role I'd been preparing for my entire life. Yet as my debut came and went, and the seasons crept by, I'd found myself disappointed not so much in a lack of offers but more so in what that meant. Now, over a dozen years later, I was no closer to the family I craved. Hence, the list I held now in my chilly, pale fingers.

Desperate times and all that.

When the new year arrived, I would put forth my last-ditch effort to *finally* have a child of my own. The twenty-two names listed here were confirmed bachelors who were often found in the company of a mistress. It was too late for me to find a husband, and after seeing the way my parents treated one another, marriage was the very last thing I wanted. Besides, the gentlemen on my list were in no need of a wife. So it seemed like an ideal situation. My hope was that a child would be the happy by-product of regular relations with someone listed here.

I'd carefully constructed the names found on this paper. They were all unmarried and most were known through regular gossip channels to take frequent mistresses and indulge in liaisons. I no longer had the need to snare a husband or produce an heir. That ship had sailed and was circling the globe. I had no expectations beyond what these gentlemen could do for me in the bedchamber. Most high-ranking aristocrats were all too happy to relegate bastards and former mistresses to the country in order to hide their indiscretions. Well, I would save them the trouble and take my child and myself to live out our happiness away from the judgmental eyes of London.

All I wanted was a family of my own—a child. The husband had never been the important part.

Women, for the most part, had their lives dictated to them. Who to marry. Where to go. Who to associate with. If a debutante was lucky, she'd go from an indulgent father's home to a tolerant husband's estate. For many reasons, I'd never been the sort of woman to follow a prescribed path. I was too loud and too brash. Headstrong, abrasive, and forthright. Too tall and too lean. Out of fashion was a kind way to describe my figure. Plain was the generous description I often heard regarding my face. My dowry had never been enough to overcome my deficits and entice a suitor. As a woman who often did things the hard way, I'd decided to harness my destiny all on my own. I'd dedicate my future to landing a liaison with one of these twenty-two gentlemen in the new year and finally get the outcome I desired.

I wasn't dim enough to think a baby was a guarantee. Despite my mad plan, I was a fairly rational and levelheaded person. I'd had lovers of a sort before. But my courses were often irregular and unpredictable. The infrequent relations I'd experienced previously hadn't been conducive for conception. But I was hopeful that with an arrangement and consistent intimacies, I'd finally be able to conceive a child—before I was too advanced in years to do even that.

As much as I enjoyed my time with Patty and her family, I'd started feeling the insistent tug of jealousy and weariness. It was difficult to be surrounded by so much unconditional love and affection. My friend had her own husband and daughter. For so long, we'd been in a similar position—me, unmarried and restless, and Patty, a bitter widow with no designs on future romance. But then, years ago, Patty met Miles Griffin. She and the Earl of Basilton had gotten off to a rocky start, but eventually, they'd fallen in love. In the midst of their happy union, they'd taken in a young girl from a London orphanage. Franny was nearly thirteen now, and exceedingly loved by her family.

Even Patty's younger sister, Emery, had found love and happiness with two small children the joyful result. And finally Genevieve, the youngest Bartholomew sibling, was in the midst of her own great love story. At three and twenty, she'd recognized the love of her young life. They were in the process of figuring everything out, but anyone could see that Genevieve and Julian belonged with one another. It was just a matter of time until she, too, was wed.

Of my close acquaintance with this family, that only left Silas Bartholomew unmarried and unattached. But that was of no real consequence however. Silas had been avoiding his mother's frequent attempts to marry him off for years.

My eyes strayed to the final name on my list of potential affairs before I huffed out a ridiculous laugh. I didn't know why I'd bothered including him in the first place. It had been in jest, mostly.

Yes, Silas was unmarried and unattached. But gossip surrounding his exploits had become practically nonexistent in the past few years. He likely didn't even have time for a mistress. He was so embroiled in all of his siblings' lives. You couldn't attend a Bartholomew outing, luncheon, ball, house party, or supper without Silas in attendance. He used to travel with much regularity to the continent and the Mediterranean, but for some reason, my recent memory could not pinpoint the last time Silas had left the country.

The eldest Bartholomew was a few years my senior and still preferred freedom to the prospect of matrimony. He lived his life unbound by obligation and expectation. And he rarely took anything seriously—a point that irritated me to no end. Our frequent interactions were often fraught with Silas's insipid teasing and constant need for attention. Honestly, the man was an exasperating thorn in my side. He simply had to have the final word in any conversation . . . and the first word and nearly every other one in between. I pitied whatever poor woman ended up beside him at the altar. Eventually, his mother—the marchioness —would have her way. Silas was the heir, after all. He'd have to settle down someday.

The thought of some ambiguous future, where the infuriating Silas Bartholomew was married with children of his own and I was still alone, made me shift uncomfortably on the bench in this chilly carriage.

Being the only unattached member of our social circle was diffi-cult, especially since it was not by choice. I wasn't longing for a love match and romantic gestures. I didn't believe that outcome was in the cards—not for someone like me. Mostly, I wanted the family that came with marriage and companionship. I wanted a child to love and care for. Seeing my closest friends move on with their happy lives while I remained behind—forever Auntie Mary —had grown more difficult to bear over the years. Events like the upcoming house party required me to fortify my heart and mind, lest my longing show openly.

Frustrated by my own weakness, I cast the list aside to the bench and reached for my fur-lined cloak instead. My thoughts were overwhelming, filling the cramped space in this cabin to bursting.

Despite the cold I felt to my very bones, I opened the carriage door and climbed down carefully, needing fresh air and room to clear my head before my coachman returned with reinforcements and we were on our way to Laurel Park once more.

It wouldn't do to be in a state when I arrived. My friends would know something was afoot. It was imperative that I shepherd these wayward thoughts and fit them back into their pathetic box where they belonged.

The air was crisp with the sort of cold that reddened cheeks and stole the feeling from your nose. But I had to admit, the snow was gorgeous. I couldn't have gotten stuck in a better spot. Beyond the snow-covered road, a fence rail stretched for as far as the eye could see in either direction. We were close enough that this was likely Bartholomew land. I didn't see any animals grazing, however. The countryside melted into fields and small rolling hills as the distance met the gray horizon. Snowflakes clung to tree branches and created a frosty outline in this beautiful winterscape.

I took a few tentative steps, and when my boots simply sank into several inches of snow, I felt confident enough to move around the outside of the carriage without slipping and falling on my arse. Both front wheels appeared to be well stuck in the surrounding muck. I pushed a bit, but they didn't budge.

Well, in this weather, at least I needn't worry about being accosted by robbers and the like. It was just me and my unreliable vehicle for miles.

And yet . . .

Approaching hoofbeats had my head rising sharply. I squinted into the direction that my coachman had gone not more than an hour ago, but the figure atop a chestnut horse was too far away to register. I expected Marshall to return with assistance. The person riding toward me now was just that—singular and unaccompanied.

As the rider grew closer, a strange awareness stole over me. I straightened uncomfortably and pulled my cloak tighter around my shoulders.

I could just make out the shape of a hat atop a head and the person in the astride position, and felt growing concern that the approximation of a man heading for me was not Marshall nor any liveried servant from Laurel Park.

That worry dissolved entirely and I fought the urge to roll my eyes as recognition dawned.

The gentleman wore his ever-present smile. One with full lips and even white teeth that he wielded like a weapon, never showing anger or complex emotions beyond his constant charm and genial nature. His muddy-brown hair was cut short on the side and was mostly hidden by his beaver hat, but I knew that the hair at his temples was sprinkled with gray—a touch premature for his four and thirty years.

His chestnut horse slowed as it approached me, and I could see the way the man's eyes lit with good humor—the tiny lines crinkling the skin at the edges.

Naturally, I couldn't simply be cold and stranded on the side of the road. I had to be punished as well.

Because my savior was none other than Silas Bartholomew.

Two

SILAS

"Damn. I was hoping for a handsome highwayman."

I let my smile stretch wide. "You'll have to settle for a handsome gentleman instead."

Lady Mary Lovelace didn't resemble any damsel in distress that I could recollect. There was no simpering or weakness present. She stood tall and proud and appeared completely unbothered by the cold and the snow that continued to fall all around us.

Nevertheless, I glanced at her ice-crusted boots and the determined flakes clinging to her dark cloak. A touch of worry for her instigated a frown. "Why aren't you waiting in the carriage?" I asked, dismounting from my horse and moving to inspect the front wheels of the vehicle.

Her coachman had caught me on my way to the stables. I'd planned on riding over to Kensworth Hall to meet with my brother-in-law, Augie, but when presented with such an opportunity as this, I could not resist. I'd advised Marshall, the coachman, to go inside and get warm, promising to retrieve Lady Mary and bring her to Laurel Park. It had taken some cajoling, but there was no point in digging out the carriage until tomorrow anyhow. Bringing out more men while the snow still fell was a wasted effort. Nothing would happen to her conveyance in the meantime, and some gallant and chivalrous part of me liked the idea of being the one to rescue the contrary Lady Mary.

Plus, I knew it would irritate her to no end to be indebted to me in any way.

Win-win.

The aforementioned lady scowled, her auburn brows lowered adorably over her vengeful brown eyes. I fought a chuckle.

"I grew tired of waiting in the carriage," she replied defensively as if I might scold her for trying to catch her death out here.

I kicked at the snow and mud that had enveloped the base of the right front carriage wheel. "Yes, but it's warm in there and snowing out here." As if to emphasize my point, I held my hand out to indicate the winter weather swirling around us. Lacy white flakes landed gently on my gloved hand.

Mary gasped dramatically. "Snowing, you say? I thought the sky was falling. I'm glad you're here to enlighten me regarding our fickle English weather patterns."

I straightened from my bent position over the axle. "Really? Because you don't sound happy to see me. I could always climb on my horse and head back the way I came."

"That is perfectly acceptable, Mr. Bartholomew. I'm sure Marshall will be along shortly to assist me."

I merely smiled.

"What did you do?" she gritted out.

It would not do to laugh at her exasperation, therefore I made a valiant effort to make my expression serious. "Well, I told your coachman that I would return you to Laurel Park and that he should head inside and enjoy a pot of tea in the kitchen. That carriage is not going anywhere, and it will be easier to dig out once the snow stops piling on top of it."

"You had no right to dismiss my coachman. We had everything under control."

I looked pointedly at the wheels currently embedded in the road.

Lady Mary growled.

I covered my mouth with my hand to avoid laughing outright and maneuvered to the door of the carriage. "Come. Let us retrieve your most essential belongings, and we can be on our way. Genevieve is eager to share her happy news with you."

"And what news is that?"

"Her betrothal to Julian."

"Oh," she said, and I turned to see a quiet smile on her face, lovely and soft. More relaxed than the typical no-nonsense woman I'd grown accustomed to over the years. Her obvious happiness for my youngest sister shimmered subtly across her features. But Mary saw me watching her and scowled. "Well, let's get on with it, then."

"Laurel Park is not far. I'll have you rescued before you know it." I grinned as I heard an annoyed sigh from behind me.

Ignoring decorum, I preceded her into the vehicle.

With my back turned, I could not see her angry expression, but I could feel it. I climbed into the modest carriage. Truthfully, I was a bit eager to get out of the weather before we journeyed the short distance back to Laurel Park. I would warm up momentarily while Lady Mary gathered her things.

With snow crunching mightily beneath her feet, Mary stomped up to the conveyance, but my gaze snagged on her abandoned blanket and what looked to be a small notebook on the carriage seat. Sitting atop it was a bit of paper. Upon closer inspection, it looked to be a list of names in two tidy columns. I reached forward and snagged the sheet.

Mary entered and ignored me, grumbling all the while. She took her seat and started digging around in a hamper by her feet as I scanned this very curious collection of names.

"What are you doing?" Mary's tone moments later had my head snapping up. She sounded alarmed, voice high and fraught. "Give that back. It's mine."

Eyes wide and frantic, she made a wild grab for the paper, but I held it aloft, intrigued by her reaction. A ruffled Mary Lovelace was not one I'd seen before. She was easy to rile, yes. We played that game all the time. But this was something else. Panic made her desperate as she lunged again for the list in my hand, ignoring her good manners entirely.

"Well, this is interesting," I teased as she practically climbed onto my lap to reach across my body. But my arm was too long, and I was highly motivated. There was something about this note that she did not wish me to see.

Shocked by her reaction and, honestly, by her proximity, I registered the heat of her as she attempted to maul me. One knee was perched on the seat by my hip while her other thigh draped across my lap. The bodice of her velvet traveling gown was pressed to the side of my face as she attempted to reach beyond me. I was indeed a gentleman, so I ignored her panted breaths and the rise and fall of her small breasts practically before my eyes.

"That is private. Return it now," she demanded, face flushed.

"All right," I said, fully intending to do just that. But as I lowered my arm, my attention caught on the very last name on the list, and I paused.

My hesitation gave Mary enough time to lean over my lap, knocking my hat askew and snatching the paper from my grasp.

She huffed an angry breath and climbed off me to return to her side of the carriage. She sat folding the list into a tiny square before shoving it unceremoniously into the valise at her side. Her cheeks were flaming and her hair—wild and unruly on the best of days—was a riotous tangle of vibrant red to rival the color staining her cheeks. Strands had abandoned her coiffure and dipped down along the column of her pale throat and several dangled in her eyes as she focused on her task and anywhere but me.

I sat waiting, one eyebrow raised expectantly. A challenge.

I knew what I had seen elegantly scrawled on that piece of paper. And I was just waiting for her to acknowledge it. The curiosity was honestly killing me, but I needed to hold myself together.

When it seemed that her traveling bag was all packed up and ready to go, Mary sighed deeply and finally looked my way.

"Wellll?" I questioned, drawing the word out.

Her brown eyes flickered uneasily to the side before she crossed her arms and regarded me once more. "Well, what?"

I grinned. "Are you going to tell me why you have that list of gentlemen in your possession and why my name is on it?"

She swallowed visibly but said nothing.

My mind worked, considering and discarding several possibilities.

Finally, I settled against the seatback, crossing one leg over the other and showing no signs of eagerness to depart. "You know, I would say it was a collection of charming gentlemen among the *ton* but Lord Mason is exceedingly dull and there is no way I would be last on the list."

Her angry expression didn't alter. "That was private."

"It was sitting out in a rather public space."

She scoffed. "I would not call a personal conveyance a public space."

"I didn't pluck it out of your journal or desk drawer. It's not as if I dug it out of your underthings."

"If you'd dug it out of my underthings, you'd have one less hand to worry about and an excess of gloves." Mary smiled sweetly, and I bit my lip to prevent my laughter. That had been a good one.

It had always been this way with us—fighting to maintain the upper hand. I wasn't even sure how it started. I was introduced to Mary Lovelace, perhaps a decade ago, due to her friendship with my sister Patty. Our relationship had fallen easily into teasing and bickering. I could recall no specific event or offense that provoked ire on either side. But my general personality had seemed to irritate her like a pesky pebble in the bottom of her boot.

Our antagonistic bantering was common knowledge among everyone at this point, and Mary and I played into the theatrics of it all. She loved to push my buttons and I enjoyed watching her neck flush crimson in irritation. But, I supposed, a part of me always thought it was for show. That Mary would know if she ever needed rescuing from the side of the road, I'd be happy to volunteer my services.

I was someone she could count on. And beneath all the blustering and public squabbling, we were actually . . . friends.

But looking at her now, I wasn't so sure.

"You won't tell me?" I questioned.

"It is none of your business. A gentleman would let this go and allow me my privacy."

I nodded easily. "Probably." Instead, I resorted to our old tricks and sought to provoke. "Is it perhaps a guest list for an upcoming event?" Mary's countenance remained stony. "Surely not. I can't imagine why there would be no ladies mentioned." I tapped my knee thoughtfully while she attempted to light me on fire with her gaze. "It looked to me like a decent collection of unmarried men. Are you finally looking to settle down, my lady?"

The flush that had momentarily receded began working its way back up her chest and into her cheeks. Her pale English skin reacted violently to what I'd said for some reason and her eyes shifted away to somewhere over my shoulder. Surely she wasn't actually considering marriage to anyone listed. I mean, I was on that list and she'd sooner bury me in the ground.

"There is no need to list potential suitors when one is firmly on the shelf, you idiot." Her words were rough and angry but there was vulnerability there in the admission.

Yes, realistically, I knew that Mary was beyond typical marriageable age, but it wasn't something I'd considered. Her skin was smooth and unlined. Her figure was willowy and lithesome. I'd never admit this to her face, but she was an accomplished dancer and entertaining dinner companion. I was unsure why Lady Mary wasn't married, to be quite honest. She was always so forthright and direct. I suppose I'd assumed it was her choice. Mary was the kind of woman who achieved her aims. I figured if she'd wanted a husband, she would have gotten one. Yet I'd never noticed her on the arm of any gentleman or courted openly.

I hadn't meant to strike a nerve. But I could see now that my words had hurt her. A twist of something unwelcome had me leaning forward, eager to draw her attention, to apologize for putting that rare look on her face.

Quickly, I attempted, "That is not what I meant."

"Don't," she snapped. "Do not pity me or offer platitudes. That is not how this works between us."

Something about the way she minimized our relationship—our friendship—had me uncrossing my legs and straightening on the seat.

"Mary," I tried again.

But before I could admit that I'd never pity anyone as strong and capable as she was, she said quickly, voice clipped and cross, "It's for a liaison."

Surprise had my brows going high on my forehead, I could feel them disappear into my hat. Lady Mary was indeed a headstrong and forthright woman, but this was extreme even for her. The implications of this list would be disastrous for her reputation and standing in society, if not handled with the utmost discretion.

I recalled suddenly the names I'd seen. The affable but clueless Lord Ashby in the number one position. Farther down was Conrad Hamilton, who could not keep a secret if his life depended upon it. And why on earth would she want a liaison with the insufferable Viscount Hornwick?

And with startling realization, my name's appearance on the list floated back to me, dead last.

Motivated entirely by pride, I blurted, "Are they ranked?"

Mary finally smiled, and it didn't look mean or vindictive. It looked like she was trying not to laugh. "Of course that would be your concern." And then she did laugh, bright and loud.

"Now, wait just a moment," I said.

She only laughed harder.

"What makes me last?" I demanded between her peals of amusement. "I'll have you know that if you were ever fortunate enough to enter into an arrangement with me—stop laughing, dammit—you would not be disappointed."

Finally in control of her faculties, Mary swiped at the moisture beneath her eyes. "Is that so?"

And while I was irritated by her disregard and the blatant assault to my masculinity and prowess, I was relieved to see this happy version of her. The one with lips tilted mischievously, her expression lovely and aglow, overflowing with mirth. Not the woman hiding from her embarrassment nor the self-conscious spinster I'd inadvertently wounded with my thoughtlessness.

"That. Is so," I said seriously.

With a smile still lingering on her full pink lips, Mary replied, "Well, apologies, Bartholomew. I did not ask for references. The positions were based entirely upon my ability to keep from murdering the potential applicant. Hence your spot in the final column."

"I'll prove it," I blurted with little forethought beyond wounded male pride.

Mary's mouth fell open. "You'll prove it? And how do you plan to go about that?"

"A kiss. Grant me the favor of a kiss, and I'll prove to you that I should not be last on your list."

She stared at me as if I'd lost my mind, but I did not care. She'd taken a battering ram to my ego, and it was suddenly imperative that I correct her weak opinion of me. We'd always been companionable adversaries—gaining and losing the upper hand in our battles with entertaining regularity. The idea of being found deficient and wanting by the one woman I considered my finest opponent was doing irrational things to my sensibility.

"You are serious."

It wasn't a question, but I answered it anyway. "Absolutely."

The way we sparred and battled in ballrooms—there was something to be said for that sort of passion. And there had been fleeting moments in the past when I'd considered Mary Lovelace's lips. Those thoughts had been predominantly in the vein of shocking her into shutting up. Our arguments often devolved into childish, petulant banter. But it was fun, and she knew it. Her brown eyes consistently sparkled when a quip landed neatly between us. I could envision her wicked smile turning up the corners of her full, sinful lips when an imaginary point was awarded in her favor. Mary liked the chase and skirmishes as much as I did. She was frightfully intelligent and quick-witted. And now I wanted her to acknowledge that I was desirable for more than antagonizing.

Mary regarded me cautiously, but something else shined behind her eyes—curiosity. She was thinking about us too.

"Do I need to steal your valise to get you to come over here and find out just how serious I am?"

Her grin was all challenge. "If you want a kiss, you'll have to come and get it."

For once, I allowed my features to convey my seriousness. "Is that an invitation? Because you're going to have to say it. I'm not going to take something that isn't expressly given."

Mary's grin fell away at my words, and I could see her turning over my statement, examining my demand for consent before she returned the earnestness I required. She nodded slowly and finally said, "Yes."

Without breaking eye contact, I leaned forward across the narrow valley separating our two seats. I braced my hands on the worn green velvet on either side of her narrow hips before lowering to my knees by her feet. My thighs slowly grazed her skirts before she spread her legs wide, allowing me to settle right where I wanted to be.

Her wide and expectant chocolate-brown eyes took in my every move. She appeared shocked that I'd lowered myself before her. Mary Lovelace had so much to learn. While we both attempted to avoid submission, to never give in or bare our throats in our public battles, in this—in proving oneself so intimately—I'd gladly get on my knees for her.

Mary sat straight and tall on the carriage bench. She was all taut lines and hard angles as I drew closer. She was also bracing, and I wanted her loose and receptive instead. So with deliberate slowness, I pressed forward, enjoying the way her breath hitched at our closeness. Never mind that her bosom had been plastered to the side of my face five minutes ago. Now, the woman was wary and tense—nervous, if I had to put a name to it. While I did wish her to be comfortable with my proximity, some perverse part of me—and there were many—relished in her dismay. It was quite a thing to ruffle the perpetually controlled Mary Lovelace.

That tremor in her inhale—I'd done that. The fidgeting of her gloved hands—that was me. The way she watched my mouth and swallowed audibly as I drew closer was infinitely satisfying. I couldn't wait to make her lose control.

Before I could do more than exhale a breath across her lush bottom lip, I angled my head and veered toward the side of her neck. She made a surprised sound when my mouth pressed warm and wet to the pulse beating rapidly there.

Her fur-edged cloak flared wide, leaving the column of her throat bare for my ministrations. I took advantage and placed slow kisses all the way up to her earlobe, dragging my lips across the sensitive skin of her neck, leaving gooseflesh in my wake.

By the time I nudged a tendril of hair away and pressed my mouth to the skin behind her ear, Mary was no longer rigid. Her back reclined against the seat, and her hands no longer clutched desperately at the velvet bench. Her labored breathing was the only sound in the carriage, and I could feel her breasts against my chest with every ragged inhale.

I smiled against her skin and leaned back to kiss her jaw and then her chin. Mary's eyes were closed, and her face relaxed.

Everything up to that point had been calculated. I'd sought to ease the tension and nervousness radiating from her, so I'd distracted her with unexpected and languid touches.

Without warning, I clutched her hips in my hands and scooted her forward on the bench until we were flush together. Her eyes opened abruptly, and she squeaked in surprise. Before she could scold me, I pressed my smiling mouth to hers.

But something happened when our lips met. The control and experience I'd planned to wield to my benefit evaporated, and Mary was no longer a passive participant in this little experiment meant to soothe my wounded pride.

Our mouths parted, and instinct took over. The kiss became heated instantly. Our tongues and teeth gnashing at one another. I was vaguely aware that she knocked my hat from my head and raked her nails along my scalp.

My hands were moving—one under her cloak and low on her back to hold her close and the other pulling her thigh over my hip.

Stopping to breathe didn't seem all that important, so we panted desperately against each other. Mary sucked hard on my lower lip in a way that had me clutching the fabric of her dress in my fist. She released me, and my abused flesh came free with a pop. In retaliation, I bit down on her bottom lip.

She made a rough sound of outrage even as she snaked a hand beneath my coat and pulled me closer. I freed her tender lip and smiled before licking into her mouth once more.

The heel of her boot dug into my backside as she moved against me, seeking contact and friction. I didn't know what insanity held us in its thrall, but we were similarly possessed. This was every bickering argument we'd ever had—each of us attempting to gain the upper hand or to drive the other to madness. But instead of the bite of our words, we were using our teeth to punish and provoke. Our bodies were doing battle, and I'd never felt so overcome. My eyes were rolling for an entirely different reason when I felt

Mary's sneaky fingers maneuver between our bodies and press against the placket of my breeches. I groaned and thrust my hips forward into her searching hand—not caring that she was a lady or my sister's best friend. I wasn't capable of being concerned with my improper behavior in this moment of reckless abandon.

I was reaching for the edge of her skirts and dragging my fingers along her wool stockings when I registered a shout from beyond the carriage.

Mary and I both froze as we listened to what was very well Augustus Ward, the Duke of Kendrick and my brother-in-law, calling out my name.

I leaned back and wide brown eyes met my own. Our breaths were ragged and I knew I had to will this erection away and go outside and speak to Augie.

As I slowly gained control of my faculties, I removed one hand from Mary's skirts and the other from her mess of hair. I honestly hadn't even remembered winding my fingers into her flaming red locks.

We hadn't spoken a word into the oppressive silence, and for once in my life, I had absolutely no idea what to say. She'd stolen the words from my tongue.

That had been entirely unexpected . . . and euphoric.

My God. I'd been ready to fuck Mary Lovelace in a carriage on the side of the road.

The realization was confounding, and, *Jesus*, could Augie stop shouting for a moment so I could think.

I rose swiftly and practically stumbled out of the conveyance. I vaguely heard Mary hissing behind me—something about a hat.

When I emerged from the vehicle, Augie was on horseback in the middle of the lane. He jolted in surprise, straightening in the saddle and pulling his mare up short.

"Augie!" I called and then coughed as the winter air hit my lungs. The snow was still falling but in a lazy and unhurried way, knowing the damage had already been done and the countryside was sufficiently covered.

I patted my chest as I worked quickly to recover my breath and noticed that two buttons were undone on my waistcoat. When had Mary managed that?

In retrospect, I should have taken a moment to collect myself and ensure my appearance was presentable. But I'd felt the need to get out of that carriage with some urgency. Recovering some semblance of sanity had seemed essential.

"Good of you to come, Augie. I apologize. I meant to send word on to Kensworth Hall about my delay in our meeting."

My brother-in-law's blue eyes were wide and horrified, but he said nothing. I watched his attention shift over my shoulder and heard Mary clamber down from the carriage.

I turned and took in her appearance. She had hastily re-pinned her hair, but it was still a mess. Her cloak was back in position and tied snugly under her chin. But, without a mirror, she hadn't seen the state of her face. And I knew Augie was seeing it just as plainly as I.

Her chocolate-brown eyes were wild, and her lips were pink, plump, and kiss-swollen from my ministrations. I could see the way the scruff on my cheeks and chin had abraded her pale porcelain skin. Mary stood staring at me, and I hoped I didn't look as proud and gratified as I felt. But I must have because she scowled at me in irritation. I noticed for the first time that she was holding my hat.

"No," he said over my shoulder. I turned back to see Augie shaking his head furiously, expression stricken. "No. I do not want to know about this."

"Now, Augie," I attempted.

"No," he repeated. "I saw nothing. I know nothing. " Without making eye contact, he clutched his reins and turned his horse, riding off as quickly as the snow on the road would allow.

Three

MARY

"Are you sure you're warm enough, Mary?"

"Oh, yes." I nodded, answering Genevieve's question a bit distractedly.

"Because I can get you another blanket. Or more tea perhaps?" She was already up off the settee and moving toward the doorway.

"Gen, stop," I said with amusement, finally turning from the fire and giving her my full attention. I had hot tea and a comfortable quilt draped across my lap already. "I assure you, I am quite well. Fit as a fiddle."

She stopped her forward progress but eyed me speculatively. The youngest Bartholomew was very perceptive. She'd known me long enough to realize something was amiss. I'd been distracted and fraught since I'd dismounted from her brother's horse half an hour ago.

After Augie had abandoned us—and honestly, I couldn't blame him—Silas had wordlessly helped me into the saddle, mounted up and settled behind me. We'd ridden the remaining distance to Laurel Park in complete silence, his chest pressed to my back and his arms around me holding the reins. Several times, I'd felt him draw in a breath as if to speak, but words had never materialized. I'd frankly been too dumbfounded to offer anything beyond muddled, bewildered sounds.

I didn't understand why my body had reacted so . . . so fiercely to Silas. If Augie hadn't stumbled upon us and interrupted, God knew what would have happened. It was as if all my frustration and irritation had built up over a decade of knowing Silas and then erupted. I'd always assumed that I would strangle the man if I ever got my hands on him. I was mortified to realize that I'd nearly had my hand down his trousers instead.

Could madness come on suddenly? Or perhaps it was hereditary on my father's side?

These were the thoughts plaguing me while Genevieve did her best to ensure I was comfortable. I owed it to my friend to focus my attention and stop thinking about her brother's lips and his hands . . . and his other parts.

She still hovered by the doorway of the sitting room, as if contemplating ignoring my assurances and going for the extra blanket anyway.

"Come, Genevieve." I patted the open seat next to me on the floral brocade sofa. "Tell me all about your betrothal. Your brother mentioned some big developments with Mr. Moore since I last saw you."

A smile broke over the young woman's face, and she drifted back toward me with a small skip in her step. But then she sobered as if realizing she'd been distracted and muttered, "Are you sure you're all right? You've been so quiet since you arrived."

I called forth a reassuring smile. "Well, I couldn't very well talk with my teeth clattering. But now I am warm and ready to chat. I am perfectly fine."

Genevieve continued to eye me, but she sat.

"Tell me," I demanded. "I'm put out that I missed it. I want to hear about Mr. Moore's proposal." While marriage was not in my future, by both circumstance and choice, that did not mean I was not eager to support my sweet friend in her lovely future.

"Well," Genevieve began, a healthy blush on her fair cheeks, "Julian surprised me here—at Laurel Park—yesterday. He had assistance from my siblings to get me out to where they're building the new stable, but instead of new construction, I found Julian waiting for me and the land cleared for our future home nearby. He brought the cat and asked me to be his wife," she concluded with a laugh as if her wide smile could not contain her joy.

I grinned at her happy news. Reaching over, I clasped her hand. "Congratulations, darling. I'm so thrilled for you both." And I meant it. Genevieve and Julian deserved this happiness.

A thought occurred. "What about his uncle and Brightleaf?" I asked cautiously.

Despite having been raised alongside Genevieve, the pair hadn't seen each other in the past seven years. Quite unexpectedly, Julian had traveled to London on business this past autumn, attempting to acquire buyers for his uncle's horse farm in Leicester. He and Gen had reacquainted and fallen in love, but there were details and family obligations that needed to be addressed.

Gen squeezed my hand in return. "He left Brightleaf Farms and his uncle to partner with Miles. They're going to have their own stable and breeding operation. Julian's uncle agreed to downsize and sell them much of his stock. The construction will likely not be complete until next summer, but we hope to marry early in the new year."

"That's wonderful news. You will make the loveliest bride, and Mr. Moore will be the luckiest man in England."

"Thank you, Mary." Gen's smile was luminous with love, and her future was so bright. I could just envision their happy union. Before long, all the Bartholomew daughters would be married.

I cleared my throat delicately before inquiring after her bridegroom. "And where is your Mr. Moore?"

I'd been surprised upon my arrival to only find Genevieve. So familiar I was with this family, I didn't require a proper welcome, of course. And the Bartholomews rarely stood on ceremony, but I'd expected more people to be about. Following our awkward horseback ride through the snow, Silas had stalked off somewhere without a word, and Gen had stumbled upon me in the foyer moments later.

"Oh, he's with Miles." She tucked a light-brown strand behind her ear. "I'm sorry Mama was not present to greet you. We were fairly certain no one would be arriving today due to the weather. She and father are somewhere, I'm sure. It was rude of me to steal you away, but I was so distracted by your arrival in out of the snow. We'll get your things tomorrow. You can borrow whatever you need to make yourself comfortable."

"Thank you, darling," I said and took a quick sip of tea.

With an uneasy glance, Gen said, "Despite being stranded in the snow, I imagine your journey alone was preferable to riding with your mother and father."

She was quite right on that front. I nodded. "I had ample time with my own thoughts. It was indeed preferable." Complicated, but the more desirable option.

Coexisting in private with my family was riddled with intricacies. It was as convoluted and treacherous as winding one's way through a briar patch.

In society, the Earl and Countess of Thisby appeared the exemplary union. However, in the privacy of their own home—or carriage as the case may be—the two were often at odds. My parents were equally resentful of their marriage. My mother was more apathetic and accepting of her lot in life. That of a woman reliant upon a demeaning and belittling husband.

My father was far more vocal and bitter. He appeared the jovial aristocrat when viewed through the lens of the peerage, but behind closed doors, he resented his unhappy marriage and his worthless spinster daughter who was nothing but a nuisance and a drain on family resources.

My parents were the reason I'd never been particularly upset by my lack of offers. Marriage was nothing beyond a prison, one I'd seen my mother and father bound to my entire life. Despite the Bartholomew daughters' loving relationships, the vast majority of *ton* unions were like my parents'—an agreement contracted between families for mutually beneficial gain. I didn't believe a love match was a possibility for someone like me, and I'd be damned if I was forced into a marriage like the one that had stolen the joy from my parents' lives.

But a family—on the other hand—that was what I sought. The unconditional love of mother and child. The idea reached into the missing places inside and gave me the courage to do something outlandish—like make a list of potential men for liaisons.

Genevieve regarded me curiously. "How exactly did Silas end up being the one to fetch you?"

I shook myself out of bitter thoughts of my parents and replied, "How Silas does anything, I would imagine." I placed my teacup and saucer on the low table before me. "He inserted himself with little forethought or planning."

Gen let out a quick laugh. "But what happened?"

I sighed. "My carriage is not far from here on the main road. Once we were stuck, my coachman rode on ahead with the horses and was intercepted by your brother who assured him that he would return me to Laurel Park and to ignore the wishes of his mistress."

"Ah." Genevieve grinned. "That sounds like my brother."

A moment of companionable silence passed while we watched the flames in the grate.

"I'm surprised you both managed the ride without killing each other."

I swallowed uneasily, refusing to think about being tucked up on horseback against Silas—his firm thighs bracketing mine securely and his sweet cigar-smoke scent mixing with the crisp winter air. And I definitely was not going to think about being overcome by madness and mauling him in a carriage.

"It was a surprise, to be sure," I finally managed.

Gen watched me from the corner of her eye for a moment before commenting dryly, "You are blushing."

I met her sly gaze. "I am still quite chilled. This is how I look when I'm cold. Perhaps you should go fetch me that extra blanket after all."

She grinned and rose from her seat. "Perhaps I shall. And I'll let Mama know you've arrived safely and may be the only guest for her annual house party."

I was, indeed, the only non-family member who arrived to spend a fortnight at Laurel Park. The letters arrived over the next several days. Due to the weather, everyone else had chosen to remain in London or at their own country estates.

Once the roads were again passable, my carriage and my belongings were retrieved and the remaining Bartholomew siblings joined us at Laurel Park.

Emery and Augustus Ward, the Duke and Duchess of Kendrick, arrived when they were able with their rambunctious children, Reeve and Beckett, in tow. Patty and Miles and their adolescent daughter, Franny, joined us from their nearby home for an afternoon of visitation.

We were all to dine together this evening along with Genevieve, Julian, Silas, and the matriarch and patriarch of the family, the Marquess and Marchioness of Northcutt.

I was eager to see everyone. But I had to admit, it had been nice to ease into festivities without the whole family all at once. Things had been fairly quiet and undemanding with only Gen and Julian as companions. Silas had been mysteriously absent since our encounter, but I was quite sure he'd make an appearance tonight. He liked to be involved in all family affairs and was never one to shy away from being the center of attention.

I didn't mind that he was avoiding me. It was pleasant to have a little peace and quiet where Silas was concerned. It wasn't as if I thought we should discuss what had happened in the carriage. That would be silly and unwise. What we'd done probably didn't even signify in the life of Silas Bartholomew.

For me, it had been a singular occurrence. I'd never found myself overcome like that before. And men did not ever find themselves overcome by me.

By and large, I found intimacies and all manner of physical inter-action to be underwhelming. That had been my experience anyway. And, honestly, that sort of halfhearted attraction was what I'd envisioned for any future arrangement I could hope to secure in the new year with the aid of my list.

But something strange had happened with Silas. Perhaps it had been the threat of freezing to death that made my biology trigger a response. Yes, that had to be it. I'd been stricken suddenly with the urge to procreate as the result of being on the brink of death. That was a fine excuse as any. And since Silas seemed disinclined to see me following our . . . survival madness, the topic wouldn't come up again, and I could simply leave it at that.

Perhaps he was embarrassed by what had happened, ashamed of kissing the spinster friend of his sister. The consistently annoying presence in his life for the past decade. I'd emerged from our carriage encounter wearing a mirrored expression of confounding shock. He'd gotten swept up just as I had. That much had been obvious. I didn't begrudge him his dismay, however.

Yet I didn't want to force the man to hide away in his own home just to avoid me. Maybe I *should* talk to him. Clear the air. I'd let him know that I had no intention of telling anyone what had happened and we could move on with our lives. No need to continue being childish. He'd been the one to demand the kiss, after all. And from the horrified look on Augie's face, I couldn't imagine he'd tell anyone either.

Silas and I had twelve more days under the same roof. No need to make things difficult. A simple conversation would set things to rights. He loved to talk, so it shouldn't be a trial. All would be well.

Besides, his siblings would notice something amiss if Silas didn't turn up soon.

In my guest suite, I took a quick glance in the mirror and straightened a few curls in my coiffure. I ran a hand along my bodice and straightened my emerald skirts a bit before settling on a shrug in the looking glass. This was as good as it was going to get.

With that, I exited my rooms and went in search of Silas. I wandered idly through corridors before taking a quick loop through the family wing on the opposite end of the floor as my own Red Suite. Smiling briefly at a maid who passed, I checked the morning room and a study on the main level before strolling toward the library on the off chance Silas was hiding there.

I'd just turned the corner when I came face-to-face with the man himself. Silas appeared momentarily startled, frozen in place in the middle of the hallway. At the end of the corridor, the window at his back outlined his tall form in cool afternoon light. His face was shadowed by the contrast, but I was close enough to see that he recovered quickly and offered a polite bow and a tight, close-lipped smile. "Lady Mary, how do you do?"

I frowned at his formality and returned it. "I am well, Mr. Bartholomew. Thank you." I cast a quick glance behind me before moving closer. "Actually, I was hoping for a moment of your time. Perhaps we could—" I broke off as I heard footsteps behind me.

Silas's eyes widened in alarm and he moved quickly to open a door and grab my hand, tugging me inside a small cupboard.

It was dark and cramped within. Light shone around the border of the doorway, but I couldn't make out the contents of the cupboard nor Silas's expression. We simply held very still, listening for the passage of footfalls.

After approximately twelve years had passed, the corridor fell quiet. Our breaths the only sounds in this overcrowded hiding space.

"Why did you do that?" I whispered.

"Do what?" came his quiet reply.

"Drag us in here."

"Well, I assumed you would not want to be seen talking to me."

I made a face at that, but of course, he couldn't see me. "Why would you assume that? *I* am not the one who has hidden away for days to avoid me. Neither am I the one who refused to even speak to me on the horseback ride here."

The silence was pronounced following my accusation. But I could still feel him there. I realized suddenly that his hand was on my waist—perhaps it had been there since we stepped within the musty cupboard. But heat radiated from his body, and the scent of cigar smoke permeated the confined space. Despite his sudden inability to speak, I couldn't ignore how very present Silas was—how much space he occupied. The awareness skated along my skin, leaving tiny prickles in its wake.

"I was not hiding," he finally said, so softly I might have missed it had I not been so close beside him.

I shook my head. "It's no matter. That is what I wanted to discuss with you before we were interrupted in the hallway."

I shifted uneasily. It was difficult to have a conversation with someone when you could not see their face.

"Careful," Silas murmured, his other hand coming to the side of my waist as well as he steadied me. "The maids store all manner of things in here while the Christmas decorations are up. I think there are a collection of candlestick holders behind you."

"Oh," I said, pressing forward into Silas's secure hold. I brought my hands up and placed them gently on his firm chest, feeling the wool of his coat and stroking the lapels with my thumbs.

I felt something brush my temple, and instead of backing away, I leaned closer. Silas's soft breath exhaled against my cheek as his nose nuzzled at my temple once more.

"What did you wish to discuss?" Silas whispered directly against the sensitive skin of my ear. His lips grazed my earlobe before he took it between his teeth, delivering a gentle bite.

I swallowed hard, my eyes closing of their own volition as my heart beat a savage pattern in my chest. "I—I wanted to . . ."

I trailed off as Silas released my ear, but then my hand was moving beneath his coat and around his lean waist, holding him to me.

Silas hummed against my skin as his lips trailed tender kisses along my jaw. "You . . . wanted to?" he prompted, but my mind was mostly blank. My hand had worked itself beneath his waistcoat to loosen his shirt, and I could feel the warm skin of his back, so soft and smooth.

"Ohh," I breathed when I felt his teeth nip the tip of my chin. "Survival madness," I mumbled just as his lips met mine.

And then all remaining thoughts of clearing the air fled entirely. It was as if we were back in the carriage, dueling with our hands and teeth. Except now, we were wrapped securely in the darkness of this cupboard. Our indiscretions and impropriety given freedom by the illusion of secrecy. And sensations heightened by the absence of light, supported by the intimacy of touch.

I scraped my nails up the flat plane of Silas's back as far as I could manage. He grunted into my mouth and turned us, pressing my back firmly into the closed door. Silas broke our kiss momentarily as he lifted me, skirts bunching everywhere as I wrapped my legs around him. I put my arms over his shoulders and held on as he supported me against the wood, his hands clutching my bottom.

His mouth returned, sucking on my bottom lip with relentless abandon. I ran my fingers along the short hairs at the base of his neck up into the longer strands atop his head. I clutched his hair and pulled. Silas released my lip with a pop, and we panted into each other's mouths.

"What is happening to us?"

"I don't know," he breathed.

And then we were kissing again—open mouths and seeking tongues, battling for dominance, feeling the urgency in the effort. I'd never wanted to gain the upper hand with Silas more than I did in this moment, but even when he advanced, I never once felt like I was losing ground.

We were so wrapped up in one another and this . . . madness that I didn't care that he was an insufferable blowhard half the time. Or that he talked too much and told the same tall tales over and over again. And he must not have minded my plain face or small breasts because I could feel him against my center, so hard and so eager through the layers of fabric that I thought I might die from being wanted for the first time in my entire life.

I wrenched my lips away to whisper brokenly, "Closer. I want more of you."

One of Silas's hands left my bottom and touched my ankle, following the line of my leg and bunching fabric as he went. "There are too many layers," he growled in frustration before lowering me to the ground and spinning me around.

My hands came up in surprise and pressed flat to the smooth wood of the door. I rested my forehead against the surface, inhaling deeply, expecting this foolishness to be over and sanity to return with regular breathing. But then I felt cool air along my backside before Silas pressed against me, so hot and firm through his trousers that I caught myself before I moaned aloud.

He'd flipped my skirts up and out of the way as his hand snaked around my hip and down to my center. Silas's lips fastened to the sensitive skin of my neck as his tongue caressed and laved. His clever fingers found the slit in my drawers, and I thought I might never breathe properly again.

I arched helplessly, pressing my backside more fully into him as his touch moved expertly between my legs. His lips faltered, and I felt his forehead rest against my hair. Silas worked his fingers against my core, dipping down to where I was wet and aching before going higher to circle the place that seemed to concentrate all my pleasure.

"Widen your stance," he whispered against the shell of my ear, and in this, I obeyed.

His finger prodded lower again, and I felt him go deeper, slipping inside me. My inner muscles were clutching and desperate and I thought to tell him I could come like this. If he simply pressed his palm flat against me and let me ride his hand. But then I felt the hard line of his cock stroke against my backside as Silas thrust against me through his trousers.

"Oh God," he moaned before pulling his length away.

I wanted to tell him to come back, that I liked feeling him hard and wanting, even through our clothes, but then his palm pressed down against that little bundle of nerves—just how I'd envisioned —and I was gasping out a broken plea against the door and cresting against his hand.

Reality returned slowly as I could feel his lips ghosting soft kisses along the column of my neck. Finally, he removed his hand from my body and lowered my skirts around me.

Aching to touch him in return, I took a moment to collect myself. I had no idea where we went from here, but luckily, I didn't have to flounder helplessly in a cupboard with Silas after he'd plea-sured me with his fingers because Augustus Ward chose that moment to open the door I was leaning against.

I felt myself falling forward, but I didn't stumble a step. Silas's arms came around me and pulled me upright in all the shocking confusion.

Augie's eyes were wide and dismayed. "I was looking for the children. We were playing hide-and-seek, and I heard a sound, and oh my God." He turned his back but stayed in the hallway.

With Silas's front pressed so closely to my back, I could feel the hitch in his breath and knew he was trying not to laugh. Then he simply laid his forehead on my shoulder and shook with amusement.

I bit my lip helplessly as Augie turned back to us, expression flat and disappointed. "You both have rooms in this house." He gestured wildly. "Do you really need to—never mind. I saw nothing. I know nothing." And with that, he marched out of the corridor and away from us.

With a hand over my mouth, I laughed helplessly into my palm while Silas worked to gain control of himself.

Eventually, I stepped out of the cupboard and into the corridor, turning to face Silas. He looked as disheveled as I felt—clothes rumpled, shirt untucked, and the longer strands of brown hair atop his head askew from my enthusiastic fingers.

"That was probably a bad idea," I said, finding it prudent to inject seriousness into my tone.

A smile lingered on Silas's lips as he watched me fluff my layers of skirts. The weight of his gaze kept me from fleeing the hallway in awkward embarrassment. "All the best ones generally are."

"I'm going to return to my room to freshen up. I would advise you to do the same," I said with a pointed look at his hair and clothing and then further south to the prominent bulge in his trousers.

"You'd like me to freshen up in your room?" he replied innocently.

I gave him a flat, unamused expression.

His smile grew. "All right. I will go and make myself more presentable. Wouldn't want anyone to know you lured me into the cupboard and attacked me."

"I did not—" I cut myself off. This was what he wanted. This was how we got into all our squabbles. He baited, and I simply could not ignore the challenge. Well, not this time. "My aim in seeking you out," I said primly as I straightened the sleeves of my dress, "was to assure you of my discretion with—with what happened in the carriage . . . and now the cupboard." I swallowed, feeling a flush working its way up my neck. "You needn't avoid your family on my account. I have no intention of saying anything to anyone."

Silas remained utterly cool and unaffected. Perhaps he dallied with women in storage rooms all the time. I could feel my brow furrow unexpectedly at the thought before I forced my face to relax.

We stood staring at one another until he finally nodded. "That is good to know." After a moment, he added hesitantly, "Should we talk about this?"

"No." Shaking my head for emphasis, I added, "Definitely not."

His curious gaze went nowhere. "All right, then. I shall . . . join everyone downstairs shortly, once I am presentable."

When I could detect nothing beyond earnestness in his claim, I nodded and turned to move in the direction of the staircase and away from whatever madness had overtaken me for the second time.

I cast one more searching glance over my shoulder before rounding the corner and leaving Silas behind. He stood right where I'd left him, watching me. Just before I moved out of view, his lips curled up on the ends.

I didn't like that look on his face. It felt knowing instead of smug —which was what I would have expected. Shrewd and perceptive were not typically characteristics I attributed to Silas Bartholomew.

But perhaps I should.

Four

MARY

Dinner that evening was a boisterous affair. Glowing candles reflected wide smiles and frequent laughter. Fresh garlands and holly berries adorned the mantels and painted a wide swath down the length of the beautiful dining table.

With all the Bartholomew family members in attendance, I was required to talk very little.

The marchioness was engrossed in her youngest daughter and determined to discuss all things related to the upcoming wedding. Julian, Genevieve's betrothed, was typically very quiet in social settings and seemed to get by now with only nodding and smiling when appropriate.

Emery was her usual engaging and entertaining self. Augie hadn't looked in my direction once. Poor man. We'd scandalized him. Miles, Patty, and Franny also joined in the conversation, and for much of the evening, the chatter and voices were louder than the cutlery and serving utensils.

It was rowdy and chaotic in the best way. So very different from the silent dinners I endured in my own home. This wild love between so many people was on abundant display among the beautiful place settings and lavish meal. I wanted this. Desperately, I realized as I sat, taking it all in. I ached for my own children settled around a holiday table, bickering and teasing while I watched them indulgently and lovingly. It was a vivid picture. One I had imagined so often in my mind's eye. And one that reflected back to me now in stark contrast to the reality of my future.

Silas's voice floated to me from across the table. I shifted in my seat and looked up. Silas had indeed straightened his appearance. His hair was freshly styled, the longer hair on top swooping elegantly away from his face. The gray at his temples shining silver in the warm candlelight. Silas had donned a fashionable waistcoat with a maroon-patterned design and elaborate stitching along the lapels.

I self-consciously touched the coil of red hair resting along my collarbone and wondered if I appeared as unaffected as he did— as if nothing of consequence had taken place that afternoon. What would it be like to feel completely at ease with one's decisions? Entirely unencumbered by uncertainty or discomfort? I suppose that was the same as asking what would it be like to be a man? Specifically, Silas Bartholomew—unaffected rascal and consummate people-pleaser.

We were seated across from one another with several comfortable chairs and the length of the table between us. He'd behaved normally—telling stories and dominating the conversation when he could wrestle it away from Emery. It was a familiar song and dance.

I'd remained quiet for the most part, chiming in here and there when appropriate, mostly to Franny who was seated at my side.

Throughout the evening, I'd ruminated over the survival madness that had instigated the incident in the carriage as well as the residual madness that had struck unexpectedly in the cupboard. I'd reached an uncomfortable conclusion. There was a *slight* chance that I was attracted to Silas. And for all his aggravating and insufferable ways, there was something to be said for the honesty that existed between us.

When I conducted myself in society, I carefully considered my manners and softened my harsh edges—the ones that were too loud and opinionated, brash and headstrong. For that very reason, I was never more myself than when battling with Silas. It felt freeing to say what I meant for once, no matter how outlandish or outspoken. I couldn't ignore the thrill I got from riling Silas up and being riled in return. Perhaps our recent exchanges were simply another version of that instigating sort of freedom.

The question remained: did I want it to continue?

A physical relationship had been the entire point of the list—the very one that Silas had spied. However, engaging with Silas would complicate things greatly. I'd only put him on my list of potential gentlemen on a lark, never actually intending to pursue an arrangement with him. He was frequently insufferable, after all. Should a pregnancy result from intimacies with Silas, it could very well end my friendships with Patty and Emery and Genevieve. They wouldn't understand. And some part of me thought Silas would never stand by while his child was raised a bastard, away from him and his family. He'd demand rights and a relationship and, in all likelihood, marriage. He was just that sort of person— demanding but also principled. It was the Bartholomew way. All of those possibilities made a liaison with the man too risky, no matter how maddeningly good he felt beneath my hands.

If I thought my suppertime reflection and solitude had gone unnoticed, I was mistaken. Halfway through the fish course, Emery called, like a heathen from two seats away, "Mary, what are you so maudlin about down there? I've hardly heard your voice at all tonight."

I paused with my fork in the air and briefly locked eyes with Silas. "Well, I was quite famished and keeping my mouth busy with eating, Emery."

The middle Bartholomew daughter peered around Patty, who sat between us, and eyed me skeptically before replying, "There are many ways to keep a mouth busy."

At this confident pronouncement, Augie spewed the wine he'd been drinking in a brilliant spray of fine red mist.

Everyone stared in stunned silence as Augie muttered furious apologies and used his linen napkin to wipe his face. Emery patted his back in concerned confusion, and Silas dissolved into laughter. I bit my lip and refused to make eye contact while also fighting the embarrassed flush warming me from the chest up.

"I propose a toast," Silas called out suddenly, drawing everyone's attention, including mine. His brown eyes sparkled as he smiled my way. "Although, you be careful over there, Augie. Perhaps you've had enough." Augie gave him a flat, unamused glare.

Undaunted, Silas continued, "A toast to my mother. The marchioness has the finest table this side of London—red wine stains notwithstanding—and it is through her hospitality and festivity that we are fortunate enough to gather for celebration and camaraderie. Thank you, Mother." He raised his glass, and the rest of us joined in, murmuring praise and gratitude.

Joy radiated from the marchioness, and conversation resumed. Augie's blunder and my atypical behavior were not brought up again. Silas's distraction had seen to that.

Silas looked my way once more, wearing a knowing smirk. He gave me a little wink that did interesting things to my middle.

I could feel my gaze linger as he turned easily to speak with his mother and father. He gestured with his hands and seemed to take up so much space, forever joyful and open with his expressions. It was difficult to imagine Silas being calculating. And certainly not for my benefit. But he had. He'd turned the attention of everyone away from me.

The feeling of gratitude was unexpected but not unwelcome. And I began to wonder what else I'd overlooked regarding this man.

The following day was once again snowy and wet. Patty and Emery remained in their own homes with their families while I wandered around within Laurel Park. Genevieve and Julian were out in the gardens, throwing snowballs at one another and just generally being adorably in love.

I made my way to the library, intent on picking out a novel— something with adventure—and whiling away the afternoon in front of a fire.

I stopped abruptly upon entering the bright space when I noticed Silas perusing the bookshelves. He was in profile and noticed me immediately.

"Good day, Lady Mary," he said with a warm smile.

I cleared my throat and took a step back. "Hello."

"You needn't go." He turned to face me and leaned a shoulder casually on the tall bookcase, crossing his arms over his wide chest. "I think there are enough books here for the both of us."

With another small step backward, I was nearly in the corridor. "I do not wish to disturb you."

His grin widened. "I am rarely disturbed. Come," he said easily. "I promise to keep my hands to myself."

I scowled at the reminder, eager to move on from his hands and his lips and the rest of him.

Survival madness. Oh God. Could the snow bring it on again?

My eyes drifted to the large windows that peered out over the white landscape as I considered. Probably best to leave and not tempt fate or whatever this was.

"Mary." Silas said my name around a laugh. "We are adults. Were you not the one yesterday telling me I was being ridiculous by avoiding you?"

"I don't believe those were my exact words—"

He rolled his eyes. "You know what I mean. You can stand to be in a room with me."

If the sudden heat in my center was anything to go by, I wasn't so sure.

I swallowed reflexively and took tentative steps into the library. That in and of itself annoyed me. I didn't do anything tentatively, and here I was, tiptoeing around Silas because I didn't trust myself around him. It felt necessary to be cautious, however. No one invited recklessness into their lives. I was simply being mindful. There was no shame in that.

In answer, I walked along the shelves, barely noting the book spines. I could feel Silas's eyes following me.

"This is a good one," he offered, holding up a burgundy cover, "if you're in the mood for romance."

I kept up my perusal, refusing to take the bait. "I am not."

"Pity," Silas murmured. I could hear him slide the book back onto the shelf.

His footsteps sounded on the wooden floors, and my constant awareness of him did little to dispel my grumpy mood or my frantically beating heart. Forcing a deep breath, I stopped and made myself look for a novel. The sooner I found something, the sooner I could escape this over-warm room.

Retreat was a version of admitting defeat, but at this moment, it felt necessary, and I'd allow it.

Silas approached my side as I examined titles. Unfortunately, I seemed to be in the section of the library devoted to farming implements and agricultural practices. Dammit.

"Can I ask you something?" He'd resumed his casual lean against the bookshelf, except this time, he was three feet away from me, his gaze fixed on the side of my face.

"I suppose," I replied as I thumbed through a volume on . . . something with crop rotation.

"Why is Lord Ashby at the top of your list?"

I closed my eyes briefly. I did not want to have this discussion. Everything had snowballed out of control with Silas since he'd found that bloody list.

"I'm not judging," Silas offered magnanimously. "Just curious what put the baron in the number one position? I haven't noticed you in one another's company."

James Letford, the Baron of Ashby, was someone I'd known all my life. We were very close in age, and our families had neighboring properties in the country. Our mothers were dear friends, and James and I had been thrown together a great deal in our youth as a result. We didn't typically congregate now, as adults, as we tended toward differing circles, but he was someone I retained a fondness for and always greeted happily as a result. Lord Ashby was, simply put, a very nice person. I didn't feel any sort of attraction to him, per se, but when I'd considered an arrangement and the potential future father of my child, his gentle smile and kind gray eyes had come to mind immediately.

But I couldn't say all that to Silas, so instead, I kept my eyes trained on the page in front of me and estimated yearly crop yields and offered mildly, "Lord Ashby and I are friendly."

"Hmm."

I ignored Silas's curious gaze and kept thumbing through the pages.

"What about Simon Edgemoore?"

"We are acquainted." I pulled out a new book bound in black cloth. Ah, animal husbandry. The secret desire of my heart.

"Lord Montcroft?"

Flipping to a random page and fixing my stare, I replied, "Rumors indicate that he is in need of companionship."

Silas snorted. "And Viscount Hornwick?"

"He has a reputation." That bit was actually true. It was common knowledge and well-gossiped that Lord Hornwick was an expert and accomplished lover. Both widows and married ladies alike claimed an enjoyable encounter with the handsome viscount. When the sherry was flowing and lips were loosened, I'd heard stories of bedsport and prowess that had even my eyebrows rising. I had not been above placing him in the top five when I'd made the list.

Silas remained quiet for a moment while I scanned the page before me with unseeing eyes. "You must know that you play a dangerous game seeking an arrangement in this manner, Lady Mary."

I paused, frozen with righteous indignation. Silas presumed too much. This was not his place, and he had no right to question my choices. My very private choices that he'd merely stumbled upon.

Of course it was dangerous and ill-advised. That was what last resorts were for. If I wasn't desperate, I would be married with a child already. I wouldn't have the need of a list at all. Or I would have been brave enough to create my own family with a child from the orphanage. Or I would have continued visiting the secret brothel in South London that catered to rich society ladies in need of male courtesans—the one I'd told no one about during my visits last year. Not even Patty.

But I found, after months of seeking intimacies in exchange for coin, I could no longer stomach the fantasy. Too many times, the men there—handsome and attentive as they were—had called me beautiful as they'd worshipped my body. But I knew the truth. Hell, gentlemen had called me horse-faced behind my back, laughed about my appearance and too-lean figure. The men at that brothel were paid to create an illusion—one that made me uncomfortable in my own skin. I didn't need trite commentary and assurances to accompany my intimacies. And that was why I'd made the list in a last-ditch effort for a future I desperately wanted.

Finally, I turned and gave Silas my attention, fully prepared to lash out about boundaries and minding his own damn business.

But his expression was solemn, troubled. "What you desire will require discretion. And after seeing Conrad Hamilton on your list, I find myself quite concerned."

It was my turn to roll my eyes. "You are one to talk."

Silas made an affronted sound, rarely seen frown lines bracketing his mouth. "I can keep a secret."

I laughed loudly despite my unease, returning my gaze to the book I still held.

"I can," he insisted, glaring at my profile.

With a side-long look, I said, "Silas, you love gossip. You're worse than my mother. And you would talk to anyone. About anything. Your mouth is nearly always at work."

He raised a brow. "I didn't hear you complaining about my mouth yesterday."

The memory of his lips dragging purposely along my throat flashed brilliantly in my mind like a firework. Heat detonated throughout my body as a result, but I frowned in response. "Go away. I am reading."

"Invested in livestock management, are you?" he deadpanned.

I slammed the book closed. "I shall take my leave. I'd rather be bored all afternoon than remain with you one more moment in this room."

"Don't let me stop you," Silas said as he pushed off from the bookcase and gestured in a sweeping motion to the doorway with his bare hand.

After sliding the book back into place on the shelf, I stepped smoothly around the giant horse's ass and walked with purpose toward the exit.

"We both know that your ranking system is faulty anyhow," Silas called out.

I whirled to face him. "Is that so?" My tone was all challenge, and I could only imagine the fierceness in my expression.

Unbothered, Silas kept his arms crossed as he closed the distance between us, coming to stand toe to toe with me. "After this week, you must admit that my position in last place is not deserved. And Lord Ashby would have no idea what to do with you."

I scoffed. "Of course this is all about your precious, delicate male pride." That was all it had been about, I realized with no small amount of hurt. "You weren't last because I thought you'd be a bore in the bedchamber, Silas. You were last because of this." I motioned between us. "We irritate one another relentlessly. We've never made it through a meal or a conversation without bickering and fighting to the bitter, bloody end."

"Well, perhaps that is why it feels the way it does."

I frowned. "What way?"

Like whiskey lit by firelight, his warm brown eyes caressed every part of my face before lingering on my lips. "When we touch. It feels like a battle—one where I am desperate to get closer, to feel as much of you as I possibly can." He raised his hand as if to touch my arm before pulling back and dropping it to his side. "All the energy we devote to fighting with one another channeled into needing more. Aching for it."

The words he spoke mirrored the thoughts I'd been having regarding what we'd done—how we'd reacted, explosive and unexpected. And hearing them spoken from his full lips so softly and reverently had my pulse thundering beneath my skin.

This wasn't supposed to happen.

We were supposed to hate each other.

My voice emerged embarrassingly breathless as I countered weakly, "It was survival—"

"Madness, I know," Silas interrupted. "You said so yesterday."

But we were already drifting closer, his lips barely grazing my cheekbone. Silas rested his forehead against mine and said quietly, "Earlier. I promised to keep my hands to myself. If you want me to touch you, you're going to have to tell—"

My body overwhelmed my good sense. The newly awakened heat between us made the decision for me. "I want you to touch me." I breathed the words against his mouth as I snaked my hands under his coat and around his waist, drawing him to me.

And then we were moving together. This kiss was different from the others. We weren't rushing and fighting for dominance. It was more like we were working together to achieve the closeness Silas had mentioned—the desperate ache to feel as much of each other as possible.

His hands cupped my jaw as the kiss deepened, tongues seeking and searching, delving within. I pressed my body as close as my skirts would allow, loving his heat and the way his hard planes felt against me.

Our movements were less frantic and hurried, but I still couldn't get near enough. In that moment, I wanted Silas to absorb me. To feel us wrapped together, warm and eager and a little mad for each other.

It felt good to be wanted. The sudden force of it made me just as desperate to keep it, to never let it go. Even if the inexplicable desire Silas felt for me ticked away like the hands on a pocket watch, we had this moment. And I wanted it.

Silas's hands left my face. His arms closed around me, enfolding me and drawing me in. I sighed into his mouth, a barely audible moan of relief.

We were touching everywhere, blood heating and desire simmering in my veins.

Silas's head snapped up suddenly, and I felt cool air rush in, filling the space he'd vacated and bringing with it blessed sanity. I heard the voices then and the reason for his swift retreat. Our eyes locked as Genevieve and Julian spoke from somewhere beyond the library, likely the hallway. No matter how isolated and consumed I'd felt in this space moments ago, the voices were a stark reminder . . . we were not alone nor were we behaving properly.

With quick movements, Silas disentangled himself and snatched my hand, leading me to an alcove in the back of the library. It was a small recess behind a pillar in the seating area. A candelabra sat atop the pillar, along with a large fern. I felt quite hidden behind the plant's fronds, but it wouldn't save us if Gen and Julian decided to enter the library for any reason. However, it would provide adequate cover from anyone strolling by the open doors of the large room.

I could feel the chair rail digging into my back as I pressed myself to the wall, attempting to make my breaths deep and even. Genevieve's laughter drifted closer as Julian murmured something low and indistinguishable. Silas still clutched my hand in his as we stood shoulder to shoulder.

My eyes cut to his, finding him already watching me. A mischievous smile lit his features, and I fought the urge to laugh. We were behaving ridiculously, hiding like children.

As the sounds of our interruption faded away, Silas released a huff of laughter. "What are we doing?"

A tiny thorn embedded itself beneath my skin at the incredulousness I heard in his deep voice. Silas had obviously realized the lunacy of our actions and regretted them.

I pulled my hand away abruptly, stung by his implications and, God help me, disappointment.

Silas's words came from behind me as I maneuvered out of the alcove, intent on fleeing. "Augie was right. We each have rooms in this house. We needn't hide in cupboards or against bookshelves. We're being short-sighted."

My feet slowed in their attempt to escape as understanding dawned. I turned to look at him. "Are you saying you want to sneak into my room?"

His smile was wicked. "Do you want me to sneak into your room?"

I stood frozen. My mind shuffled through scenarios and ramifications if this—this whatever this was between us—went any further. What we'd done thus far hadn't hurt anyone. Well, save Augie.

Silas and I could forget our unbelievable lapse in judgment had ever happened and still keep our strange, antagonistic relationship intact. No one would know. No one would be hurt. Patty and Emery and Genevieve would never find out that I'd had several moments of weakness with their brother.

The thought of sitting across from Silas Bartholomew at a dinner party years from now and not knowing how deep this well of attraction really went was suddenly unfathomable. I had never felt as truly desired as when Silas was holding me and kissing me.

Could I be selfish in this? Allow myself to experience what very well might be the only enjoyable lovemaking I'd ever know?

Bravery couldn't exist without fear. Staring at Silas now and the playful tilt of his lips and the mischievous twinkle in his eyes, I'd never been so afraid. He was temptation and poor decision-making in a gray wool suit. He was also the only person who'd ever made me feel wanted in my entire life.

So, I overlooked my instincts and better judgment. Cast aside my misgivings and ignored the warnings shouting from within.

I met Silas's warm brown gaze and nodded once, decisive and intent. "Tonight."

His amusement fell away in fragments, not all at once. The suggestive gleam in his eye softened and the challenging purse of his mouth relaxed into sincerity. He straightened imperceptibly and confirmed in a reverent tone, "Tonight."

Bravery carried me out of the library. It made my gait even and my steps unhurried. I could only hope it wouldn't abandon me when I needed it most—tonight.

Five

SILAS

Twenty-two minutes to midnight.

I picked up the clock from my bedside table and held it to my ear. The ticking hands appeared to be functioning correctly, but for some reason, the last hour had felt like the length and breadth of a Sunday sermon at the village church. Vicar Edmonds had always been painfully monotone and, unfortunately, consistently thorough.

I lay back on my bed, arms crossed behind my head, staring straight up at my canopy.

I'd wait until the quarter-hour chime. Just to ensure that the majority of the servants were abed, and I wouldn't, Lord willing, run into Genevieve in the guest corridor—sneaking into Julian's room.

I shuddered at the thought. There were just some things one did not wish to see of one's baby sister. I frowned, considering how Genevieve and I were separated by a dozen years, yet she was old enough to be betrothed. She and Julian would be married in the spring. They'd start a life together and presumably a family. Their very recent engagement would see all the Bartholomew daughters —all three of my younger sisters—settled happily.

And here I was, in my old bedchamber in my family's home. Alone.

Reaching up, I loosened the fabric at my neck, willing away the tightness I felt when I considered being the lone, unattached Bartholomew—the one with no obligations or responsibilities, no one relying on me, and no courtesy title or reputation to uphold.

I craned my neck.

Twenty minutes to midnight.

I rose and walked to check the mirror above my chest of drawers. Removing the cravat entirely, I straightened my sleeves and smoothed down the fabric of my scarlet embroidered waistcoat. I wouldn't need a cravat where I was going anyhow. The fabric parted, revealing the skin of my throat and the day's growth accumulated on my jaw. I took a comb and brushed back the longer strands atop my head. I needed a trim. If it got any longer, it would start to curl.

With a glance at the bedside, I registered the time and took a deep breath. I met my eyes in the mirror and, not for the first time, wondered if I was making a huge mistake.

Dallying with Lady Mary had felt right at the time. In fact, it felt bloody perfect. I'd never experienced such full-bodied attraction before. And I'd had my share of wild nights, youthful indiscretions, and the occasional mistress over the years. But nothing of this magnitude. No encounter resembling the urgency and intensity I felt with Mary.

The overwhelming desire to rip her clothes off was layered oddly upon the urge to make her scowl. We weren't known for being delicate with one another. I wasn't surprised to realize we'd nearly mauled each other when overcome with this insane craving.

But *this* was different. My hands weren't on her right now. We weren't even bickering in a dining room and riling each other up. We'd done that earlier—between nearly getting caught together in the library and now.

Tonight.

I'd offered it in challenge. And Mary had called my bluff.

Nothing about this was instinctual or impulsive. Tonight would be planned. Tonight would be premeditated. And the location for our calculated madness ensured that we would not be interrupted.

Perhaps, even now, Mary might be sitting at her dressing table wondering what she was getting herself into. It was impossible to know. She wasn't exactly an open book. And she was far more likely to bluster through something than admit to anyone—but especially me—that she was uncomfortable.

It was all right for her to change her mind. I'd spent the last hour considering all the ways this could go horribly wrong. Oh, it would feel very right in the moment. I just knew it. Fucking Mary Lovelace would be a revelation.

I didn't get the sense that she was some untried virgin. She'd moved confidently and boldly. There had been no stilted, hesitant touches, no jolts of surprise as our bodies teased and played with one another. And when I'd made her come in that cupboard, she'd known exactly how to get herself there.

Besides, women didn't make lists of potential liaisons if they were guarding their purity for marriage.

Even if she was not ready to further intimacies with me—if she chose not to cross that final barrier—that would be all right. We needn't be joined to enjoy ourselves. That was what I had lips and hands for. I would follow her lead.

The quarter-hour chime.

Time to go.

I decided to forgo my boots and walked quietly on bare feet through the dark hallway. Rounding the corner of the family wing, I passed the top of the staircase and took the first corridor on the right toward the Red Suite, Mary's room for the duration of her stay.

There was no one about, and I breathed a sigh of relief.

With quiet intent, I raised my hand and tapped lightly on the door.

But a moment passed before it flew open, and Mary dragged me inside. I caught a flash of white silk nightgown before she was on me, wrapping her arms around my neck and muffling my surprised grunt with her perfect pink lips.

I held my arms aloft as if I was being confronted by footpads and pulled my mouth away to suck in a breath. "Wait a moment. Shouldn't we talk about this?"

"No talking." Mary shook her head, her flame-red hair free and loose, falling around her slim shoulders and down her back.

The sight of her—wild and unbound—slowed my thoughts for a moment before I regrouped and managed, "I think it would be wise if we had a discussion."

Her lips explored my neck and the skin visible in the absence of my cravat. "When have you ever cared about doing what was wise?" She hardly paused in her ministrations, and the insult vibrated the delicate skin she'd uncovered on her persistent voyage.

Mary's tongue dipped into the base of my throat, and my eyes rolled back before I caught myself and caught her as well. I gently grasped her shoulders to stall her progress any farther down my body. "Mary." It was a reprimand and a plea all at once.

Her lips paused against my chest, but she didn't move to step away. I felt her sigh, warm and heavy through the fine lawn of my shirt.

"I didn't come here just to get this over with," I said gently, pressing a tender kiss to her hair. "If you've changed your mind—"

"I haven't," she said quickly. So quickly that I took a step back to put distance between us.

I was surprised to glance up and see that she'd dragged me halfway to the bed when she'd pounced on me upon entry.

Frustrated brown eyes landed on mine. They held accusation and something else . . . knowing, perhaps. Mary looked at me as if she expected me to back out on tonight's arrangement. She confirmed it when she snapped, "I'm surprised you showed up at all. If this wasn't what you wanted."

I kept my expression and my voice deliberately even. She expected me to rise to her bait. What she didn't realize was that I'd already been caught and hooked straight through. "I do want this—want you. I just need you to be sure. And I don't intend to rush. Every moment together thus far has been hurried and inter-rupted." I took a step closer, reclaiming the space I'd intention-ally put between us a moment ago. "I want to take my time with you."

Mary examined my face. It was impossible to know what she was looking for—sincerity, signs of falsehood, worthiness.

But I couldn't make this decision for her. She had to want this —*want us*—all on her own.

"There should be rules," Mary finally said, eyebrows still drawn in consternation.

"All right."

"Don't say that I'm—don't lie to me. Don't say things in the heat of the moment because you think I want to hear them. No false compliments or platitudes. Just . . . be honest with me."

My mind wandered across uneasy terrain, wondering what had happened in her past that she felt the need to stipulate such a command. Regardless, I nodded. "I won't lie to you."

"Good," she murmured around a hard swallow. "And this has to stay between us."

I nodded, content to be her dirty little secret.

"Any more rules?" I asked as I carefully brushed her long hair back over her shoulder.

She seemed to hesitate for a moment at my innocent touch before finally saying, "Just make sure you withdraw when the time comes."

"Of course."

An impish smile tilted the corners of her lips. "You know, I always assumed that you taking your time with me would involve all manner of medieval torture."

I allowed my smile to bloom. "We can try that if you'd like."

That enticing flush I enjoyed so much started working its way up her chest and across her collarbones. I traced the progress of her heating skin with my eyes before following along with my fingertips.

Stepping closer, I skimmed my touch up the column of her throat, enjoying the contrast between my sun-kissed hand and her milk-pale skin. I whispered, "Where else can I make you blush, I wonder? Hmm."

Bold brown eyes met mine as I finally cupped her cheeks. "I guess we'll find out," she replied.

Leaning in, I brought my smiling lips to hers.

For the first time, our kiss felt less like a battle and more like a dance. We nipped and teased, circled and melted into one another. We worked together instead of pulling apart. Finally, our goals were one and the same.

Impatient hands unbuttoned my waistcoat. I assisted by removing my shirt, only breaking the kiss to let the fabric pass over my head. Mary's tentative fingers found the line of my sternum and the hair on my chest. She stroked slowly over the planes of my pectorals down to my stomach. An involuntary jolt had our lips disconnecting as she dipped curious fingers below my waistband.

But I wanted to feel her, too.

Reaching down, I gathered the smooth fabric of her nightgown and pulled it up until she was bared to me. Her hair settled in a wild tangle on her naked flesh as I tossed the gown aside. Several rebellious strands fell across the pale skin of her chest—one distracting curl landing on the tip of a rosy nipple. Her breasts were small—perfect for my eager mouth. And the fiery thatch of hair hiding her womanhood was nestled between two slender thighs that my fingers ached to part.

While I looked my fill, marveling at her long lines and impossibly smooth skin, I noticed Mary shift uncomfortably from foot to foot. My eyes snapped to hers. She looked so uncertain and anxious that I abandoned my visual exploration and pulled her close. Our chests pressed flush to one another, and the relief and feeling of her skin on mine had a sigh escaping my lips.

"Boring you, am I?" she inquired cheekily. I could feel her voice vibrating against me—the bare intimacy so unexpected that I couldn't reprimand her smart remark with my suddenly tight voice. So I reached down and pinched her bottom instead. Her surprised yelp and subsequent laughter made me smile into the delicate skin of her throat.

Once I was there, I trailed my lips down to her shoulder. Mary's laughter cut off on a quiet moan as my tongue traced an aimless pattern over her sensitive skin. She angled her head to the side, giving me more room and providing access to continue my ministrations.

And continue I did.

My lips and tongue and teeth traversed a meandering path, lazy and unhurried. I guided Mary to the bed and settled over her, continuing my leisurely exploration as her hands roved my back and shoulders. I became intimately acquainted with the stark edges of her hip bones, the pert tips of her nipples, and the delicate skin of her inner wrist. The latter of which elicited a surprising sound of pleasure, so I made note to return to the spot often.

The lavender scent of her skin welcomed me with the warmth of a summer day. Sweet and fragrant as the gardens at Laurel Park.

Mary's hands were busy in return, tentative at first, then bold in their exploration. After unbuttoning the falls of my trousers, she pushed them down my hips. Her fingers lingered on the return trip, nails scoring my ass and causing me to thrust forward without meaning to. She was hot and wet as my cock pressed against all her soft, secret places, and it took everything in me to pull away. It wasn't time. I wasn't ready for this to be over.

I eased back, kissing my way back down her body. I ran my nose from hip bone to hip bone breathing her in until she squirmed against me, tugging me higher until our lips were on each other once more.

"Now." She breathed out an impatient sound. "I can't wait any longer."

I smiled. "But I wasn't done torturing you."

Her eyes narrowed and the retort was poised there on the tip of her tongue. I could see it as plainly as an arrow nocked, quivering and ready to fire. But then an errant lock of my hair fell forward between us. Mary's brilliant eyes followed the movement. In her distraction, she reached forward and so very gently brushed the strand back into place. The touch—so simple and benign compared to the other ways she'd touched me this night—had me leaning into her, pressing close to her hand, eager for the caress to extend. Instead, her eyes caught on mine, and we shared a long look rife with tenderness and longing and feelings neither of us were prepared to voice.

The moment passed, and she repeated, "Now." It wasn't as plaintive as a plea, nor would she ever be one to beg, but I could tell from her tone and her expression that I'd pushed her as far as she'd allow.

Lady Mary would need to get used to the idea of being romanced.

Releasing some of the tension holding me back, I settled more fully against her. Mary's legs widened farther in response. Her breathing quickened as I pushed forward. Closing my eyes, I dropped my forehead to her shoulder and groaned. She was tight. So snug and warm. And I needed a moment.

As we breathed together, we waited for our bodies to adjust to being so intimately connected. I forced myself to pause until she was ready for more, but my body ached to move, to demand, to conquer.

Finally, I felt Mary's hips tilt—a tiny questioning thrust.

I raised my head and said, "All right?"

Her smile unfurled slow and wicked before she nodded once.

Time and space compressed. Our movements simplified to the most necessary elements—heavy breaths and essential touches. Slow, drugging kisses that matched my deep, grinding thrusts. I could feel Mary winding tighter and tighter, seeking and searching. And when our movements became hurried—her thighs high on my sides and her hands clasped behind my neck—I reached between us to relieve the tension pulling her muscles taut. I caressed her center in small circles. That extra touch, just where she needed it, had her back arching and her mouth dropping open on a forceful exhale.

As my pleasure consumed me soon thereafter, I had a moment to appreciate the incredulous journey that had brought us to this point.

My own foolish, stubborn pride had instigated all this. I'd wanted to prove something in that carriage. Instead, I'd been taught a valuable lesson.

Never underestimate Mary Lovelace.

After a slight hesitation, I rapped my knuckles in an upbeat pattern to the door of my father's study.

"Silas, come in!" he called, already knowing it was me.

I pushed the door wide and entered the large room. The Marquess of Northcutt sat behind a wide oak desk wearing a warm smile I matched with one of my own.

"How are you faring today?"

I cleared my throat and sat in one of the upholstered chairs facing my cheerful father. "I am well. Eager for some clear weather to escape outdoors."

Father chuckled knowingly. "You've never been one to sit still."

I smiled through the comment. It wasn't intended as a slight—simply a fact. But my father's words caused my mind to snag, like an unexpected splinter beneath my palm.

Shifting in the chair, I replied after a moment, "That is true."

My father wasn't wrong. For many years, all I'd wanted was to travel and see the world—taste exotic foods, meet new people, experience anything and everything beyond the borders of England. After university, I'd been constantly on the move with only occasional visits to see my family at Laurel Park or Patty in London. My mother had been intent on marrying me off, and that, admittedly, had contributed to so much time away. I didn't want to be badgered about finding a bride every time I set foot in Hampshire. With Emery's marriage to Augie, Mother had calmed her matchmaking tendencies quite a bit. And now she was fully invested in Genevieve's upcoming wedding. A brief respite awaited me in her meddling ways.

But I realized, as my siblings grew, how much I enjoyed being a consistent fixture in their lives. We were a close bunch. And I knew how rare that was among the aristocracy. However, I genuinely enjoyed spending time with my sisters and their husbands, being an uncle to my nieces and nephew. The prospect of visiting the Mediterranean held less and less appeal as my relationships grew closer.

And part of me thought, it was, perhaps, time I settled down.

Even my baby sister had found her future. She'd discovered her other half in Julian, and something about that notion left me feeling like the odd man out.

The Bartholomew voted least likely to succeed.

"Was there anything you needed, Silas?" My father's voice dragged me from my unexpected personal reflection.

"No, Father," I answered automatically, but then backtracked. "Actually, I wanted to see if I could be of any assistance. With the estate or any of your duties."

My father did not speak, but his brow furrowed in confusion.

I leaned forward in my chair. "Is there anything at all?"

He laughed lightly in response. "No, Silas. I can't think of a single thing. You'll be marquess one day, and then you can be saddled with correspondence and solicitors and land managers and investors and stewards and neighbors."

"But surely, I can be of some help."

"While I greatly appreciate the offer," my father began, "you should enjoy your freedom. You haven't taken a trip in a while. You could escape this moody English weather and head south. Perhaps that would make you feel better."

I hadn't said I felt bad. Just a bit at loose ends.

I didn't possess the responsibilities or obligations that often took up Miles's and Augie's time. With no courtesy title to see to or investments to manage, there was little in my day-to-day life that went beyond amusement. I received an allowance from my father's estate . . . like a child. I didn't even possess my own lodgings in London. I stayed with my siblings while in town. I was practically a vagabond.

Perhaps my father noted my awkward silence because he removed his spectacles and clasped his hands together, leaning forward on his desk. "Or perhaps Miles and Julian would like a consultant for Owensby Stud Farm. I'm certain you could find any number of things to occupy your time."

Nodding absently, I considered how little help I could possibly be on a horse farm or in the planning stages of said horse farm. Young Julian was the real brains and experience behind that operation. Miles was the motivation and the capital. I really only knew how to ride a horse. I couldn't imagine they'd need me for that.

Ignoring Father's helpful suggestions, I said, "I think I should like to acquire a home in London."

"That is a grand idea, son." My father's enthusiasm for such an uninspired aspiration made me feel like a child again. It was as if he was exclaiming over a particularly heartfelt squiggle and calling it art. "Feel free to ask Mr. Hodges for assistance. I'm certain he'll have knowledge of several wonderful properties."

Mr. Hodges was our family's long-time solicitor.

I nodded. "Thank you, Father. I will visit him upon my return to London."

Establishing my own household could be the first step in settling down. The first very literal step, but progress nonetheless.

Perhaps it was time I found a wife. I was four and thirty after all. The idea of marriage had never really appealed before mostly due to my mother's insistence and constant expectations. But with age came responsibilities. I would approach spouse-hunting the old-fashioned way. With courtship and familial connections, a marriage contract and a dowry. As opposed to how my sisters had done it—by falling in love. The idiots.

I would dance at balls and pay calls and find an appropriate match —the way it is typically done.

And be the rascally Bartholomew son no longer.

Everyone had to grow up sometime.

Yes, that was a capital idea. It would make my mother exceed-ingly happy should I find a beautiful, well-spoken, and demure young lady to be marchioness someday.

The thought of the perfect debutante had my mind drifting to a very different sort of woman.

Mary had left for London two days ago. My mother had invited her to stay on and spend Christmas with us since the house party had effectively been ruined by the weather. And with her own mother away, Mary hardly had a family celebration to go home to. But she'd said she needed to return due to obligations at the orphanage. I knew of her involvement with Patty's home for chil-dren in Bethnal Green, but I was surprised to realize that the bulk of Mary's charitable giving was her time. She apparently took great pride in delivering presents and spending time with the chil-dren on a regular basis.

Part of me wondered if she'd felt the need to escape.

We'd spent our nights together for nearly a fortnight, but we hadn't discussed it at all. We'd simply fallen into bed together. I'd never experienced anything like it, and the thought of this newfound connection being severed left me confused and at loose ends.

Both everything and nothing had changed. We'd lived a secret, separate life for the duration of Mary's stay in Hampshire. During the day, we behaved normally without avoiding each other. We still squabbled and bickered as was our way and what everyone expected. But at night, I'd tiptoe to her guest suite, and she'd be waiting at the door in her silk nightgown, and one very memorable night, in nothing at all.

The thought of her standing tall and proud, her long red hair covering her breasts while she held a single candle and a wicked expression had blood rushing toward my groin. I shifted uncomfortably in my chair and reminded myself that I was still in my father's study.

It didn't matter that we hadn't discussed this odd arrangement. I wasn't hurt that she hadn't asked for more or even invited me to sleep in her bed through the night. I knew Mary could be calculating and mercenary when needed. One didn't have a list of potential gentlemen for liaisons without a pragmatic approach to life.

I refused to allow her departure from Laurel Park to bother me. Nor did I fret over her lack of a goodbye. If I was a touch disappointed, then that would be my own problem. We'd had our fun together, and I wouldn't be the needy bastard demanding more of her.

Clearing my throat, I thanked my father for his time and rose to standing.

He eyed me curiously, but before he could reply, I said happily, "I believe Emery and Augie and the children will be here shortly. I'm going to indulge my niece and join her in her efforts to acquire a puppy."

Father laughed, as I'd intended. "Good luck. But no bloodshed at the dinner table. Your mother hates when Emery throws cutlery."

I laughed as well, thinking how entertaining it was to annoy my sister—how enjoyable it was, in general, to be a part of my siblings' lives. I'd made the right decision to discontinue my travels. Being a supportive brother and beloved uncle brought me more joy than the beautiful and wondrous things I'd seen in my youth.

And now, the time for becoming a respectable and reputable gentleman was upon me.

Six

MARY

"Lady Mary! Come see my drawing!"

"Of course, darling," I said with a smile and moved to sit beside little Jeffrey.

The great hall was warm and cozy today despite the chill of the late December day. And the Watford Home for Children was abuzz with energetic and excitable children. I'd delivered their Christmas gifts, each thoughtfully selected by Patty and myself.

"What a beautiful horse you've drawn. I must have this artwork for my sitting room."

Jeffrey, the little boy of seven, beamed happily, displaying his missing two front teeth. "Would you really hang it on your wall, Lady Mary?"

I smiled, fighting a rush of emotion at the delight I saw reflected on his sweet face. "I would be honored."

There hadn't always been joyful Yuletide celebrations for the children here. Patty had acquired the orphanage over a decade ago with the funds she'd inherited from the death of the old duke per her marriage contract. She and I had visited the facility in Bethnal Green before she'd become the owner. Before the building had been renovated. Before there were classrooms and tutors and music lessons and the sounds of happy, well-fed children within its walls.

My friend had changed lives for the better all those years ago while I'd simply stared on in horror. The reason for our initial visit had been my idea. In my desperation to have a child, I'd begged Patty to come with me. I'd been foolhardy and determined to raise a child on my own if I couldn't land a husband. Looking back, I could see how poorly I'd reacted to overheard gossip. I'd listened to women call me "firmly on the shelf" and gentlemen mock my appearance. As a result, I'd concluded that the traditional methods of gaining a family were no longer available to me.

However, upon arriving at the dilapidated and understaffed orphanage—then called the Kellerman Asylum—I'd felt nothing but despair. How could I choose one child to bestow my love and affection upon when there were so many in need? My barely constructed plan for ruination and scandal had wilted under the weight of hopelessness.

But not Patty. It had merely hardened her resolve. She'd bought the orphanage and began an extensive renovation to make it a place where children were educated and cared for. A place where they had a future. I'd joined Patty in visitations—slowly and carefully at first. And now that Patty and Miles and Franny spend so much time in Hampshire, I'd become a sort of advocate for my friend. I visited the children weekly and conducted any Watford business while Patty remained in the country. I worked closely with the headmistress. And I'd finally found something that brought me joy and gave me purpose.

What started as a painful reminder had become my life's work.

I was making a difference for all the children, not just saving one —as I'd seen it all those years ago.

And perhaps my current plot to have a family was just as reckless as the original.

Thus far, nothing had gone as planned.

First, Silas had discovered my secret, and then we'd become a secret of our own.

Despite his name being on my list, I hadn't ever truly considered Silas for the role of lover.

There were too many complications. And that was why I'd asked him to withdraw every time we'd been intimate. Establishing rules would keep us out of trouble.

Using Silas to achieve my aims felt wrong. I wasn't his mistress, and he wasn't my protector. There were no expectations in our arrangement, whereas gentlemen who kept women knew the ever-present risk of pregnancy.

Additionally, there was the very real fear that I could ruin my friendships with the Bartholomews. They would likely be horrified by what Silas and I had done. Continuing on in some sort of arrangement would only increase our chances of being found out and for potential feelings to become involved. We hadn't discussed any sort of future meetings. In fact, outside of the Red Suite, we'd pretended nothing improper was happening. Deep down, we both knew that persisting with this . . . this madness was entirely unwise.

I had no problem being someone's secret. That was ultimately my goal—just with someone else. Someone from the list.

Someone less complicated. Someone who was not Silas Bartholomew.

I hadn't changed my mind. I would pursue an arrangement with one of the gentlemen I'd indicated on the paper hidden within my journal. The incidents with Silas would be forgotten. It didn't truly matter how remarkable our encounters had been. And they had been shockingly fantastic—each time better than the last. Yet it hadn't always been frantic lovemaking. Some nights had been teasing with just as much laughter and smiles as breathy sighs and low moans of pleasure.

Other nights, it had been slow and tender while Silas had kissed every inch of my body with single-minded determination. I had marveled at those times the most. His focus and concentration. The way he was so intent on me, my body, and my pleasure alone. Those laugh lines near his temples went entirely unused. His serious, unsmiling mouth softening only to drag along my skin. The rough scrape of his jaw on the skin of my thigh. I fought a shiver at the remembered sensation.

Seeing another side to Silas had me questioning, once again, the face he wore for polite society. Always jovial and consistently good-humored. I knew what it was to don a mask for the masses. I'd watched my father do it all my life, only to return home and criticize my mother's every misstep. How much of the Silas I'd witnessed had been the real thing? And how much was the person he wanted everyone to see?

My connection with the Bartholomews made things messy with Silas, and it wasn't as if there was a future there anyhow. We'd only end up hurting each other and everyone around us.

Scanning the tables in the great hall and observing the children only made the longing grow deeper. I didn't wish to be on the outside looking in. For that reason, in just a few short days, I'd see to my plan in the new year and pray that someday I'd have a child of my own.

~

Hours later, I was sipping soup in the formal dining room with my father. My mother was still away, so I braced for criticism directed solely at me.

"Where were you today, Mary? Shopping on Bond Street?"

I bit the inside of my cheek. "No, Father. I was at Watford House today visiting the children."

He just barely withheld an eye roll, and my hand tightened around my soup spoon. "I don't know why you waste your time there. The Duchess of Cawthorn sees to all of their needs. They don't require you parading around, pretending to mother them. It surely gives them false hope."

My father continued eating, some of the broth clinging to his thick gray mustache. He'd said his piece and was apparently done with this part of the conversation.

I should just let it go. I would only provoke his ire. It truly did not matter what he thought about the orphanage. Voicing my opinion would do no good in this situation.

And yet, I cleared my throat. "I don't think it gives them false hope, Father. I think it is important for the children to know that they have people who care about them beyond their instructors and Watford staff. And besides, my visits there likely enrich my life substantially more than the children's."

It was this same argument—repeated often over the years—that had deterred me from running away to the country with a ward from the orphanage. That initial visit to Kellerman Asylum for Orphans had weakened my resolve, yes. But years later, when I was regularly visiting the children of Watford House and acting in Patty's stead, there were times I considered taking in a child in such a manner. But my father would have never understood, and I could not afford to be cut off by my family.

"I suppose it does not matter what a spinster does with her time. You are in no danger of attracting a match this season. Not with the crop of young debutantes on the marriage mart."

I gritted my teeth and ignored the familiar insult. The fresh batch of elegant young ladies did not matter. In the privacy of our home, I received the same setdown every season. I would never be enough to attract a husband.

My father's words hardly dented the armor around my heart. Rage simmered instead. I'd never treat a child with such contempt. If only the future I'd envisioned could come to fruition. I could have a family born of love, not resentment. Even if my reputation was tattered and I was forced to spend the rest of my days in the country raising my child, it would be worth it.

I knew Patty would support me—financially and emotionally— with whatever I decided. She was more than my closest friend. She was my sister in all but blood. But a part of me worried I'd always be trying to earn my parents' approval—to make up for the fact that they had been saddled with a daughter that no one wanted to marry. An obligation. A failure.

And somehow I knew that my family would have an easier time accepting a bastard born to their ruined daughter than a child from the orphanage.

My father signaled a footman for more wine.

Our meal devolved into silence and continued that way until it finally concluded, and we bid each other an awkward farewell.

The Viscountess Westbrooke reserved nearly all of her holiday celebration, it seemed. Her grand event was on the eve of the new year and began just after the clock struck midnight. I'd been told that the Lady Westbrooke had welcomed her first guest—the dark-haired and handsome Lord Hornwick—at the door, ensuring his had been the first feet to cross her threshold. The superstition foretold prosperity and good health in the upcoming year as Hornwick had gifted the viscountess Scottish whisky and a large arrangement of greenery.

I'd arrived after all the ceremony and foolishness to an elaborately decorated ballroom and festive wassail and hot mulled wine.

I supposed, the viscountess had done her utmost to ensure a prosperous future. I couldn't begrudge her, for I was doing the same.

Her celebration this night would provide ample opportunity to lay the groundwork for my plan. Several high-ranking gentlemen on my list of potential affairs were in attendance, and I was ready to make myself charming and available. I would need to be discreet but suggestive, alluring yet seductive. I didn't want to scare them away with ideas of marriage and purity. Rather, I wanted to draw them in with the promise of corruption.

The night started off well. I spotted the friendly and affable James Letford, the Baron of Ashby, right away and made my way toward him.

"Good evening, James!"

"Hullo, Mary! Always a pleasure to see you, my dear neighbor," he replied with a wide smile. His drink sloshed a bit over the rim of his glass, but he hardly seemed to notice. "How is your family? I know my mother has been eager to call upon yours."

"They are well, thank you. Mama is away at the moment in Dorset visiting her sister. But I'll mention your mother in my next letter."

James nodded enthusiastically before his eyes drifted briefly over my shoulder.

With a quick glance, I noted several well-dressed young ladies march by with fluttering fans. They paid us no mind. I wondered what had drawn James's attention—or who.

I turned back to find the baron with a blush high on his pale cheeks. He brushed an awkward hand over his golden curls before clearing his throat.

"Well, James, you must tell me how you've been. I don't think I've seen you since the autumn. And I am eager to catch up."

He took the lifeline readily and told me about the horses he'd purchased recently—from Brightleaf Farms, I was happy to hear —and his father's recent travels. I encouraged the conversation and asked pertinent questions, and it was all very natural. James and I got on well. He was like a cousin to me.

And that was part of the problem. Despite his position in the number one spot on my list, I didn't know if I could successfully pursue an improper arrangement with the man. He was perhaps too kind. James would undoubtedly be scandalized by any arrangement I might propose.

The baron continued speaking with a wide grin and large hand movements while I listened along, feeling as seductive as an old boot.

This would never work with James.

Movement beyond the gentleman's gleaming hair caught my notice. Of course Silas would be in attendance. He stood with a group of young men, jovial as ever.

I didn't know why his friendly nature bothered me so much. My own current conversational companion was the human equivalent of a happy hound, and I found Lord Ashby nothing but charming and pleasant.

But something about Silas's constant cheerfulness put me off. At times, it felt like a performance or a role he played to put everyone else at ease. Part of me longed to see him on a bad day —to see the real Silas Bartholomew.

Or perhaps I just longed to see him lose his temper for once. I'd done enough over the years to provoke a reaction. Part of the fun was getting one. The sudden flash of reluctant humor. Exasperation hovering on the edge of his features. I wanted to watch him unravel.

I wanted to unwrap the merriment he swathed himself in and get to the very heart of him.

That wayward thought heralded another. Slipping the buttons free on his waistcoat and peeling the fabric of his trousers down his strong thighs.

"Would you care to dance, Lady Mary?"

Lord Ashby's words shepherded my errant thoughts and drew my gaze away from where it had snagged inadvertently on Silas.

"Yes, of course," I replied too brightly.

But James didn't notice or mind my distraction. He simply smiled his easy grin, teeth gleaming, and led me to the dance floor.

The remainder of the event was not nearly as successful. After bidding James a fond farewell, I managed a reluctant waltz from Lord Montcroft. My ramblings about the delightful music and talented string quartet gained me another unenthusiastic dance partner in Lord Hornwick. But when I sought to continue the conversation following our turn about the dance floor, he practically winced and begged off, insisting he saw someone he needed to speak with right away.

The night felt like a failure as I made my way past a group of giggling young ladies in the process of Bible dipping in order to predict their futures. My tired feet led me to the refreshment table, where I seriously considered calling for my carriage and making my way home at this late hour.

While I was pouring a fresh goblet of mulled wine, a low voice spoke suddenly from my side, "That is a fierce frown you're wearing."

I only just managed not to spill the dark liquid all over my vibrant watered silk gown.

In a low voice, Silas murmured, "Is your plan not going well, then?"

I stiffened. "I am quite sure *that* is none of your business," I said without meeting his gaze.

Silas ignored me. "You know, scowling is no way to attract a gentleman."

I cut him a look but said nothing, choosing instead to turn and face the assembled crowd. I caught the fine cut of Silas's black jacket and an elaborately stitched pale blue waistcoat before I forced my eyes forward, intent on ignoring his insufferable presence.

He turned with me.

My resolve crumbled nearly immediately. "I suppose you're here to tell me that I should smile more?"

I could see Silas shaking his head on the edge of my vision. "No. I have three sisters. I would never advise a woman to smile more." With a lean in my direction and a whisper, he added, "I like my bollocks right where they are."

His proximity and his infuriating exhale ghosting the shell of my ear had me fighting an involuntary shiver. The mention of his bollocks probably didn't help either. I tried valiantly not to picture them . . . right where they were.

"Your cheeks have gone quite pink," he mused delightedly. "You're imagining me nude, aren't you?"

I turned to glare at him. "You are behaving abominably. Can't you refrain from acting like an adolescent for one moment?"

Silas's features arranged themselves into something bordering on contrite, but his whiskey-brown eyes sparkled deviously. "You're right. I apologize profusely, my lady. I shall be obliged to make it up to you. Shall we have the next dance?"

I raised a brow. "I'm not sure how that signifies as a debt you are repaying."

"You do enjoy dancing, do you not? I believe I've seen you with several gentlemen this evening, looking elegant and amused on the dance floor. I, myself, am an excellent partner."

I scrutinized his seemingly innocent expression. There was an edge to his words, however. He'd noted my movements this evening, and I wasn't sure how I felt about that beyond . . . oddly squirmy. Surely, Silas wasn't acting the part of a jealous lover. Perhaps the idiot actually thought he could absolve his bad behavior by gracing me with his presence on the dance floor for the next waltz.

I rolled my eyes and released a gusty sigh. "Let's get this over with."

"Just what a man longs to hear," he replied brightly, completely unbothered.

We made our way from the refreshment table, across the ballroom, and toward the musicians. Due to the thinning crowd, we managed a spot near the center of the dance floor.

I curtsied, and Silas bowed, and suddenly, we were dancing—touching for the first time since Laurel Park. Since he'd been pressed hard and naked against me—inside me.

Shaking myself inwardly, I forced away the images of damp, sweat-slicked skin and his soft lips moving hungrily against me. Warm hands molding to my pale flesh.

Now those hands I knew so well were turning me in time with the music. I had trouble ignoring all our remembered touches and concentrating on the innocence of Silas's fingers along my back, my shoulders, meeting palm to palm. This was just a dance. We had gloves on, for God's sake. I could feel the heat working its way up my chest, painting a telling flush for all to see.

His whispered words from weeks ago came back to me then, making me nearly falter my next step.

"Where else can I make you blush, I wonder? Hmm."

I was playing a dangerous game. I'd been so sure I could ignore everything that had happened between us. I'd been intent on behaving normally and never addressing our nights together in the Red Suite. But now, in the candlelight of the ballroom, with Silas's hands and attention focused solely on me, never deviating, I wasn't sure I could ignore anything.

Moments later, the song ended, but my inner turmoil was just beginning. Panic made my heartbeat loud and forceful in my chest. Surely, Silas could hear it.

He executed a perfect bow while my body trembled its way through a passable curtsy. But suddenly his brown eyes weren't crinkled in amusement. They'd lost their teasing light, and in its place was something heated.

Without saying a word, Silas took my hand and placed it on his arm and led us through the remaining crowd. I didn't protest. I didn't feel capable of speaking with this strange urgency and awareness thrumming between us. He moved behind a pillar and through a doorway as I shuffled along next to him, the rustle of my skirts barely audible over the blood rushing in my ears.

This seemed like a dire fight-or-flight state of affairs, and I was tired of battling Silas. It felt natural to escape with him instead.

Once we entered the empty corridor, Silas shifted, lacing our fingers together and guiding me around two corners. We passed no servants nor guests in the passage, dimly lit with wall sconces and burning candles. When we reached the end of the hallway, I stopped abruptly before a dark window. Silas wasn't deterred by the apparent end of our journey through the Viscount West-brooke's home. He opened the second to last door on the left and pulled me within.

We were once again in a cupboard, and from the angle of the ceiling, the cramped space appeared to butt up against the servants' stairs. On one of the high shelves sat a single taper burning in a candlestick holder.

I spun to face Silas, who pulled the door closed behind us and crowded close to me. Any closer and I would need to crouch to fit beneath the underside of the stairs.

"Did you plan this?" I whisper-hissed as his hands gently guided my back to rest against the closed door.

He spoke quietly into my ear, "With you in that dress, dancing with other men all evening . . . it was inevitable."

Silas leaned back to meet my undoubtedly dumbfounded expression, but my hands were cradling his jaw, and I had no memory of doing so.

Our lips found each other softly at first, pausing between kisses to breathe the same air. The madness rolled over us slowly this time, but it was no less consuming. My frantic hands ended up clutching Silas's dark hair while he groaned quietly into my neck, placing wet, sucking kisses to the delicate skin there.

"I don't understand," I gasped as his hands went to my bottom to pull me more solidly against him. "I thought—thought it was just Hampshire. Just survival—"

"—madness. I know," he finished for me.

"Why is it still like this?"

I felt him shake his head in answer before dragging his tongue along the column of my throat.

His lips closed on the skin beneath my ear—a sensitive spot he'd discovered in our time together, one he used to his advantage. Silas brought with him the smoky, sweet scent of tobacco, and my muscles relaxed in response.

"Earlier this evening," I gasped, "I wanted to strangle you with my bare hands."

"I know," he replied easily.

"And your mouth," I groaned.

"Tell me more."

"You never stop talking." My breath hitched as he bit the lobe of my ear in retribution. "You're always telling me—"

And then he was gone, cool air rushing in and filling the space he abandoned. My eyes snapped open, wide and alarmed.

"Down here, Mary darling."

I looked down to find Silas kneeling before me, a devious, knowing grin lighting up every one of his features. He appeared youthful and wicked as the soft candlelight painted him in warmth and diffused edges. He looked like he was up to something. I had to swallow hard against the sight.

Since that very first kiss—snow-stranded in a carriage on the side of a country road—the image of Silas Bartholomew on his knees appealed to every indecent part of me. The ones that longed to battle him and provoke, to dominate and prevail. His utter willingness to surrender, like this, had heat flooding throughout my body and wetness gathering between my thighs. It was absolute seduction and ruination—and thoroughly unexpected.

His hands became very busy with my skirts, but his eyes never left mine.

Silas murmured, "Hold these," before unceremoniously shoving fistfuls of pleated silk and petticoats into my hands. Thank God I'd skipped the caged crinoline this night. I'd known Lady West-brooke's event would be a crush, and I would have been barely able to maneuver with such a large hoop beneath my gown.

With all of the fabric clutched to my chest, I couldn't see Silas anymore. But I could feel him untying ribbons and sliding my drawers down my legs. His hands briefly caressed my thighs in their lace-edged silk stockings before I felt his breath at my center.

That was all, just cooled air blowing over my most sensitive parts. I felt exposed and wanton. The sensation and the expectation had my back arching off the door. My body bowed like a question mark—seeking, searching, and desperately awaiting a response. It came suddenly in the form of Silas's mouth—hot and wet against my center.

My eyes closed, and my mouth dropped open, but the sound that emerged in the tiny cupboard space we occupied did not come from my lips. Silas groaned as he continued to feast upon me, the vibrations of which had my crisis fast approaching.

I couldn't widen my stance as far as I'd like, constricted as I was by my undergarments around my knees, but no matter. Whatever Silas was doing with his lips and his tongue felt amazing. I was rising with every sensual movement against me. One of his hands gently stroked the back of my knee, but before I could focus on how strangely erotic it felt to have him touching me there, he sucked hard at the apex of my thighs, and all the tension fled my body at once.

Pleasure flooded me in waves as I leaned boneless and spent against the door, so awash in sensation that I didn't realize Silas held me steady with his hands wrapped around my thighs.

My breathing was loud in the small space. I could see the candle flame wavering with the force of my exhales.

"Can you stand?" Silas's disembodied voice drifted up to me, and I managed to straighten away from the door in answer.

I could feel him maneuver my drawers back into place and gently tie my garters. Finally, he stood, meeting my gaze squarely as he disentangled the fabric of my skirts from my desperately clutching hold and smoothed them down back into place.

I reached for him, the hard line of his cock straining and visible in his breeches. But just as my hand met the heat of him over the smooth fabric, Silas's hand gently encircled my wrist, halting my intent.

He shook his head slowly. "If you touch me now, I'll be ruined." His words had a very far-off warning bell jingling in the distance, but I ignored it as he continued. "Now is not the time or the place for what I would want to do if you touched me."

Some rebellious part of me that dwelled beneath the surface and consistently managed to stick her head above the water said, "What would you do?"

Silas's eyes went dark and focused. "I wouldn't be able to be quiet, for one. And neither would you." With deliberate slowness, Silas raised the hand he still clasped to his lips. He pushed the fabric of my glove aside and placed a warm kiss to the sensitive skin of my inner wrist before carefully lowering my arm back to my side.

The thought of being even more undone by Silas had arousal settling low and insistent despite my very recent and enthusiastic release. I was disheveled and wrinkled beyond repair as it was, certain that my hair was unsalvageable. I would need to exit the ball immediately.

But Silas watched me as if we had all the time in the world. I could see the amusement enter his features in bits and pieces. The way his eyes smiled first, sparkling in the dim light while the tiny lines fanned out near his temples, crinkling agreeably. His lips came next, pursing slightly before giving in and stretching wide.

I felt myself returning his grin. I couldn't have stopped it if I'd wanted to. And, for once, I didn't. The moment was too ridiculous, and I was too loose from his seduction. Augustus Ward could have pulled open the cupboard door right then and the smile would have stayed firmly on my face.

"What?" I asked, for he obviously had something to say. Silas nearly always did.

"Just curious," he replied, hands coming up to stroke the wayward hair away from my temples and behind my ears. "What was that you were saying about my mouth?"

I did my utmost to quiet my laughter, but my words still emerged uneven and tinged with poorly concealed happiness. "Your mouth . . . is perhaps, acceptable. In certain situations. I suppose."

Silas's grin was unrepentant. And just this once, I let myself share it. No battle to be won. We were on the same side, comrades in arms, bonded over our shared experience.

He leaned in and placed his smiling lips against my own, so gently it felt like a dream. "Perhaps I should call on you tomorrow?"

I was too buoyant from our clandestine encounter to be alarmed at Silas's suggestion. Instead, I shook my head and whispered against his lips, "Remember the rules."

For once, Silas didn't argue. He just nodded and kissed me softly again.

I didn't let myself think about the mistake we'd just made. Or about how continuing these encounters in London would ruin everything.

I wanted to be selfish. Impossibly irresponsible. I was desperate to make a decision for myself, one that heated my blood and beat a frantic warning in my chest.

I let myself have this moment of wild and reckless freedom.

And a man looking at me like I was the only thing in the world he wanted.

Seven

SILAS

February

There were four men in my receiving room waiting to interview for a valet position.

Actually, three grown men and a boy in a too-large jacket.

I dubiously eyed the scrawny child of no more than sixteen. I didn't want to consider where he'd stolen that wool suit coat from.

Mr. Hodges, my father's long-time solicitor, had indeed been instrumental in acquiring my new home. Barely six weeks since I'd broached the idea with my father and here I was, settling in quite nicely in my very own lodgings in Belgrave Square.

My housekeeper/cook and maid had been recommended from Patty's household and seemed to require very little input from me in maintaining the townhome. It all suited me nicely.

It felt good to have my own space—to no longer be dependent on the hospitality of my sisters. Mealtimes were a bit lonely, and I did find the house altogether too quiet. But I was sure, in time, those bothersome aspects of independence would fade.

I'd wanted to interview the recommended candidates for valet myself. I needed to ensure we got on well, considering I would see the man nearly every day.

I frowned again at the boy staring goggle-eyed around the room. Best not to leave him too long near the silver candlesticks.

"You there," I called.

The boy jumped, turning toward me with wide blue eyes under a mop of dirty blond hair. "Yes," he fairly squeaked. After clearing his throat, he attempted once more in a fractionally deeper tone, "Yes, sir."

I stared for another moment as the youngster fidgeted under my attention. The three older men watched the exchange with varying degrees of disapproval. They were well-dressed—appropriate for our meeting—and seemed firmly in their third or fourth decade of life. It was clear they viewed the boy in their midst as an interloper.

But something about that overly large black coat on the child's too-thin frame kept me from dismissing him outright.

"You'll go first," I said quickly. When he just stood there staring, I motioned him forward. "Well, come on, then."

All of his limbs seemed to react at the same time, expressing instant urgency as he followed me out of the front receiving room and down the narrow corridor to my study. I heard frantically shuffling feet and assumed the boy was trailing me.

I entered the study and sat behind my large mahogany desk, indicating that the boy should occupy the wingback chair facing me. He sat gingerly where I indicated and took in the space with wonder. It wasn't anything special. This room was honestly the one that needed the most work. I'd yet to move my personal journals and favorite travel volumes from Laurel Park. The bookshelves lining the walls were fairly barren for the time being. Two large windows emitted pale gray February light, and a fire burned happily behind me.

"So, what is it that you think you are doing here?" I asked mildly.

Blue eyes snapped back to mine. His mouth opened a few times and finally his youthful voice emerged. "My name is Basil, sir. And I'm here to be your new valet." I raised a brow. "That is, if you decide to hire me. I'd be an asset to you, sir. I'm quick. I follow directions well. My mother says I've always been a good listener. I would do whatever you asked—whatever you needed. And in a timely manner." Basil ended his heartfelt speech with a wide smile. Surprisingly even white teeth greeted me.

My eyes trailed over the smudge of dirt on his left cheekbone and the way his hair hung limp and dirty, brushing the collar of the borrowed jacket. "How did you hear of this available position?"

His gaze circled the room, clearly shuffling through responses. He must have landed on one because he replied, "I . . . saw the advertisement. And came at the appointed time."

There had been no such advertisement, and even if there had been, I doubted this boy would have been able to read it.

Mr. Hodges had recommendations for the three men in my receiving room from other households. One was the brother of a valued member of Augie's staff.

"I see," I replied, nodding.

The boy appeared relieved by my response, shoulders sagging and smile growing even wider—stretching his pale skin tight. He looked impossibly young and very undernourished.

"Pardon me a moment." I stood and walked toward the kitchens at the back of the house.

When I returned a few moments later, Basil was still staring after me. He seemed to remember that he was supposed to rise after I'd already sat and a strange up, then down, then up again resulted.

I waved away his mumbled apology and motioned impatiently for him to sit. Leaning forward, I rested my forearms on the desk. "Basil, why don't you tell me about yourself?"

This seemed to encourage the boy, and he sat up straighter. "Well, I am the eldest. I have three sisters. I enjoy horses and boats and —and working hard for my employer." The last added as if he remembered he wasn't just here for a nice visit.

I was willing to bet Basil had never been atop a horse nor on a boat in his short life, but I offered a small smile in his direction. "And which household did you valet for previously."

His enthusiasm dimmed a touch at my question, but he rallied admirably. "Well, honestly, sir, my previous position was not as valet."

"You don't say."

"It's true. And I worked for the—the Abernathy family, sir."

There was a prominent chimney sweep who made his rounds in London by the name of Abernathy.

Before I had the opportunity to question young Basil further, my maid, Cora, entered with a tray.

I indicated she should place the offerings upon the desk. "Thank you, Cora. I'm happy to pour for myself and Mr. Basil. You may go."

I turned to study the boy's reaction, but his eyes were fastened to the thick slices of bread and the glistening slabs of butter smeared atop their surface. I placed three on a plate and passed them over. "Here you go, lad. I always say it is better to conduct a meeting over tea and a full stomach. My housekeeper is an excellent baker. I wouldn't want all this to go to waste."

To his credit, Basil didn't fall upon the bread as a starving animal might, but I could see the careful restraint in his well-mannered bites. Honestly, he had better comportment than my youngest sister at that age.

I poured tea and added cream and sugar as he indicated. Basil ate purposely and efficiently while I prepared my own cup.

When two of the three slices had been sacrificed to the boy's yawning hunger, I set my cup down on the desktop and said, "All right. Why don't you tell me what you are really doing here?"

Basil's face fell but honesty rose up. He admitted to overhearing two of the men currently in my front room. They'd been on the street corner discussing this afternoon's interview. They seemed to think it would be a fairly easy assignment as I was an aristocrat of means and only ever out and about for recreation. Basil confessed that he followed them to the entrance of my home as if he belonged and gave his name to the housekeeper as "Basil. Here for the valet position."

He told me about his home in White Chapel with his mother and three younger sisters—all between the ages of five and fourteen. Basil himself was seventeen years old and, despite being small for anyone that age, had grown too large to climb and sweep chimneys for Mr. Abernathy—a position he's held since the age of seven. He'd been trying to find work to support his mother and sisters since his father left them before the birth of his youngest sister, Elodie.

I listened patiently as the boy recounted his story around bites of bread—two additional slices—and three cups of warm tea.

"Where did you get the coat?" I asked while the boy chewed on the last bit of bread from the serving tray.

"It was my da's. Thought it made me look more professional." He reached down to brush the crumbs from his lapels. "It's the only thing Ma kept. She sold the rest of his things after a time."

I nodded. "And your name? It's not really Basil, is it?"

The boy looked sheepish but he returned my smile. "I'm sorry for lying, sir. I thought Basil sounded a bit more refined. Like a name someone should have for working in a fine household for a fine gentleman."

"What's your real name, then?"

"It's Jamie, sir. James Hartt."

Jamie seemed to realize our meeting was coming to a close. I watched as he moved his cup and saucer back to the tray and tidied the crumbs from the edge of my desk. "I thank you for your hospitality, sir. I'll shove off so you can get on with your appointments."

I watched as an embarrassed flush stole over the boy's cheeks. He refused to meet my gaze.

I'd felt many things while Jamie had relayed his tale—explaining how he'd ended up in my receiving room this afternoon. I thought about my own three sisters and what I would do to protect them and ensure their safety.

Clearing my throat, I said, "Would you be able to get here from White Chapel every day? Except for Sundays. Those would be your off days."

Jamie regarded me with a shocked expression. "Yes. Yes, I can manage that easy enough, sir."

I nodded. "Then you start tomorrow."

I'd hadn't seen Mary Lovelace in a month. Not since I'd dragged her into a cupboard at the Westbrooke Ball.

Despite my painful erection that night, things had ended pleasantly between us. I'd never seen Mary smile at me that way. She'd been radiant and open. Her grin so damn beautiful, I'd felt as if I'd won a prize, or more accurately, I'd felt as if I'd earned it. My happiness had been reflected back at me.

Honestly, I wasn't sure where we went from there. She'd hidden behind her rules to prevent anything real from developing between us. No calls. No courting. Only secrets. I'd abide her rules . . . for now. But there was something happening between us. Something more than either of us had bargained for. And the prospect of seeing her again had filled me with an odd sort of anticipation.

Ignoring Mary's demands and paying a call to her in her father's home had not seemed like the correct path forward—no matter how much I wanted to. Our secrets were our own, and I had a feeling that shedding any sort of light on our relationship would most definitely have Mary shying away like an irritated horse.

So, I'd been patient and ignored my desire to seek her out. I'd seen to my own burgeoning responsibilities in London.

In truth, I'd been busy for the past month. First, with viewing properties with Mr. Hodges. And then I'd been meeting with workers and craftsmen and settling into and furnishing the home I'd acquired. There hadn't been time for balls and musicales in the new year just yet, no chance for another cupboard encounter or even a dance, should Mary allow it.

But tonight, after weeks apart, I had the pleasure of watching Mary from across Patty's elaborate dining table.

My family was back in London. My sisters and their husbands and children had returned from the country—all but Genevieve who'd remained behind with Julian to finalize their wedding plans for the following month.

Mary wore a shimmering gown in gold. It caught the candlelight as she shifted and made it difficult to look away. The bodice was low and, as was typical for Mary, several rebellious red strands of hair had escaped their confines and touched the delicate wings of her collarbones. I wanted to brush them aside and replace them with my lips. She sent me a knowing grin when no one was looking, her fingers toying with the ends of her hair.

A sense of anticipation joined the slow-simmering arousal I'd been managing throughout the meal.

Granted, it could have been my body now associating her with the most astonishing sex of my life. But who was I to argue? We were unbelievably compatible in the bedroom. And in the cupboard. And the library.

It was as if our decade-long acquaintance had been preparing us for future intimacies. Ten years of foreplay that made every encounter better than the last.

"Silas, when will you host an event at your own home?" My sister Emery's voiced emerged, drawing my attention reluctantly.

I frowned at her question. While my household was growing comfortable in the weeks since I'd moved in to Belgrave Square, it wasn't ready for my family to descend and cast judgment.

"Not that we're not always happy to have you at our table," Miles added helpfully. "But when can we expect an invitation?"

I ignored my brother-in-law's cheeky grin. "I'm still getting settled."

Mrs. Fullerton, my housekeeper and cook, and my maid, Cora, seemed to have everything well in hand. And Jamie, well . . . the boy was trying. He'd shaved me for the first time this very afternoon with minimal damage. That felt like a cause for celebration.

Still. Surely, there was a time when my residence would feel like a home—with memories and favorite spaces. I didn't even know where the light hit just right in my study for optimal reading yet. I couldn't be expected to entertain in a space that was hardly my own. I needed more time.

"Right, but we're your family, Silas," Emery argued. "We don't need a fancy event. We're nosy and want to poke around."

"Well, I don't want you poking around until it's ready," I insisted with finality.

Naturally, my family ignored me, and started speaking over one another. I signaled a footman for more wine while Emery squawked in affront and Patty assured me they were all just curious. Miles and Franny cut in as well with only Augie and Mary remaining unbothered and quiet.

My eyes caught on Mary who studied me with an odd expression. Finally, her brows rose, and I rolled my eyes before throwing back the contents of my newly refilled goblet.

"Fine!" I fairly hollered to be heard over the commotion. "I will host an event—something small. A dinner party in April and you can all see my home then."

Mary hid a victorious grin behind the rim of her wineglass.

Two months felt like enough time to get my act together. I would need to hire a gardener to tend the property, but everything should be lovely and green by April. And perhaps by that time, I might be well on my way to a respectable status. I could even be courting an appropriate match by then. Mother could assist in hosting a small gathering. It felt like a good decision—a responsible, adult decision.

"Two months!" Emery called, incredulous. "What more could you possibly need in order to get settled? Can we not simply drop by for tea?"

I ignored my high-handed sister and announced, "And everyone besides Emery is invited to supper next week."

Chuckling, I dodged the hard roll aimed at my head.

~

"Did you hear that?" Mary whispered before stopping suddenly in the middle of the hallway.

I only just managed to keep myself from barreling into her. With a hand braced on the wall of the corridor, I looked behind us to ensure we hadn't been followed.

"No, I don't hear anything," I said quietly beside her ear. "Hurry, before we're missed."

I stepped ahead and guided her toward the formal receiving room that was never used. Patty used to receive morning callers with some frequency back when she was a sought-after wealthy widow. Miles grumbled about how much he hated that room and all it represented, so they decided to retire the space. Only the maids visited.

Once inside, I closed the door behind us. It was dark and chilly within. There were no candles and no fire laid. Only dim gray moonlight shone from the windows and the warm outline of the doorway we'd just entered gave off minimal illumination. But I didn't have time to worry about the dark or the cold.

Mary's arms came around me, pulling me close. Our lips met in a feverish flurry. We knew we were behaving recklessly and had little time to spare.

We'd stumbled upon each other in the hallway following the evening meal. I'd been on my way to join Augie and Miles for cigars and brandy in the study. Mary had been returning to the dining room for dessert with the ladies. We'd stopped abruptly, two feet apart, before she'd whispered, "Come on," and had taken my hand.

Now we were on one another in a secluded room in my sister's house.

As we kissed with shuffling, stumbling steps, Mary dragged a finger across the nape of my neck and up behind my ear. She paused, pulling away, withholding her lips.

I chased after her, but she held her finger up between us, squinting into the darkness. "What's this?"

Struggling to focus my attention, I sighed. "It's shaving soap. My valet. He's . . . learning."

The bare light glinted off Mary's teeth as she smiled at me before backing slowly away.

I followed as she climbed onto a tufted settee that looked horribly uncomfortable.

"What are you doing?" I asked as she positioned herself facing away from me.

"This way I'll keep my hands out of your hair and your clothes. We'll be easier to piece back together afterward."

I wasn't sure all of my pieces were going to survive whatever this was.

While on her knees and with her hands braced on the rolled arm of the furniture, Mary regarded me from over her shoulder. "What are you waiting for?"

I stared dumbfounded for a moment longer before I correctly interpreted her intent and her position. "Right," I murmured, unbuttoning the falls of my trousers while she gathered her layers upon layers of skirts. I crowded close behind her, assisting in leveraging the fabric up and over her bottom . . . her very bare bottom.

"It appears your underthings are missing, Lady Mary," I whispered into the skin of her neck, pressing my body against the back of her thighs.

"Funny that," she replied a touch breathless. "Perhaps you can conduct a thorough search and uncover their location."

I smoothed my hand across her unbearably soft skin as she pushed against me, eager and waiting. The fingers of my other hand ghosted gently up the inside of her thighs until I found her center.

"I'm ready," she insisted, shifting her backside against my aching erection.

"I know," I breathed against the shell of her ear, an errant curl clinging to my lips. "I can feel how wet you are for me." I sank two fingers inside, stretching her slim body. I knew she wanted hard and fast, hidden away and forbidden as we were. But I needed to know she was ready. I didn't want to hurt her.

She moaned as I curled my fingers down and used my thumb to massage the tiny pearl at the apex of her thighs. Moving swiftly, I replaced my fingers with my cock and gave her the hard and fast she was searching for. Her cries muffled against the upholstery as she found her release a short time later. With a quiet groan, I folded my body over hers, pulled out, and spent on her thighs as pleasure claimed me as well.

Moments later, when our breaths were still heavy, and we worked quickly to clean up and set each other to rights, I blurted out rather inelegantly, "You could come and see my home, if you wanted."

Mary froze in the darkness from where she'd been shaking her skirts back into place.

She didn't speak, and I thought about what I'd foolishly offered, unsure if my meaning had been clear. "We would still need to be careful and discreet, but we'd have more than five minutes on an uncomfortable settee."

She'd yet to answer. In truth, I hadn't heard her breathe.

I wondered if my abrupt proposition had been utterly foolish, wincing slightly as the silence stretched into something fraught.

Finally, her voice emerged, firm and unyielding, "The rules would still apply."

Right. Only secrets and absolutely no lies.

"All right," I agreed. Because, honestly, I would have agreed to anything. Even if she'd declined clandestine meetings in my bedchamber, I would have said yes to forbidden trysts in cupboards or darkened drawing rooms. I feared I would even climb a trellis into her father's house, if need be. I seemed to be desperate for more of whatever this was between us.

I wasn't a fool. I knew that the way forward—the future in which I wanted to be respected and taken seriously—did not involve a non-arrangement with Mary Lovelace. But I still had time to settle down—to become the man I was meant to be. There were months left in the season. I could still find a wife when the time came. And if I recalled correctly, Mary had her own plans and the list to prove it.

Eight

MARY

April

"Will you stay?" Silas asked from his place among his white bed linens, unconcerned with his nudity.

It wasn't the first time he'd asked me to stay following intimacies in his home. We'd been meeting regularly for nearly two months now, and he asked me to stay at least once per week. Some part of me wanted to accept. To stop piecing myself back together as the sweat cooled on my skin and simply curl up in his big bed with Silas's warm body behind mine. But the larger, louder, and more opinionated part of me knew that those were dangerous things to want and a slippery slope indeed.

I was doing up the side closure on my dress and trying to remember where I'd put my earrings. Ah, there on his desk. With candles burning on nearly every surface, he'd set me atop that desk and gone to his knees when I'd first arrived tonight.

I moved to gather my jewelry and threw Silas a glance over my shoulder. He was frowning. It was still startling to see anything but a smile on his handsome face.

"I can't. You know that," I said, turning away and placing one earring back in my ear.

"But it's early yet," he argued. "Stay and have dessert with me. Or a drink." I heard bedcovers shifting as he rose.

Warm lips pressed to the side of my neck. "You have time." He sucked gently on the exposed slope of my shoulder. "You could stay."

I couldn't. It was too dangerous . . . for many reasons.

"I'm sorry. I must get back."

A warm sigh gusted over my sensitive flesh. "All right."

I continued facing away and replaced my other earring. I could hear Silas moving about the room. Probably retrieving a dressing gown to escort me down the back staircase to the rear entrance where my carriage waited to return me to my parents' home.

I gave up on the state of my hair and simply plaited it down my back. Beneath my fur-lined hood, it wouldn't be visible anyhow.

We made our way down the stairs and through the kitchen, embers glowing in the grate. Silas was oddly silent.

I reached for the doorknob, but Silas was there first. He pulled my hand in for a brief kiss on my knuckles before saying quietly, "I could call on you, you know. Or we could go for a ride in the park. The weather has been fine. Perhaps, a walk?"

Frowning, I met Silas's earnest gaze. Why was he bringing this up again? He knew everything about our arrangement hinged on secrecy. I didn't want to hurt anyone. His sisters could not know of our association. But neither did I wish to hurt Silas.

I feared my hand might tremble and so I pulled away slowly. I made my voice soft and pleading. "Silas, you know the—"

"Yes. I know. Your bloody rules," he interrupted, looking away. "Forget I said anything."

"Silas," I attempted, but he was already opening the door to the garden and the drive beyond.

"I'll see you at Drakefield's event?"

I nodded, regretting the reminder of the rules. But not ready to examine too closely everything that was happening between us.

Silas pressed a quick kiss to my cheek before standing sentry by the open doorway, not meeting my eye. He was all stiff lines and restraint, and I hated that I'd made him that way.

So I went up on my toes and pressed a kiss of my own to the underside of his jaw. My lips lingered against his rough stubble. Silas softened by degrees, his head tilting into my touch—seeking and following.

I saw Silas at Drakefield's two days later. We greeted one another cordially before bickering among his family.

Afterward, I joined him in his bedchamber at Belgrave Square at two o'clock in the morning. He welcomed me with sweet, slow kisses that heated my blood into an inferno. It all devolved from there, and we fell upon one another with a frantic, frenzied fervor. Later, when we'd caught our breaths, he didn't prop himself up in bed and ask me to stay.

And as he, once again, escorted me down the back staircase to the rear garden entrance, he didn't stop me with a hand on the door or ask to call on me. Silas simply gave me one more slow-simmering kiss to see me on my way.

If I felt the loss of his words, it was my own fault. I had no one to blame but my rules and my own expectations.

So I pushed it away and focused on the here and now.

I wasn't ready for anything to change between us. Change meant the unexpected and the unknown. Right now, I was happy. Right now, *we* were happy. And I wouldn't wish any foolish imaginings to take that feeling away.

A few weeks later, the sunshine warmed my skin beneath my shawl. It was very newly spring, and green buds dotted the shrubbery and pale flowers swayed in the breeze on the cherry trees. The scent of renewal was as sharp and fragrant as lavender drifting through the air. Patty's garden party at Cawthorn Hall was widely attended, aided no doubt by the fine April weather. The air was cool but the sun was a comforting weight, brightening the dreary gray winter London had been plagued by for months.

Bonnets and fashionable hats shielded fair English skin, but I found myself discreetly seeking the warmth and tipping my chin to the sky.

I opened my eyes to see Silas watching me from his position a few paces away, a small smile tugging at the corners of his lips. The moment passed quickly as if his attention hadn't rested on me at all. He faced Miles and continued their conversation with no one the wiser.

But I'd noticed, and I liked the way he'd looked at me.

Patty's elbow jostled the arm holding my lemonade. "Are you all right?"

I turned to my friend and smiled easily. "I am. Why? Don't I look it?"

Her attention was heavy. Blue eyes thoughtful and piercing. "You do look it. Happy, I mean."

I grinned. "Well, mystery solved. I'm quite content."

"What she means is," Emery interjected, peering around her elder sister's shoulder, "that you're abnormally happy."

"What is abnormal about it?" I could feel the smile fighting to remain in place as my eyebrows lowered in confusion.

Patty opened her mouth, then closed it.

No matter, because Emery continued on, obviously voicing their combined opinion. "Just that it's so unlike you. You are not a turn-your-head-to-the-sun-and-smile sort of person."

She was right. I knew this. I was behaving oddly and out of character. I didn't want to examine the motivation for my abnormal happiness—as she'd referred to it—especially when the reason for my strange mood stood five feet away and shared their ancestry.

My smile had all but dissolved by now but I blustered on, "Well, today, perhaps I am *that* sort of person."

Augie was standing on Emery's other side. He was quiet but watchful. The knowing in his gaze had me shifting uneasily. We hadn't discussed what he'd witnessed back at Laurel Park. True to his word, it was as if he'd seen and heard nothing. Now, in the gardens of Cawthorn Hall, he tracked my discomfort, and when Emery attempted to further question my motivations, he placed a tender kiss on his wife's temple and asked if she'd heard from her mother since we'd all been in Hampshire last month for Genevieve and Julian's wedding. An event that had seen Silas and I, once again, meeting in secret and continuing our liaisons at Laurel Park.

Taking the bait easily, Emery announced, "Oh, I have indeed heard from Mama." Her volume and enthusiasm was enough that Miles and Silas turned their attention toward her, leaving everyone in our standing lopsided circle facing the middle Bartholomew daughter. "She and Papa are excited to return to London next week for Silas's first social event in his new home."

"I wouldn't call it an event," Silas said around a laugh. "It's a dinner party, and the guest list is mostly you lot and a few of Mother's friends."

Emery's brown eyes sparkled. She obviously had a bit of gossip on her brother and looked forward to making him squirm. "And what interesting friends she has invited."

"Emery." Silas's sharp tone had several heads turning his way in surprise—mine included.

But she was unwavering, a hound on the hunt. The strange panic in Silas's eyes just made her sibling delight that much more determined. "Mama is overjoyed that Silas has finally consented to introductions. It seems brother dearest has decided to take a wife. I never thought I'd see the day . . ."

Emery kept speaking but the words were indistinct, going fuzzy at the edges as I watched Silas's jaw go rigid and his cheeks heat.

But he didn't look my way. Not once. That realization was a blade, slipped quick and sharp right between my ribs.

I was continually surprised that Silas Bartholomew was such an adept actor. In the nearly two months since we'd been meeting at his home in Belgrave Square, we'd never once been questioned or caught by a servant or family member. We behaved normally in public and among his family, no one ever the wiser to our frequent nighttime activities. He'd adhered to my rules: never lying to me or offering ridiculous proclamations of beauty or love, he always withdrew from my body as I'd instructed, and he'd gone above and beyond to ensure our secret meetings were protected.

Looking at him now, you'd never know that he'd been sharing intimacies with the woman standing opposite him twice weekly for several months now. One would just assume he was an irritated brother having been teased mercilessly by his younger sister. Just a man on the cusp of entering the marriage mart, not one refusing to make eye contact with the woman who'd left his bed barely twelve hours ago in the cover of darkness—one he'd kissed up against the door to the back garden before watching her climb carefully into a carriage and return home.

Silas Bartholomew was better at hiding things than I ever imagined. And now I knew I wasn't the only secret he'd been keeping.

Anger and hurt propelled me into motion. I drained the lemonade in my glass and mumbled to Patty that I was off for another. Forcing calm into my steps, I traversed the cobblestones, skirting the large circular fountain in the middle of the garden. I didn't let myself think about Silas's plans to marry. I ignored the sharp ache beneath my ribs and what it meant. My attention was singularly focused on getting as far away from him as I could.

Foolish. Foolish, Mary.

I'd grown too complacent in our arrangement—too content. In the months since we'd taken up with one another, I'd become lax in my plan to seek out anyone from my list. I could see now what a mistake that had been.

With a deep inhale through my nose, I slowed my pace. I was grace and composure as I bypassed the covered tent filled with tables of refreshment and liveried servants.

I would call for my carriage and send word with a footman that I was suddenly feeling unwell. Everything would be fine.

I was all genteel poise as I guided my skirts carefully up the stairs to the stone terrace and the interior beyond.

I was no longer the abnormally happy woman with her foolishly optimistic face turned toward the sun. Emery had been right. That woman wasn't me. It had been a daydream, as fanciful and insubstantial as the cool breeze on a spring day. There one moment and stealing your breath the next.

The dark interior of the house welcomed me. I passed a footman on his way to the kitchens with an empty tray and requested my carriage as soon as possible. My satin slippers were approaching the foyer and the front door was in sight when a hand clutched mine in earnest. I closed my eyes and resisted the urge to jerk my arm away like a petulant child. But it was better this way. I could safely stow my emotions—even the sudden, surprising ones that indicated I was more affected by Silas's news than I had any damn right to be.

I took a deep breath in an attempt to calm my racing heart. No one liked a hysterical woman who slung insults and truths with unfailing accuracy.

Silas's smoky, sweet scent washed over me as he guided me to the left of the opulent gilt entryway and into an empty receiving room —not the one we'd been intimate in months ago, I noted bitterly.

We turned to face one another, and I was quietly enraged to realize my hand clung helplessly to his. I severed the connection and let his hand drop back to his side.

"I was going to tell you." He shook his head. "I only just agreed to my mother's guest list. Emery's big mouth and incessant needling are poorly timed."

I kept my face impassive as Silas ran a frustrated hand through his hair. The strands on top were longer than I'd ever seen them, the brown locks curling slightly on the end. He still didn't trust Jamie to do more than trim the sides. I'd learned that Silas was a vain creature in regard to his hair. I'd fanned the dark strands across his down pillow and teased him just last night.

I cleared my throat delicately, willing the tightness to loosen enough to allow me to speak. Finally, I said, "It's quite all right, Silas. To be expected. You're an heir to a marquessate."

It was always so strange to see him wear a frown. He was forever smiling. And by now, I could tell the difference between his entertaining smiles and his polite society smiles and the soft ones he wore in the middle of the night, lazy and tired and secret. The ones just for me.

But Silas was definitely frowning now. "Right," he said slowly, scrutinizing my features. If he was waiting for a reaction, he'd be waiting a good long while. Finally, he sighed. "I didn't mean for you to find out that way. I wanted to have a conversation. Make you understand."

"Make me understand what exactly?" I worked to ensure my tone came across as curious rather than judgmental. If he thought I'd continue with our *private meetings* while he courted some debutante, well, he was mistaken.

Silas took a fortifying breath. "I am tired, Mary. Tired of not being taken seriously. Tired of being the rascally brother or the wayward heir. My father treats me like a little boy—no responsibilities or obligations. And my sisters . . ." His hands went to his hips as he searched the room for the right words. "I envy them."

I lost the careful hold on my emotions and narrowed my eyes in confusion. "What?"

"They are all moving on with their lives. Far beyond me. Even Genevieve. She's married, for God's sake. My baby sister. And she'll likely have a family soon. And I will be alone in that house in Belgrave Square."

He wasn't alone there last night. Had he forgotten?

When I said nothing, simply stood knee-deep in shocked silence, Silas went on. "It's time for me to grow up and settle down. Make an appropriate match. Find someone who I can have a future with. Someone who actually wants me."

The implication nearly pushed the air from my lungs. But I held steady and firm.

Silas wanted a wife. Someone appropriate. Someone to be marchioness someday. Someone young and beautiful. Someone to give him heirs and carry on his name.

Someone who was not me.

His eyes were pleading, begging me to understand. Full of so much sympathy and pity that I had to look away.

It was wrong of me to feel such bitterness and anger, such crushing hurt at the realization that I was simply not in the running for Mrs. Bartholomew. We'd had an arrangement, and it had suited us both. We'd shared our bodies, and I'd been very careful to keep all the rest boarded up. But clearly something had gotten through because my heart ached with the unexpected truth of it.

It wasn't fair to blame Silas for my unforeseen lack of control, but there he was, looking at me like he felt sorry for me. And I couldn't abide that.

I nodded and pulled my gloves a little higher along my wrists. My eyes tracked my shaking grip as it closed around the pale fabric. I watched as Silas's warm hand interrupted my movements, capturing my hand and holding tight. "Mary," he breathed. "I'm sorry. This was not how—I didn't want it to—"

His apology was cut off by a throat clearing behind us in the open doorway. I dropped Silas's hand as if it was on fire. Turning, we saw Augie standing just inside the room. Only this time he didn't appear scandalized or horrified by my proximity to his brother-in-law. He looked like a lifeline.

"Lady Mary, your carriage has arrived," Augie said evenly. "I've come to escort you to the front drive."

I didn't question how the duke had come by this information or why he'd felt the need to play the part of rescuer on this day. I simply nodded, relief weakening my knees. "Thank you, Augustus."

I stepped forward, ignoring the way Silas called my name.

Meeting Augie in the doorway, he guided my arm through his and patted my hand gently before leading me from the room. We made our way down the front steps to the circular drive where my coachman waited.

Augie handed me into the carriage, looking into my watery gaze. "I'm sorry, Mary. If Emery had known, she would never have announced her mother's plan so thoughtlessly—"

"It's all right," I interrupted, unwilling to hear more. "There is nothing for Emery to know."

Not anymore.

One week later and fueled by pettiness and poor decision-making, I strode up the front walk of Silas's home in Belgrave Square for his intimate dinner party.

I'd never been weak and refused to be a coward, but this past week had tested the limits of what I'd allow. I was finished with feeling sad and lonely. Hiding away would do nothing but prove that I had something to hide from. Avoiding Silas would give too much away. And, frankly, I couldn't quite wipe the look of pity he'd worn on his face from my memory.

Propelled to his door by a healthy dose of stubbornness and determination, I gave a firm rap with the doorknocker. A child in a man's suit opened the door with a bright smile, and I immediately knew this was Jamie.

Silas's references of the boy were frequent in our time together. I'd talk about very little, for the most part. But Silas had enjoyed discussing his day, occasionally mentioning his ongoing progress with his unlikely servant. It was easy enough to see Silas becoming caught up in his valet's life, but I'd never commented on the oddity of their relationship. It clearly made Silas feel accomplished to have his own loyal valet. It hadn't seemed necessary to mention that aristocrats didn't typically donate their gently worn clothing to their servants or arrange fresh food deliveries to the homes of those in their employ.

Here on this chilly evening, Jamie remembered that he should offer a polite bow and released the door. Shifting to grasp his hands behind his back, the boy lowered his head as the door swung back toward my face.

"Oh, no!" He lunged forward to keep the wood from slamming before me and breathed out a sigh of relief. "That would have been a right disaster." His smile was so relieved that I found myself returning it.

"Indeed."

We stood smiling at one another for a long moment before I inched forward, "Might I come in?"

"Oh! Right. Of course." Jamie pulled the door wide once more. "Apologies, m'lady. I'm to escort guests to the parlor. Typically, I act as Mr. Bartholomew's valet," he said proudly.

"You don't say." I walked beside Jamie as he led the way. I noted the art on the walls, paintings I'd never before seen in this part of Silas's home. Something bitter twisted in the pit of my stomach, and I didn't feel very hungry at all.

"Yes, ma'am. For going on two months now."

"Well, congratulations on a job well earned," I said, mustering up a grin for the boy.

Jamie nodded happily as we inched closer to where I could hear voices. "Thank you, ma'am." He peeked at a shiny new pocket watch on his waist. "You've made it just in time for supper. Mr.

Bartholomew will be leading guests into the dining room any moment."

"Fashionably late, I'm afraid." Although in truth, I'd timed my arrival very carefully. Hoping to avoid pre-dinner conversation and mingling, I'd dallied for nearly an hour before summoning my carriage for tonight's festivities—the first of the heralded matchmaking events and the first formal gathering in Silas's new home.

What was I even doing here?

It wasn't too late to turn back. But something bitter and determined kept my feet moving forward.

Finally, Jamie stopped at the entrance to the receiving room and cleared his throat. He opened his mouth to announce my presence, then seemed to recall that I hadn't given my name upon arrival. Despite visiting this house in the dead of night for months, the servants had no idea who I was. I certainly wasn't mistress of Silas's home. And now, I was even less than that.

I leaned close and whispered, "Lady Mary Lovelace."

Jamie recovered and announced me to the room in a voice that was suspiciously lower than his own. I was grateful for the distraction before I stepped within. I wasn't sure who or what I'd see tonight, but I knew it would be enough to rile my irrational anger and fuel my hurt.

No matter. As long as I appeared unfazed, I could get through the first night of Silas's newly constructed future—where he sought a wife and entertained guests in his home. Where he was taken seriously as an heir and grew beyond our meaningless affair into the man he'd decided to become.

The formal receiving room was full of bodies—most I recognized. My eyes found Silas's first. He glanced up in surprise from where he was speaking to his mother, dinner guest Lady Gravely, and her youngest daughter, Sophia. I swallowed hard and looked away quickly as Patty and Emery made their way to me.

I chatted momentarily with my friends before Silas announced supper and led us all into the beautifully appointed dining room.

As we settled around a long oak table decorated with embroidered table linens, fresh flowers, and a sea of candles, I noted the presence of three matrons and their daughters. Lady Gravely and Sophia, of course. Viscountess Stottenham and her fair-haired daughter, Jane. And the enterprising Mrs. Crawford accompanying her eldest daughter, Annabelle, who could not be more than seventeen years of age.

In addition to the marriage-minded women all clustered around Silas and the Marchioness Northcutt were his family members— Patty and Miles, Emery and Augie, and his father, the marquess, as well. Daly and his wife were also in attendance but were seated too far from me to make pleasant conversation. I enjoyed Daly's wife very much. She was incredibly shy but a very calming presence at these rowdy Bartholomew events.

As the meal progressed, I made conversation with Patty on my left while Augie eyed me warily from his place across the table. I wanted to shout at him that I wasn't quite so breakable. That it would take a lot more than Silas's potential brides picking at their plates while their mothers extolled their virtues in a pompous show of one-upmanship to cause me to snap.

Occasionally, my gaze would snag on Silas. He was the consummate host and lived for this sort of socializing. He listened attentively to the mamas and worked to include the young ladies in their conversations as well. I couldn't fault these debutantes. It was likely awkward to be talked about as if you weren't there and only your accomplishments in Latin or music made you marriageable. Only the young Annabelle Crawford seemed undaunted by the attention. Her high, melodious voice drifted down the table many times throughout the meal. Silas would nod along to whatever she said, grinning his polite society smile.

I felt my stomach turn over and pushed the food around my plate for the remainder of the meal.

My glances and attention rarely strayed after the second course.

I felt like a fool for donning my most flattering emerald gown and asking our maid to pay extra attention to my wayward curls.

What had I been trying to prove coming here tonight? That I was unaffected by the end of our relationship? That Silas was missing out on something by brushing me aside?

He didn't care about any of that. Silas had his own strategy for the future—one that did not include me. I should have been relieved that I could move on with my own plan to secure an arrangement.

My experience in Silas's home had been limited to his bedchamber and the back staircase. I looked around this foreign dining room and tried to remind myself that it was I who'd demanded secrecy. I'd been the one to make the rules. The realization sat like a stone in my stomach. I couldn't look at Silas much less consume any more food.

"Mary." Patty's voice came from far away despite her proximity.

I blinked and forced myself to focus on my friend. "Apologies, darling. I am distracted."

Patty's blue eyes were concerned. "Are you all right? Has something happened?"

I pressed a hand to my stomach. "I find I'm feeling unwell. I think I shall bow out as soon as the meal concludes."

She eyed me carefully. "You can leave now, if you wish. I shall make your regrets."

I shook my head quickly. "No. No need. I can survive another quarter hour."

It was perhaps the longest quarter hour of my life.

But shortly after dessert, I escaped with barely mumbled farewells as the rest of the guests reconvened for drinks and conversation.

No one followed me out.

~

May

I sifted through correspondence and invitations before stacking them neatly on the corner of my dressing table.

I would decline Abigail Markwood's event, I decided as I dragged the coarse bristles through my damp hair. Abigail was friendly with the Bartholomews, so they were sure to be in attendance. For the same reason I would send my mother along with my regrets to the Countess of Drakefield's spring luncheon.

Patty's letter sat accusingly on the top of the pile. I eyed it distractedly as I prepared for bed. There had been no demands in my friend's elegant handwriting, nor had she been nosy and questioning. But I could read between the lines. Patty wondered what was wrong. She wanted to make sure I was all right. Even if she didn't come right out and demand to know why I'd been out of contact for nearly a month following Silas's dinner party, I could infer the meaning behind her correspondence.

I would pen something tomorrow. Something benign and ambiguous. Truthfully, I'd felt an odd twinge the other day. Perhaps that would inject enough truth into my response that I wouldn't feel guilty over it. I couldn't very well tell Patty the truth.

I couldn't admit that I'd been such a fool to attach myself to her brother—behind her back, in her very own home. It had been monumentally stupid to allow my feelings to get involved. All those nights, sneaking in and out of Silas's London home. The home he'd been preparing for some respectable future. For a faceless bride. Someone young and beautiful and *appropriate*.

I set the brush aside and took in my appearance in the mirror of my dressing table. There were dark smudges beneath my eyes and shallow grooves bracketing my frown. I forced a smile and watched tiny creases fan out near my temples. Men didn't want a face that had been lived in. To wear your emotions was to age yourself. They wanted unlined and unmarred, rosy cheeks, and someone objectively lovely. I supposed Silas wanted someone like that too.

Ignoring the image in the mirror, I focused on my hair and began plaiting. The room was too quiet for my persistent thoughts.

I should have kept the nature of my relationship with Silas in perspective. We didn't have an arrangement. I wasn't his mistress. I'd been a secret and nothing more.

But hadn't I asked for that? Demanded Silas's secrecy and his honesty.

Perhaps *that* was the part that hurt the most. He hadn't told me of his plans. I'd been blindsided at Cawthorn Hall last month by the news.

And then I'd tried to pretend everything was just fine at Silas's dinner party. I had been a prideful fool to attempt such a move.

I couldn't do this. Couldn't pretend. I wasn't nearly so good an actor as Silas. I wasn't as strong as I thought I was either.

And so, I'd stayed away. Declined invitations and begged off teatime or horseback riding with Patty and Emery or any combination that might see Silas Bartholomew in attendance.

It was a bitter pill to swallow that my relationship with Silas—knowingly unwise and risky—had affected my friendship with his family after all. I'd thought I could keep whatever was happening between us separate. I'd allowed myself to be selfish for the first time in my life and look where it had gotten me.

I'd loved the way it felt to be with Silas. Freedom and pleasure and raw honesty, not to mention the thrill of such secrecy. And I'd loved the way he'd looked at me, how he smiled into my sweat-slicked skin, the laughter and joy and fun he brought to my life.

I shook my head, forcing the memories away, finger tracing the edge of Patty's note once more. I would answer her, assuage her worries over me. Everything would be fine. I just needed more time apart—away from painful reminders and my own foolish regrets. I wasn't ready to see Silas dancing with debutantes and charming their mamas. After reading the gossip rags, I knew what to expect. And I knew myself well enough to know I wasn't prepared to stomach that in public.

Perhaps, in time, it wouldn't hurt so much. Soon enough, I would be ready to continue with my own plan—the one cut short by my relationship with Silas. I would consult my list and try again. I felt more determined than ever to get the family and the child I so desperately wanted. Silas had been a distraction, and I'd been foolish to allow my plan to be derailed for so long.

Shifting Patty's letter aside, I pulled out Abigail Markwood's invitation. It would be a crush. Her husband was the Baron Oakley, and he was wealthy beyond belief. No expense would be spared. Abigail would have the social event of her dreams. And half the *ton* would be in attendance to enjoy the fine spread—including most of the gentlemen on my list of potentials. The ball was in one week. I could pull myself together by then. I could ignore Silas and in all likelihood avoid his family.

And that was exactly what I would do.

Nine

SILAS

May

"Mr. Bartholomew, we must prepare you for this afternoon's event."

I groaned at Jamie's attempt at a stern reprimand. I wasn't ready. I didn't wish to attend Lord and Lady Gravely's garden party complete with insistent matchmaking. I wanted to hide in my study or do literally anything else besides prepare for this event.

Over the months, Jamie's responsibilities now included drawing my bath, shaving, and dressing me. It had been a slow and bumpy start, but I could trust him now not to draw blood.

Also, in the time of his employ, we'd been working on conquering other tasks. "Jamie, wouldn't you rather we have another lesson and read the next chapter in that adventure novel together?"

The boy wavered. It had been a low blow to tempt him with the book we'd been painstakingly reading together. He was a fast

133

learner and very bright, and he gained twice the practice when he repeated our reading lessons for his sisters in the evening.

Finally, he managed, "No, sir. The weather is fine, and you shouldn't keep Lady Sophia waiting. She could be the one, you know."

Sophia Huntsford, daughter to the Earl of Gravely, was not going to be *the one*. I had no intention of marrying the girl. Or any of these girls.

My mother had taken her duty to introduce me to every well-bred young lady in London very seriously. Since the night of my first dinner party weeks ago, she'd had me promenading in the park and paying regular calls alongside her, attending every event day and night. And I'd danced with, conversed with, or been introduced to every eligible young woman in Mayfair and surrounding areas.

None of them were right. Not Sophia Huntsford who was too shy to even look at me. Not Jane Bexley who never laughed at my jokes. And certainly not Annabelle Crawford who was but a child.

Of course, they would be perfect partners someday for someone else. I wasn't expecting love or even strong feelings to accompany meeting these women, but there had been nothing. No spark. No connection. They were too young or too serious or utterly silent at their mothers' sides.

I met the expectant gaze of my valet, wondering who else might be attending the Gravelys' garden party today.

It was wrong and selfish, but I hoped Mary would be there. I just . . . wanted to see her. Argue and bicker like we used to do. She was like a ghost these days. A phantom I would see for but a moment in passing. I'd spy her dancing or conversing with someone from her bloody list—like I had at Oakley's ball last week—but she never made eye contact and never got close enough to greet, let alone touch. Mary had declined all of my family's invitations since she'd found out that I planned to marry. Since I'd driven her away.

I couldn't blame her for being angry. If our roles had been reversed, I would have been seething. But I had never intended for her to find out in such a manner. Despite my intentions, guilt consumed me for how things had ended between us. I had wanted to tell her of my plans for marriage and end our . . . whatever we were, privately.

Lines had been blurring in the months we'd seen one another in secret, and spending our evenings in my bed hadn't been enough. She kept leaving, putting on her clothes before the sweat had cooled on our skin. Some nights I could draw her into conversation, but it was usually while she dressed. I always followed her down the back staircase and kissed her against the door, prolonging our time together. I'd wanted her to stay, and that proved to be a dangerous thing.

Mary wanted furtive meetings after dark, and I couldn't afford to be someone's shameful secret for much longer. I'd wanted to tug her back down and curl around her and beg her to stay until morning. But she was a proper lady, not a mistress. And she'd made it plain enough that a physical relationship was all she sought with me—all I'd been good for. She'd rejected outright any mention of an outing in public or paying a call. I'd been forced to acknowledge that there was no future for us—no matter how I hoped for one. Because she simply wouldn't allow it.

So I'd made the painful decision to end things and use the rest of the season to find a wife. A decision I was growing to despise.

"Sir," Jamie said expectantly from the doorway. "We best get on with it."

"Fine, all right." I rubbed my whiskered jaw in frustration and stood, determined to put on a pleasant face for this gathering. It was what I'd asked for, after all.

~

"Mr. Bartholomew! Oh, Mr. Bartholomew! You'll be in this group," Lady Gravely called grandly, waving me over. "With Lord Ashby, Lady Mary, and my dear Sophia, of course."

I worked hard to keep the charming smile upon my face and not scan the area as I nodded to the hostess of today's event. I hadn't seen Mary in the garden since my arrival nearly an hour ago. I'd endured refreshment—weak lemonade—and idle chitchat in the wide garden behind Lord Gravely's grand Mayfair home.

The weather was fine on this sunny May afternoon, and after a light repast, it seemed the exercise and activity portion of the garden party was set to begin on the open green space in the rear of the property. Lady Gravely read from a list of groupings for croquet.

Normally, I would have been very happy to participate in yard games. Croquet was especially popular with our set, and I enjoyed playing with my siblings in Hampshire in the summer months. But my sisters and their husbands were not in attendance today. The guests and conversation had been decidedly uninspiring. Even my mother had sent her regrets. I was on my own with Lady Gravely and her extremely shy offspring.

However, my interest in the afternoon's sport went up exponentially at the prospect of being joined by Mary.

"I'd be happy to, Lady Gravely," I replied, a genuine smile lighting my features as an expressionless Mary finally—*finally*—came into view. She wore a gown in bold peach stripes with a shortened hem. It looked as if Mary had been made aware of the sporting plans for Lady Gravely's event. A matching hat sat at an angle on a nest of unruly red curls. There was a strand grazing her cheekbone as the spring breeze moved through the garden. I realized I'd been staring a beat too long when her face hardened, and she looked like she'd prefer to use my head instead of a ball for croquet.

"Mr. Bartholomew, perhaps you and Sophia on the left and, Lord Ashby, yourself and Lady Mary on the right." Our hostess indicated each side of the area of play, which had already been prepared with ten arches and the starting and turning stakes.

Ashby gave a jovial affirmative and escorted Mary to their starting positions.

What had Mary said about the baron when I'd questioned his presence on her list? They were acquainted or close family friends? Neighbors perhaps? Well, they appeared friendly enough just now, standing close to one another, sharing smiles and whispered conversation.

The reminder of her bloody list had my fists clenching. It was wrong to begrudge her her own plans—if she was indeed still pursuing them. Her comfortable manner with Ashby certainly indicated she was. Wasn't I seeking my own future just the same?

But the thought of Ashby's hands—anyone's hands—on Mary's body had me fighting a grimace.

I stared after them feeling unjustly annoyed before Lady Sophia cleared her throat at my side. I startled, having forgotten she was nearby, before offering a polite smile and holding out an arm to find our places.

The game started off . . . poorly.

We chose our mallets and Lady Sophia seemed daunted by the prospect of swinging hers. She insisted I act as leader for our pairing while I noticed Mary assumed the role opposite me.

"You can swing first, Lady Mary," I offered congenially. I thought it best to forgo the ceremony of winning first position. She could have it. I would not pose a challenge.

"How magnanimous of you, Mr. Bartholomew," she replied, tone flat and unimpressed.

She took her first swing—a solid thwack that had her ball sailing through the first arch. Ashby congratulated her, and she beamed a smile to his insufferable face.

"Well done!" I felt compelled to say over the sound of Ashby's continued applause.

Pausing his ovation, Ashby lifted his head. "What was that, chap?"

Fighting a glower, I enunciated, "I said well done."

The baron buffoon smiled widely. "No, Mr. Bartholomew. That was Lady Mary's shot, not mine. She deserves your praise."

"I know," I replied in frustration. "I was complimenting her. Not you."

I caught Mary's stifled laughter just before she took her next swing, propelling her ball through the second arch. More clapping from Ashby.

She cleared the third arch before her turn was over, and my play was to commence.

I took my swing and easily maneuvered the ball through the first arch. With a quick glance, I noted that Mary and Ashby were in conversation and hadn't even noticed my shot. Lady Sophia was playing with the ribbons on her straw bonnet and gazing longingly to the grouping of four playing adjacent to us.

I rolled my eyes at my utter ridiculousness and strolled forward to take my next swing. Just as I brought my arm back, I heard Mary laugh loudly from behind me. My mallet struck the side of the ball and had it veering wildly off course.

"Bad luck, that," Ashby remarked with what appeared to be genuine empathy.

"Yes. So sad," Mary agreed with a solemn nod.

Lady Sophia whispered, "It was a good attempt, Mr. Bartholomew."

I resisted the urge to sigh.

Ashby took three arches before it was Lady Sophia's turn. Fearful of her mallet, she merely pushed the ball the short distance to the first arch.

Ashby called suddenly, "Ho, now, Lady Sophia. Surely, you can put a solid hit on the ball."

The young woman smiled prettily. "Oh, Lord Ashby, I'm ever so afraid of striking my foot by mistake."

"That is natural," the baron replied easily as he and Mary came closer to observe. "Simply stand a bit to one side and swing your arm clear of your body."

I rolled my eyes at his overeager and helpful manner. Mary caught the movement and raised one perfectly arched brow. Despite my annoyance with her companion, I felt a warmth move through me at her notice—the teasing on her face.

"Like this?" Lady Sophia called. She gave a halfhearted swipe and then blushed, giggling at her attempt.

Turning to watch this impromptu lesson, I placed the head of my mallet on the ground and leaned against it. "Lady Sophia, perhaps you should envision the boot of someone you find irritating and aim a solid hit in that manner."

The young lady paused her swinging arm to regard me curiously. "Why ever would I want to do that, Mr. Bartholomew? I couldn't imagine wanting to strike someone." She appeared unbearably disappointed in me.

I felt Mary lean in my direction, and I fought the urge to wrap my arm around her waist and haul her close. The heat and lavender scent of her skin taunted me.

"Clearly, she hasn't spent enough time around you, or the idea would be more appealing." Mary's muttered words were for my ears alone, as was the self-satisfied grin she wore.

I spared an amused look in her direction before mustering a winning smile for Lady Sophia. "I was only jesting, my lady."

The young lady's expression remained perplexed before she once again gripped the handle of her mallet and swung with enough force to hardly wound a blade of grass.

"Go on, Mr. Bartholomew," Mary said brightly, "show her how it is done."

I frowned in confusion, but once our party's attention had turned my way, I stepped back and took a practice swing of my own.

"No, no, no." Mary laughed. "Show Lady Sophia the correct way to hold her mallet and position her body." Mary made a shocking motion as if wrapping her arms around some invisible object. "Surely, you can demonstrate the appropriate force to use as she hits the ball."

She couldn't mean . . . to position myself behind Lady Sophia and grasp her body? Surely not.

"I don't think I understand."

"Come now, Mr. Bartholomew. We're all sportsmen and women here." Mary came around behind me and applied light pressure to the blades of my shoulders, urging me over to Lady Sophia.

I looked back to see Mary's gleeful expression. I could only imagine my confused and panic-stricken face.

"Here we go," Mary exclaimed as we approached Sophia and her mallet. "Mr. Bartholomew will set you to rights, Lady Sophia. I have no doubt."

I wondered at Mary's intent—her obvious effort to force my hand and make this entire exchange painfully awkward.

I very suddenly had no idea what to do with my hands. I refused to ignore propriety for the sake of some silly game. And honestly, I didn't want to put my arms around Lady Sophia. Instead, I approached haltingly and grasped the handle of her mallet— placing my fingers above her own.

Smiling in encouragement, I said, "You want a firm grip." And to demonstrate, I swung the mallet awkwardly behind our bodies before pausing. "And do your best to keep your eyes trained on the ball. It will be instinctual for your arm to follow your line of sight."

Lady Sophia wore a frown of utter concentration that I could not believe was actually warranted. But she dutifully followed my direction and locked her gaze on the ball by her feet.

"And then bring your arm forward with feeling and follow through." As the mallet passed beside my body, I released my grip. Lady Sophia's hand remained in place, and her swing continued toward her target with a satisfying thwack. Her ball sailed through the first arch and rolled with force, colliding with my own ball and sending it beyond the border of our field of play and out of bounds.

"Oh, well done!" called Ashby, who was back to inane clapping.

Lady Sophia turned to us with a wide grin before she jumped up and down in excitement. I nodded and smiled in her direction while Mary applauded merrily from my side.

"Wonderful job, Lady Sophia," Mary said sweetly.

The young lady continued her turn and managed another solid strike but missed the arch. It was then Mary's opportunity, and she successfully passed through wickets numbered four and five before narrowly missing the sixth.

Hoots and happy laughter followed Mary's successful turn, and I fought my irritation at everyone else's enjoyment. Ashby was smiling so brightly I thought his face might split in half.

I walked stiffly to where Lady Sophia had knocked my ball beyond the boundary and returned it to the edge of the green. With concentration and effort, I managed to pass through the second wicket. And then the third, fourth, and fifth.

Mary, Ashby, and I remained in close contest over the next quarter hour. We gained the midpoint in rapid succession, and each struck the turning stake. Lady Sophia had improved greatly but was several arches behind as the game progressed. Ashby's swings turned a bit wild during the second half of the game. Before long, it was down to myself and a determined Mary in her peach-striped gown.

The cheers of accomplishment dwindled as the game took on a serious edge. Ashby and Lady Sophia seemed content to chat amiably between alternating turns while Mary and I played against one another for the win. When only the tenth and final arch remained for us both, our balls collided. I could have taken the shot, cleared the arch, and struck the starting stake, but instead, I met Mary's determined gaze and smiled, slow and taunting. She'd grown quiet as the game wore on. There hadn't been teasing remarks or further attempts to foist me upon Lady Sophia. I ached for Mary's attention—for her eyes on me.

And now, I had it.

With my sudden delight, those gorgeous eyes narrowed. "You wouldn't," she said.

This was how we'd always behaved—even before everything had become complicated. I teased, and she sniped back. Her sharp expression settled something within me. Something I'd desperately missed.

I felt happy and free—like I could take a deep breath for the first time since we'd been apart. Maybe, after this, we could talk. Maybe she'd stop avoiding me.

"I think I might," I challenged, surveying the field.

Abandoning my final play, I turned and directed my attention to Mary's orange ball. With all my focus, I aimed and swung. My ball struck hers with such force that it rolled clear across the green and nearly to the turning stake opposite our current location. I'd sabotaged her play and ruined her positioning.

She stood across the green, exasperated and shaking her head. And her attention was all mine. Some selfish, undeserving part of me relished it.

Ashby approached with a shocked grin and raised eyebrows. "Perhaps a gentleman would have let her win."

"You must not know Mary very well if you think she'd want that." I didn't look away from the woman of whom I spoke, so I saw the change that came over her. The tight, irritated lines of her face fell into nothingness. And I was once again out of her orbit.

"I actually do know her quite well," Ashby said easily. I dragged my attention away from Mary to study his face. *What did he mean by that?* "We've been friends since childhood, and while I'd wager she enjoys a challenge, I don't know that she'd fight dirty in order to win."

I frowned as Ashby clapped me on the shoulder and stepped forward to take another shot. Lady Sophia followed suit.

Then Mary took a solid swing to put herself in better positioning for her next play.

But it wasn't enough.

I was the first through the final arch. With a skillful attack, I cleared the wicket and struck the starting stake, securing victory for my side.

Looking up, I sought Mary. I wanted to see her reluctant grin—the way her lips would turn at the corners before giving in and stretching wide. I'd seen it enough times in my bedchamber. I could plot the course and map her affections with ease.

But she wasn't watching me at all. She was beside Ashby, turning away and placing her mallet in the box. I couldn't see her face but instinctively knew she wasn't smiling.

"Thank God that's over," Lady Sophia murmured to herself before abandoning the remainder of the match and walking toward her mother who was in the middle of her own game.

"Well done, everyone," Ashby called as he tucked Mary's hand into the crook of his arm with ease and led her back on the garden path.

All the relief I'd felt at being near Mary again ceased. The air stalled in my lungs, and the brightness of the afternoon dimmed in her absence.

I no longer felt like I'd won anything at all.

Ten

MARY

"You played so well, Mary. I had no idea you had such talent with a mallet," Ashby said. He seemed to be genuinely impressed with my play. It was sweet. *He* was sweet.

I forced a quick smile. "Thank you, James."

"I'm sorry you didn't win."

"It's all right," I murmured. And it was. I was proud that I hadn't taken Silas's bait. I'd controlled my emotions—my anger and hurt —and kept my head about me. That wasn't something I was historically able to do where Silas was concerned.

There had been a moment there in the garden, with the golden afternoon light highlighting his goading smile, where I'd almost fallen back into our old habits. The bickering and the arguing— the energy and comfort of it. But I knew better now. That way lay infuriating heartbreak. Weakness.

I was moving on, and I refused to allow myself to be hurt by the presence or the absence of Silas's attentions ever again. It didn't matter how good it felt to see him and be close to him, to tease him about Lady Sophia—a woman who was so obviously not a love match that it bordered on painful.

I'd seen them together before, watched them dance or converse in our brief moments at corresponding events this spring. It had all been rather stilted and awkward, but Silas seemed determined to continue with his plans to marry this season. If not Lady Sophia, then some other appropriate woman.

No matter. He was no concern of mine.

Ashby and I continued our stroll through the Gravelys' gardens. It was a large and well-tended space, and the weather was fine indeed. With everyone distracted by croquet on the back lawn, we had a bit of privacy as we walked.

James cleared his throat before slowing us even further. "Mary, I wondered if I might ask a favor of you."

"Of course," I replied instantly. James and I had been spending more time together. I still didn't think I could broach the subject of an arrangement with my childhood friend, but he was a fine dance partner, and his presence now in my life was a kindness. I'd been lonely, missing Patty and her family. It had been painful to decline invitations and stay away from the Bartholomews. But the risk of seeing Silas was too damning. Events with them were unpredictable and, as a result, intolerable. I didn't think I could abide a chance encounter or Silas simply popping by for tea, so I'd stayed away.

And if the hollowness I felt now as a result of my latest encounter with the man was any indication, I'd been wise to refuse the company of the Bartholomews.

My friend smiled. "You are too kind."

"What is it? How can I be of assistance?"

A grimace claimed his features just as an embarrassed flush crept up his neck. "I'm afraid I find myself quite infatuated with Miss Louisa Gregory."

"Oh," I replied, surprised by the admission. I could not remember a time when I'd seen the young lady in Ashby's presence.

"Unfortunately, I find myself too nervous to speak with her." After an uneasy glance, James continued, "I'm hopeless at conversing with women. My hands grow damp in my gloves, and I can feel my heartbeat jumping into my throat, impeding all my words, all the things I want to ask her. All the things I long to know about her."

I smiled sympathetically, squeezing his arm gently beneath my hand. "How can I help?"

Returning the gesture, James patted my hand gratefully. "Perhaps you could join in conversation with Miss Gregory, and if I approach, you could lead the discussion to topics that we had pre-arranged, ones that I could practice. I want to get my thoughts organized so I don't embarrass myself. I don't want her to think I'm an idiot."

"She could never," I assured him. "I like your plan. If we practice in advance, you'll grow more comfortable. It's easier to feel at ease when there are no surprises in your path. And once you two are acquainted, Miss Gregory will be helpless to resist your charm."

James's blush was fierce now, fully encompassing his ears. "I doubt that."

"This will work. Have faith, my friend. We could start today. Is she about? I admit, I dallied indoors and avoided the garden as long as possible upon my arrival."

If James thought my admission odd, he didn't question it. "No, Miss Gregory is not in attendance today. But she accepted Mother's invitation to our event next week. You'll be there, won't you?"

I smiled. "Yes. My mother and I are attending. And we can put our plan into motion. Shall we use the remainder of our time today to discuss potential topics for conversation? I'll try to think about what I know of Miss Gregory and what she might enjoy chatting about."

James stopped on the graveled path and turned to me. "Thank you, Mary. Your agreement and immediate offer of assistance are a kindness. Truly. If there is ever any happiness my friendship could offer you, please, will you let me know?"

I thought of my goals and the child I sought—the family of my own making. Would James truly be willing to help me accomplish such radical aims? Could I trust him with the desires of my heart and ask for his support in this?

"I will consider it," I replied finally. "But for now, let's focus on your own happiness."

The Baron of Ashby was panicking.

The man appeared just moments away from heaving into the potted palm in his mother's gilded ballroom.

We were supposed to approach Miss Gregory separately in just a few short moments to enact the beginnings of our plan. But James wasn't ready.

Declining the liveried footmen bearing ratafia, I smiled and excused myself through the crush of ladies and gentlemen in attendance tonight.

James had stepped behind the greenery and was taking deep breaths and shaking out his hands. I approached quickly and glanced over my shoulder to ensure that the young lady we sought was still positioned across the ballroom. My eyes snagged unexpectedly on Silas. He wore a startling glare and watched me from a spot nearby to Miss Gregory.

What was he doing here?

I looked away quickly and focused on James and keeping him from casting up his accounts. This was no time for distractions. And Silas was nothing if not diverting.

"James," I hissed.

My friend noted my appearance and turned wide, panicked gray eyes my way. "Mary, thank God. I don't think I can do this. The nerves are starting—worse than ever." He held up a shaking hand in an elegant white glove. "Look!"

"It will be all right, I assure you. If you find you truly are not prepared, you can simply say hello, and I will control the conversation. You can nod along and smile when appropriate."

James appeared relieved as I spoke, his face regaining a bit of color. "Yes. Good plan," he choked out.

"But," I said softly, "I think you should take a moment to center yourself, and perhaps the words will come."

I quickly scanned the ballroom to ensure our odd behavior wasn't being noted and saw Silas Bartholomew watching me still, an unreadable expression on his face.

I swallowed uneasily and sought to distract James before he could argue. "Let's dance. It will take your mind off the conversation ahead, and we can practice your lines."

James nodded, looking a bit steadier.

Smiling, I held out my arm. "Come on, then."

The baron huffed a quiet laugh, his eyes losing some of the fear that had claimed his features only moments ago. "Okay. Yes. Thank you, Mary."

We made our way to the center of the dance floor, and memory took over, leading our steps in time with the music. I used the minutes to whisper words of encouragement and prompt James with our practiced conversation.

By the time the musicians played their final notes, James looked determined rather than ill.

"You're ready, and your young lady awaits," I encouraged as I curtsied. "Remember to smile. You have a lovely smile."

The severe line of his brow eased immediately, and he offered me a grateful grin as we turned away from the other dancers taking their place for the following waltz. "Mary, I can't thank you enough—"

James's words were cut off as he collided with a solid form.

"Apologies, Ashby. I didn't see you there," Silas said with a surprisingly serious face. It seemed he'd lost a bit of his charm tonight, even for the host of the ball.

James simply laughed off the interruption. "Bartholomew! Good to see you."

"Yes," Silas replied noncommittally. I fought the urge to roll my eyes at his unprovoked rudeness. "I was actually coming over to invite Lady Mary to dance. I didn't intend to interrupt."

He had most definitely intended to interrupt. The cad.

And why did he want to dance with me anyhow? Any occasion spent with me was a waste of his precious matchmaking time. Lady Sophia was in attendance with her mother. He should be over there charming them into submission. My stomach churned uneasily at the thought, and I placed a hand discreetly against my bodice.

"I'm afraid I am unable to accept your generous offer, Mr. Bartholomew. I see my good friend Miss Louisa Gregory, and I have been meaning to speak with her all evening."

"Your good friend?" he questioned.

"Yes," I confirmed, smiling with every single one of my teeth, pushing down my sudden nausea.

Silas frowned. "Well, perhaps another time."

I held eye contact for a beat before replying, "Perhaps. Good evening, Mr. Bartholomew."

His brown eyes looked frustrated and something else I couldn't name. He was typically so jovial and charismatic at society events, it was unusual to see him this way. I'd always hoped to get a rise out of him when we sparred in public . . . before.

It didn't feel as satisfying as I'd imagined to see the charming gentleman lose his luster.

Turning away from Silas was less of a challenge than it had been at the garden party the prior week. But I had a job to do this night. James needed help that required my focus and attention. And standing here mooning over Silas Bartholomew would get me nowhere.

I nodded to James, signaling we should part and then reconvene near Miss Gregory.

And then I forced my thoughts away from Silas.

Miss Gregory was too polite to question my sudden appearance at her side. We'd been introduced earlier in the season, but we were hardly more than acquaintances.

Undaunted, I bid her and her mother a good evening and asked how they were enjoying Ashby's event. Manners ingrained since birth had both women replying courteously. We discussed their travel plans for the summer, and it was as we were reveling over attending next month's Ascot Races that Ashby approached.

"Oh, Lord Ashby. What a lovely event. I do thank you and your mother for the kind invitation," I said with a smile.

"Lady Mary," James replied stiffly with an elegant bow.

I made introductions and watched Ashby light up in Miss Gregory's presence. I led the conversation easily, and James followed along, voice firming up the longer he spoke.

Louisa and her mother were obviously charmed by his affable nature.

We found a surprising topic that interested Louisa when James went off-script and mentioned how much he enjoyed our croquet match at Lady Gravely's recent event.

"Oh, I adore croquet!" the young lady said enthusiastically. "We must play together." And then she paled as if suddenly realizing how forward she'd been in her statement.

Ignoring her mother's horrified wide eyes and the girl's faux pas, I replied instantly, "That is a capital idea. Ashby's gardens are perfect, and the weather has been so grand. I am sure his mother would love to host you both."

"Yes, of course," James said happily, his grin wide and earnest. He appeared unable to look away from Louisa. Her grateful expression was so warm and admiring.

I felt confident that these two were well on their way to a happy future. It wouldn't even be a hardship to endure another croquet match in order to watch young love bloom.

And this future game had the added benefit of Silas's absence. The wayward thought had my focus slipping precariously down an icy path. My eyes searched the ballroom against my will.

The sounds of music and merriment faded. The anticipation of finding him watching me rose slowly before falling abruptly.

There was no trace of his laughing brown eyes anywhere.

He wasn't here. And he wasn't mine.

I needed to remember that.

Our paths had diverged. I couldn't rely on Silas, couldn't seek him out or depend on his smiles.

I'd never owned any part of his heart. But I'd realized too late he held all the pieces of mine.

∿

June

. . .

The carriage jostled once more and I clutched helplessly at the velvet-covered bench at my side. My stomach roiled with the motion, and I fought my mounting irritation. That hadn't even been a particularly pronounced bump.

I was going to have to ask my coachman to stop again, though. This journey to Berkshire and the Ascot Races was nothing short of misery. My eyes were watering with suppressed nausea. I closed them and took a slow, deliberate breath in through my nose and released it slowly through my mouth.

Oh hell.

My eyes flared wide as I rapped hurriedly above my head.

I flew out of the carriage as it reached a frantic stop. Wild eyes took in the tree line, and I rushed forward just in time to expel the last remnants of my breakfast.

This never happened. I had a decidedly strong constitution, and carriage rides had never bothered me before. What was different about today? Well, more than just today, now that I considered it.

I used a trembling hand to pull a handkerchief from my hidden pocket. Wiping my mouth, I straightened and made to return to the carriage. Only my nausea didn't abate even though I was standing on firm ground.

Turning, I hurried to the nearest tree and braced a hand against the rough bark, heaving once more. Nothing remained, yet my insides still protested vehemently.

This odd sickness had come and gone in waves over the last fortnight, leaving me frustrated and unwell.

Fortnight, I thought suddenly. We were well into June, and I . . .

Ignoring propriety and the hovering concern of my young coachman, Marshall, I leaned my back against the tree and thought hard. My body quivered, going both cold and damp with unease and what I knew to be true.

My courses had always been irregular, but I'd never gone so long without them showing up. I couldn't recall the last time I'd bled.

I'd been . . .

Oh.

Oh no.

It had been weeks ago, the end of March. Back when . . . Silas and I . . .

I'd refrained from visiting him in secret that week. He'd pouted like a child. He was so utterly ridiculous and cajoling, insisting it didn't matter. I'd stolen away to his home in the night anyway, and we'd dined together on sweets in his rooms instead of taking pleasure in each other's bodies. We'd eaten and drank and talked for hours. It had been the longest I'd ever stayed. I'd only arrived home a half hour before the servants had risen. And two days later, when my courses had finally abandoned me, I'd returned to Silas's bed.

And then a few short weeks after that, I'd found out he wanted to marry someone else—not even a literal someone else, just the idea. It turned out that even a hypothetical young lady was preferable to the very real version of me.

I swallowed against the hot rush of tears that threatened. Nose stinging, I tilted my head back and stared unseeingly into the green canopy of leaves above me.

What was I going to do?

I'd been reckless. Foolish to think that because Silas had carefully withdrawn from my body each and every time, that we could avoid pregnancy.

And then I fought the urge to laugh through my tears. Because it seemed I'd gotten what I'd always wanted—a child, after all. But with the one person whose involvement would ruin everything.

My breath came in pants, and the ground swayed beneath my feet. The sturdy tree at my back was the only thing keeping me upright. I couldn't think about Silas and the implications of his fatherhood right now.

What may have been moments or hours later, Marshall stood before me trying to gain my attention.

I opened my bleary, watering eyes to see his lips moving and sound coming from very far away.

"My lady," I finally registered. The concern on his face was troubling. "Please come and sit down. I am worried you will fall and hurt yourself. We can pause our journey as long as you need to gather your strength. Would you like something to drink?"

I shook my head vehemently as I let him lead me back to the carriage. The thought of eating or drinking made me want to retch once more. "No, I cannot."

"I apologize if my driving caused you distress, my lady."

"No," I rushed to say. "No, Marshall. I'm unwell. It has nothing to do with your driving. You are an excellent coachman."

He didn't look as though he believed me. "What would you like to do?"

Curl into a ball and cry. Be vulnerable for once. Allow myself to fall apart in private.

I felt a different sort of weakness now. My stomach seemed hollowed out and empty but steadier as the nausea abated. I feared I was in emotional distress from my realization rather than physically ill any longer.

"We should continue on," I said instead. "My sickness has passed for the time being. We are not far from the racing grounds."

Today was important for Julian and Genevieve and Miles and Patty. The Royal Ascot was a horse racing event over several days, and a strong performance from their horses would help establish Miles and Julian's stud farm. The races would provide connections and help drive buyers. Placement in the Royal Ascot would ensure the success of their new venture. I wanted to support my friends. I'd missed them desperately these past few months. It was important to me to be there for them today. As a result, the risk of seeing Silas had been manageable when I left London early this morning.

Now, it was catastrophic.

"Are you certain, my lady?"

I gave my very best attempt at a smile. "Yes, Marshall. I promise to rap on the roof if I'm overcome again."

But I didn't think I would be. The morning's effects had seemed to wear off, as was common with pregnancy.

Because in all likelihood, I was pregnant. With a child.

For the first time, something beyond fear and panic made itself known. There was a very small surprised and hopeful tug just behind my ribs.

I nodded once more to Marshall and let him hand me into the

carriage. I faced forward and settled myself gently as the conveyance rolled slowly into motion.

With a shaking hand, I tenderly touched the fabric covering my still flat stomach.

A baby. My baby.

My eyes filled again, but I bit my lip to keep my tears at bay.

Tentatively, I pushed with my hand, eager to feel any difference in my body. But my belly seemed just the same as it had always been.

I let my fingers splay wide across my abdomen. "Hello, in there." I waited a beat, but of course there was no response, inwardly or otherwise. After a moment, I said quietly into the small space, "If you could stop making me feel poorly, I would appreciate it."

The sounds of the carriage were all I could hear. I shook my head at my silliness.

I thought of the years I'd spent hoping, first as a young lady, eager and hopeful on the marriage mart. Then older, as a desperate and reckless woman with plans to achieve her aims. My fingers carefully stroked the bodice of my dress.

One single tear fell.

"I promise to love you and protect you. You are all I've ever wanted, and I swear to do everything I can to deserve you."

Eleven

MARY

The morning sickness returned as I was exiting the carriage despite it being hardly morning any longer. The sun was high and bright, a rare cloudless blue, that I could not enjoy with the threat of vomiting.

Ignoring the renewed churning in my stomach, I exited the vehicle and straightened the skirts of my lovely copper gown. Today's horse race was as much an opportunity to draw attention to fashion as it was to showcase horses. I reminded myself that this feeling—this illness—would pass. It wouldn't last forever. And it would hopefully leave me by the time I found my friends.

With slow, deep breaths, I retrieved my elaborate and decorative hat, complete with jeweled accents and a veritable plume of feathers. The Ascot Races gave society—especially ladies—a grand excuse to wear ostentatious and elaborate things.

My coachman hovered anxiously nearby.

I smiled weakly. "I am fine, Marshall. I shall make my way to the stands and find the Duchess of Cawthorn. I will be in good hands."

"Yes, my lady," he replied, still appearing unsure. But he went on his way, and I went on mine.

Soon, I was amid the bustle of spectators and able to ignore the discomfort I felt. I spotted Patty, Emery, Genevieve, and Silas seated in the center of a bench, and my stomach gave a hard lurch for an entirely different reason.

I'd known that Silas would be here, but seeing him so soon after realizing I was likely carrying his child was overwhelming. I forced myself to climb the central aisle of the grandstand, eyes never straying from my feet.

I could do this. I would sit on the opposite end and ignore him. Silas wouldn't be able to tell I was with child just by looking at me.

Well, not yet anyway.

Panic threatened, but I beat it back forcibly.

And then my nausea made itself known once more, and I could not stay. Turning abruptly, I bolted back down the stairs. My feet carried me away from the commotion of the vendors and observers until I found a grouping of trees and bushes in a fairly secluded area. I darted behind the tree and bent over, losing my precious hat in the process. I'd thought there had been nothing left, but I had apparently been mistaken because I expelled the remaining contents of my stomach.

From my twisted position, I heard Patty call my name.

Oh hell. They'd followed me. I prayed Silas wasn't standing behind me right now.

I turned carefully, bracing a hand on the sturdy tree at my side.

Patty and Emery stared at me with wide eyes.

I let loose a relieved breath.

He wasn't here. Thank God.

"Hello, ladies."

"What in the hell, Mary?" Emery called with a frown. "We haven't seen you for months. You've been declining invitations and avoiding us all. And now you physically run away from us? What is going on?"

Patty wasn't quite so forthright and demanding as her younger sister, but I could see the hurt lingering in her pale gaze, accusing me all the same. "Are you ill?"

I tried for a smile, and judging by Patty's worried frown, I didn't quite succeed. "A bit under the weather, I'm afraid. But I knew how important today was for Miles and for Julian. I wanted to be here." I eyed both sisters, hoping to convey all the things I could not say.

I missed you. You are my family. I was hurting, and I am so sorry.

Another wave of unease roiled through my midsection, and I felt my eyes water. I scraped my fingers against the bark of the tree, desperate to distract my body from this misery.

"What's going on?" I heard the question called and could identify the speaker as Genevieve Bartholomew, who apparently followed us from the viewing area. But I couldn't see her, as I'd forced my eyes closed, praying this bout of nausea would pass.

When that didn't work, I returned to the bushes and retched again.

I heard someone step up behind me, twigs crunching underfoot before Patty's elegant hand extended toward me, holding an embroidered handkerchief. My eyes focused on the carefully sewn blue border before I accepted her offering and passed the fabric over my lips with a shaking hand.

I straightened and faced the women—my friends—with a deep breath before noting the damage I'd done. "Dammit, my hat fell off."

Genevieve took a step forward. "We can get it back."

I raised a hand, urging her to stay back. "Don't bother. It fell off as soon as I leaned over. Then I cast up my accounts all over it. It's done for."

"It was a grand hat, Mary. I'm sorry," Genevieve replied sadly.

"All those feathers," Emery murmured helpfully.

I shot her a look.

"Genevieve, will you go and fetch some water for Mary?" Patty said impatiently.

The youngest Bartholomew straightened immediately. "Of course. I apologize. I should have thought of that."

I remembered Marshall's offer of sustenance during our last stop and the resulting churn in my belly at the thought. "No. Don't. I won't be able to keep it down. I can't eat or drink anything when it gets like this."

Patty appeared alarmed, and I knew I'd said too much. I wouldn't be able to keep this from her. From any of them.

"What's going on?" Emery said. "Was it the carriage ride?"

Genevieve argued instantly, "Mary doesn't get sick on long carriage rides."

The knowledge of the baby I carried sat heavily on my shoulders. I didn't know what to do. And the thought of continuing to avoid these women—whom I loved dearly—made a wave of loneliness and grief rise within me. Everything was about to change, and I didn't know if I could do this on my own. Despite my plans and my bluster and my arrogant independence, I was terrified.

I looked among them: Patty's dawning comprehension freezing her features, Emery's confusion, and Genevieve's sweet-natured concern for my well-being.

I shook my head and felt the sting of tears.

Their panic at the sight had them moving toward me and calling out all at once.

"What can we do?"

"Should we get a doctor?"

"Do you think you are?"

Patty's final question drew Emery's gaze and her comprehension. She gasped out my name and the first hot tears tracked down my cheeks.

"What? What is everyone going on about?" Genevieve hadn't yet realized the implications of my sudden illness, and Patty and Emery looked toward her expectantly, perhaps unsure how to respond. "Why can't you just tell me? What would make Mary sick like this repeatedly and—oh my God."

"Now she's got it," Emery murmured. "Gets her intelligence from Silas, this one."

The ground beneath my feet wobbled unsteadily as a wave of dizziness came over me. My stomach lurched once more, and I pivoted to find my place in the bushes where I stayed until the feeling passed.

Hours later, I was seated in the Duchess of Cawthorn's carriage with a lemon ice from the refreshment stand.

After my bout of sickness, I'd shooed my friends away to watch the races. I wouldn't allow them to remain with me when it was such an important day for their family. Patty had only agreed to return to the grandstand if I went to rest in her carriage, as it was the largest and the most lavish. She and Emery and Genevieve had threatened to accompany me if I even thought about leaving.

So, I'd taken the fan that had been pressed into my hand by Emery—who was wearing the largest hat I'd ever seen. And the lemon ice that Genevieve had insisted upon retrieving for me. And I was embarrassed to say I'd indulged in a long nap in the back of Patty's carriage while I awaited their return.

I'd woken to Patty and Genevieve quietly climbing into the vehicle, while Emery had been forced to remove her hat in order to fit through the doorway. We'd all laughed at the middle Bartholomew daughter and her over-the-top fashion. And it had felt good to laugh with my friends.

Emery had pressed a fresh ice into my hand and told me to sip. They'd reported that Miles and Julian's horse—Lark—had taken first in the Gold Cup, earning the notoriety they'd hoped for for Owensby Stud Farm. The men remained on the racing grounds with Silas and Augie and the farm's head groom, receiving congratulations, inquiries, and well-wishes in their new business.

I was so happy for their victory. The farm's success would ensure a happy future for Julian and Genevieve. Without a title or family money to speak of, Julian would be supporting his new bride through his own hard work and savings. His involvement with Owensby Stud as partner and head trainer would be much more profitable if the operation did well. And with the performance of their stock today, they were well on their way to becoming a lucrative investment.

With all the updates from the afternoon provided, my friends eventually fell silent.

Now they were all staring at me waiting for the truth of my situation to fall from my mouth. I looked down at my lap unsure of what to say or how to begin. It wasn't shame that held my tongue, although there was a bit of that. Silas was their brother, after all, and everything we had done had been behind their backs.

What kept me from spilling all my secrets was the realization that these women—with their love matches and devoted partners— could never understand my decisions. And the thought of not being seen or accepted by the women I loved and respected most in this world made me reluctant to reveal my truth and face their admonishment or, worse, their pity.

"Did the lemon ice help?" Emery asked quietly. "I had terrible sickness with little Beckett. The only thing that helped was tart food. Tea with excessive lemon. Orange marmalade piled on toast. Grain mustard on nearly everything. It was a trying time, to be sure."

I managed to lift my gaze to hers and nod. "It did help to settle my stomach. Thank you, Em." Whiskey-brown eyes, so much like her brother's, stared back at me with sympathy and tenderness. Her quiet smile said we had something in common, and for a moment, I didn't feel so alone.

Patty cleared her throat, drawing my attention. "Would you . . . like to talk? Now that you're feeling a bit better?"

An awkward silence descended as I thought of what I could admit. I would not tell them about Silas. I feared some wounds were too deep to ever recover from. My deception would end our friendship, and I wouldn't survive that.

"I—I had a plan," I managed, focusing on Patty so I could get the words out. I could give them this much. "I devised a plan to seek an arrangement. I hoped to have frequent relations with a gentleman from my list. And in my heart of hearts, I hoped that those trysts and encounters would result in a child."

"That's where you've been?" Genevieve asked cautiously. "You were someone's . . . mistress?"

Despite all my objections, that *was* all I'd been to Silas—a genteel mistress without compensation or protection. He wasn't a part of my plan, not really. But the outcome had been the same. Why mince words now? So I nodded in response, conceding to the simplest version of events.

"Did you tell the gentleman that you were using him to get with child?" Emery's sudden question startled me as did her severe frown. She was one of the most independent women I'd ever met. Emery had a career as an artist, and her fierce confidence was almost blinding in its brilliance. I would not have ever imagined that she could be so offended by my perceived deception.

What choices were women given in the bedchamber? It was the wife, the mistress, or the seduced who became the sole focus for indiscretions. Men lived their lives free and clear of unwanted bastards. Women were blamed, ruined, and shunned. And once married, a lady's duty was to produce heirs through no choice of her own.

I'd simply sought to make my own bed. I wouldn't apologize now for lying in it.

"No, Emery," I replied, finding the wherewithal to meet her accusing gaze. "I didn't ask permission, if that's what you mean. But our . . . arrangement wasn't about that when all was said and done. However, the consequences of intercourse are well established. It was a risk we were both willing to take." And because I couldn't stand the way she was looking at me, I admitted, "And he withdrew from my body every time. Hence my initial surprise."

Emery blinked, startled.

"*Your* surprise?" Patty questioned. "He doesn't know?"

"Our arrangement ended. Weeks ago," I confessed. "I didn't realize what was happening until the carriage ride to Berkshire this morning. I've been feeling ill at random intervals and with increasing severity over the last fortnight. My courses have always been irregular and unpredictable, but today, I realized just how long it had been."

Genevieve shifted on the bench across from me, leaning forward and clasping my hand. "But, Mary, if you wanted a child so badly, why wouldn't you simply find a husband?"

As if it were as easy as plucking one out of a tree.

I looked at this young, beautiful girl with her porcelain complexion and her unlined face. Her blue eyes bright and concerned as she awaited my answer. I wasn't angry with her naivete, simply resigned to admit the truth. "No one has ever offered, darling." Her frown was confused and indignant on my behalf. I fought the urge to comfort her. I did offer a sad smile. "I am firmly on the shelf, Gen. My dowry is not enough to tempt a match and neither is my figure or my face."

"But—but that is absurd," Genevieve managed in a dignified fluster.

I risked a glance at Patty who met my gaze—knowing and perceptive. We'd discussed my prospects many times over the years as well as my disdain for my parents' society marriage.

Closer to my own age, Patty knew from where my frustration over the marriage mart stemmed. She'd comforted me through being ridiculed and overlooked. And she'd been the only person I'd ever confided in.

I wasn't surprised that Genevieve looked so surprised by it all.

Genevieve, with her kind heart and a youthful disposition, implored me with her gaze. The world hadn't hardened her yet. And I hoped it never did. "You are—you are, Mary. So clever and entertaining. The perfect companion and a graceful dancer. And you're beautiful, Mary."

"Sweet girl, I am not beautiful."

I thought she might cry. "I hate that you feel that way about yourself. Why don't you see yourself the way we see you?"

"You view me through the lens of friendship," I replied easily. "It is with different eyes that a man views a potential wife."

I would never be anyone's prize, and forcing them to present me on their shelf would only make it that much more painful.

"Well, who is it?" Emery demanded. While the subject was not one I would have chosen, I was grateful for the shift in conversation. I didn't want to argue with Genevieve. "Who is the father?"

Before I could even begin to figure out how to answer, Patty cut in sharply, "That is none of our business."

Emery snapped, "It is if the cad won't marry her. If he turned her aside."

I laughed, drawing their incredulous stares. "He doesn't wish to marry me, Emery. And I am not about to force his hand and, now, my child on someone who does not want me—does not want us." I placed a protective hand over the tiny life growing within my womb. There was not a bone in my body that would accept a pity marriage for my future or an obligated father for my child.

"Well, sometimes men need a little encouragement," Emery supplied with a firm nod.

I nearly laughed again, thinking of her husband. Neighbors since birth, Augie had loved Emery their whole lives. Emery had only needed to finally notice him as more than a friend in order to fall.

"It doesn't matter," Patty interjected. "Mary is entitled to her privacy."

"You are right, Patricia. The father of my child does not matter. He never asked for this, and despite our precautions, the result is the same. I will love this baby just as well all on my own."

"You won't be alone," Patty said firmly.

"She's right," Emery agreed. "You'll have us. You can come to Hampshire this summer. We'll take care of you."

I looked at my friends in turn. Grateful. So damn grateful for their unwavering support.

"I do not know what I should do yet. This is all so new," I admitted. "With the season ending, it would make sense to travel to my family's home in the country and tell my parents there."

"In Northumberland? You might as well be in Scotland. We'll never see you," Emery groused. "We won't know what's happening with you or the baby or how your parents will react."

"Would they turn you out, do you think?" Genevieve asked quietly with a grimace.

I thought about my mother, who was disappointed I'd yet to marry. Then I considered my father, who was aloof at best. Neither of my parents understood me, but they tolerated me still living in their household and supported me financially. Would they consider me their daughter if my reputation was ruined? If they were forced to support a grandchild outside of marriage?

I shook my head. "I don't think so. They certainly would not be happy. They would want me to find a husband—anyone—to save my reputation. But, no, I cannot imagine my mother would let my father turn me out. That would be gossip too difficult to weather." Emery opened her mouth to respond, so I quickly amended, "But I will think on it. I won't go to Northumberland until I've decided."

Emery looked like she wanted to say more but resisted.

"What are your plans? Are you going back to London or traveling on to Hampshire?" I asked the carriage at large.

"Miles and I are returning to Hampshire. Franny is already there with Miles's mother. Genevieve and Julian are accompanying us," Patty replied.

Emery said, "Augie and I are returning to London. Gansey and Anders are minding the children, and we should return before they burn the place down. Silas is traveling with us. Though I might abandon him here. He's been in such a foul mood of late."

I endeavored to keep my expression passive at the mention of Silas and his unexpected temperament. I hadn't seen him since that strange night at Ashby's ball several weeks ago. Our paths hadn't crossed again, but everything I'd read in the gossip rags seemed to indicate he was still wife hunting, though there had been no mention of a betrothal or any one particular lady who'd snared his attentions. The season was practically over. I didn't let myself think about what that meant for Silas's aims. He could be planning a proposal this very moment.

"Regardless," Emery continued, "I imagine we'll be journeying to Laurel Park within the week." She eyed me. "You could come with us, Mary."

"I'll think about it, I promise."

And I would. I would think of nothing else but how to manage this unexpected outcome.

Going to Hampshire with my friends would solve several problems but create several more. The prospect of Silas in Laurel Park would be unavoidable, and with my body increasing, I wouldn't be able to hide my situation for long. Silas was many things, but unfortunately, an idiot was not one of them. He would realize that I was with child, and he would put together all the pieces.

He would want to do the right thing. He'd want to marry me.

I couldn't let that happen.

I'd meant what I'd told Emery. I wouldn't be an obligation—neither would my child. Silas had a plan of his own. He wanted an appropriate bride, one fit to be marchioness someday. He hadn't wanted me before. A baby wouldn't change what was in his heart.

The Bartholomews were all good people. The Marquess and Marchioness Northcutt had raised a respectable son and three good-hearted daughters. Silas would force himself to marry me because of his innate sense of right and wrong. His principles, his scruples, would demand it. And Silas would grow to resent me.

There was something to be said for duty and responsibility. But when you so desperately wanted to be chosen, a burden was the last thing you ever hoped to be.

Twelve

SILAS

I listened as Jamie carefully sounded out the words on the page, lending a patient ear and only stepping in when the boy requested it.

In the months since my valet and I had been reading together, his overall comprehension and writing ability had greatly improved. Instruction wasn't something that came naturally to me. Not at all. In truth, I'd discreetly approached the governess my sister had hired for her small children and borrowed several primers to assist my early alphabet work with Jamie. I'd considering bringing on a governess as well, but the oddity of the request would likely generate gossip, and I didn't think Jamie would take to anyone else assisting him.

After near-daily lessons for the better part of four months, Jamie had accomplished so much, and he was a handy valet as well. He still liked to chat. And occasionally forgot the correct form of address, but I rarely had gatherings in my home aside from family, so it mattered very little. Emery had teased me for hiring the boy, saying I'd just been lonely and needed someone who liked to talk as much as I did. But I'd caught her bringing him a small painting to take home to his middle sister, Miriam, who loved cats.

Jamie spoke of his family often and was happy to report that he'd been passing along his lessons, and now all three sisters were reading too. They were proud of their accomplishments as well. He often traded out books from the library here to share with them in the evenings after his work was done for the day. Patty had provided a trunk of some of Franny's old books to send along with Jamie to White Chapel. I hadn't commented on the new condition of many of those books or the dresses that had found their way in among them, but I loved my sister for it.

As a result of my efforts with Jamie's literacy, an idea had simmered in the back of my mind these last few months, and it was something I was eager to speak with Patty about. There were friends and neighbors of Jamie's in White Chapel who could benefit from learning to read. I wasn't qualified to help anyone. I could barely take care of myself. But Patty had respect and experience. And perhaps she had the wherewithal to further her reach and impact more lives. It was something I wanted to discuss with her in due time.

"I'll likely be spending much of the summer months in the country," I began, unsure how Jamie would react to the news.

He used the ribbon to mark his page and gave me his full attention. "Sir?"

"You are welcome to join me at my family home in Hampshire for a few months. Or would you prefer to remain in London?"

I typically stayed at Laurel Park with my mother and father when I visited the country. My housekeeper and maid would remain behind in London to look after the house, but Jamie wouldn't be needed in Belgrave Square on a daily basis any longer. I wanted to give the boy the option to travel with me if he desired. He'd never been out of London, as far as I knew. His mother was a seamstress and worked out of her home on mending and sewing. I was curious if he felt comfortable leaving his family for the summertime.

Jamie seemed to consider the idea. "I could go? To Hampshire and attend to you there?"

I nodded. "Yes. Although there won't be too much attending. There will be minimal events, and it is unlikely I'll be present at any house parties." There was one such invitation on my desk currently from Lady Gravely asking me to attend her annual gathering in nearby Wiltshire for a fortnight next month. I was fairly certain she was hoping for a betrothal to be the result of that event.

While I'd spent time conversing and dancing and paying calls to several young ladies this season, Sophia Huntsford had been thrown in my path by her mother more often than anyone else. I had no doubt that the countess hoped for a match between myself and her daughter; however, our personalities didn't suit, and I didn't think I could spend the rest of my life married to someone who could hardly speak in my presence. She was quiet and shy. More importantly, I did not truly believe she wanted to be married to me.

"You would have your own room among the staff," I further explained. "But in your off-time, you could go to the village or enjoy the grounds. It's a beautiful place to spend the summer." Jamie looked unsure. "Speak to your mother tonight. Think about it. And let me know. I don't plan on traveling to Laurel Park for another week or so. Your position is safe here, Jamie. You do not have to come with me. You could remain in London and resume your duties when I return."

He nodded. "Yes, sir."

I was already dressed and ready for my outing, so I said, "Why don't you take your book and go on home. I'm leaving to join Augie and Daly at the club within the hour. I imagine I will supper there and remain late into the evening. You are free to go."

"Thank you, sir," Jamie replied, standing and remembering to offer a small bow. "I'll talk to my mum about Hampshire and let you know straightaway."

I smiled as he excused himself and exited the library, book in hand and a spring in his step.

The thought of the summer months stretching out before me didn't give the same sense of excitement I typically felt. Of course I wanted to spend time with my family, and recreation in the country was always enjoyable. But I still didn't quite feel like myself. What had I actually accomplished this season? Yes, I had a new household, but not much else had changed.

Genevieve and Julian were married and absorbed with one another and their newly built home adjacent to Laurel Park. Owensby Stud Farm was staffed and operational. Miles and Julian were beginning that busy chapter of their lives. Emery and Augie would be spending time with the children, enjoying the slower pace of the country.

It would be another bachelor summer of showing up for dinner and spoiling my nieces and nephew. I'd hoped to have some direction for my life by now or at least feel more settled—not less.

Ever since things had gone all wrong with Mary, something restless lived beneath my skin. My stomach twisted when I thought of her. I could feel my typically jovial attitude drying up and blowing away on the breeze. I was unsettled. And I hated that she was avoiding my sisters—her friends—as a result of our falling out. All the secrecy had been for nothing, and she must be hurting without their companionship. Although, her closeness with Ashby persisted. Perhaps she didn't mind.

I worried I'd broken something within me when I'd ruined us. The way Mary looked at me now. It made me ache. It made me long for complications and secrets despite the path I now found myself on and the reasons I'd left that all behind.

I didn't know how to make things right between us, but I knew it would never be the same.

"Why are you glaring at Glenfellow?" Daly murmured from my right.

"I'm not glaring," I argued, still very much glaring in the man's direction.

Glenfellow and Brannigan had been playing cards loudly and obnoxiously with two other men at a table across the way. The gaming room at the club was fairly full. Cigar and cheroot smoke were thick in the air, and the sound of conversation and laughter filled the large lamp-lit space.

"Or is your ire directed at Brannigan? I can't tell," Daly said thoughtfully. "What do you think, Augie?"

I splashed another healthy serving of whiskey in my glass before throwing it back. The liquor burned a trail down my throat that hardly rivaled the anger churning within.

"I think," Augie said slowly, "that Silas can't kick his own arse, so he's looking to kick someone else's."

I ignored my friends. My focus was on the wastrels across the room and the anger consuming my thoughts.

Tonight, Glenfellow and Brannigan were in my sights for the first time since the Ascot Races, since my sister had mentioned what they'd done—what they'd said about Mary.

We'd been sitting in the grandstand in Berkshire, awaiting the Gold Cup race when Mary had appeared among the audience. It seemed that she was on her way to join us for the event. But instead, Mary had made it four steps before turning and bolting away. Emery had teased me, saying Mary had run away in order to avoid me. My sister hadn't known how right she'd been. I'd agreed in an offhand comment to Genevieve, saying the lady had bolted faster than a racehorse. Gen had rounded on me so fast that my head had spun. My baby sister had accused me of cruelty and mocking. When I'd remained confused by her scolding, Genevieve had explained that she thought I was referencing the bit of gossip that circulated last season when Glenfellow and his cronies had called Mary horse-faced and mocked her appearance. The moniker had apparently been whispered and repeated many times over.

And two of the men who'd facilitated those rumors—who'd fueled that old hurt—were in the same room with me.

As I seethed and plotted my plan of attack, I noticed the Baron of Ashby stroll through the doorway. The man seemed content to walk on by, but Glenfellow greeted him, drawing Ashby's attention and hesitation at their table.

"I must say, Ashby, I am quite surprised to see you so taken with Lady Mary," Glenfellow said at full volume—so loud I could hear him from my position, tables away. The others around us had quieted. Perhaps they could scent coming drama and wanted to give their full attention as spectators. "Always dancing and leading her about. Can't see that she's worth the effort."

I had but a moment to register the surprise on the baron's face before I was up.

Pushing back from the table, I placed my glass down hard and started toward Glenfellow and the others.

I heard a muttered, "Ah, Christ," from behind me, but I kept going, twisting smoothly between tables and chairs, ignoring calls from acquaintances.

They would not speak of her in my presence. I wouldn't allow it. I'd make them regret it.

I heard the sharp sound of Brannigan's laughter. "Agreed, gents. How could you lower yourself, Ashby? She's frightfully plain and —" Brannigan saw me coming and broke off his insults to call out, "Bartholomew! You up for a friendly game?" He tossed his cards on the table and gave me a challenging grin, his lips twisting around the corners of his invitation.

I couldn't wait to shut him up.

"Yes, Bartholomew, join us!" Glenfellow added distractedly while he gathered the cards and shuffled.

I'd neatly distracted the men with my arrival. Ashby had been forgotten and summarily dismissed. He looked at them gathered round the table, a hard frown on his typically jovial face, before stalking away. It was better he was gone for this anyhow.

"I'm afraid I'm in no mood to be friendly, gents."

And then I reached for the bottom of the chair closest to me—holding Glenfellow—and tipped it back. The man landed hard, but I stepped over him and right up to Brannigan.

He'd stood immediately as Glenfellow went down, as had the two other men at the table, but my quarrel was not with them. They hadn't been on the list of offenders my sister provided.

The room erupted in shouts. Bodies surged to get closer—to witness the spectacle.

One swift swing had Brannigan stumbling back, clutching his bleeding nose and wailing something about his father and making me pay for this. But I was already turning, focused and intent on Glenfellow who was just climbing to his feet. He wouldn't be there long.

Augie and Daly were pushing past bodies, rushing up to the scene I'd created.

"Keep them off me!" I shouted to Daly, indicating the two other men at the table who looked ready to defend their friend and come for me. I didn't want a knife in the back or a bottle of liquor over the back of my head.

I didn't bother waiting to see what my friends would do. Daly was a bruiser. Bigger and burlier than any duke had the right to be, but he was loyal and he'd have my back. Augie was the one I'd have to watch. If he got to me, it wouldn't be to help. He'd drag me out of here to keep me from hurting myself or to prevent me from getting called out. Augie would end this fight before I got what I wanted.

Glenfellow deserved to be punished. He'd hurt the woman I— he'd hurt Mary. Spread hurtful gossip and called her names. He was a bully, and he used his position in society as a wealthy aristocrat to belittle women for sport. Someone should have put him in his place long ago.

The liquor blurred the lights in the room, but all my focus was on the man staring at me with wide, disbelieving eyes.

"What's all this now, Bartholomew?" Glenfellow questioned, hair askew. He was nearly my age. Old enough to know better.

I didn't provide an explanation. I rushed him, and we both hit the floor, my shoulder landing with a jarring thud. I heard the chair snap somewhere beneath us, but then we were rolling. The carpet scraped roughly against my cheek as we grappled. But I came up on top and started swinging. Men were shouting, and glass was breaking. Glenfellow was bleeding beneath my fists. I felt something crack and fissure in my left hand, but I didn't stop, just gritted through the pain. And then it was over.

What felt like an eternity was probably done in seconds. Glenfellow was still conscious and breathing, and I was airborne.

Daly and Augie pulled me off, one of them grabbing each arm while Glenfellow lay cowering on the floor.

"Time to go," Augie said calmly as I struggled to get my feet under me.

In a hazy, drunken rage, I stumbled out to the carriage with my friends escorting me. Augie told Daly to go on, and that he'd see me home.

I cradled my hand to my chest as we rode in silence to Belgrave Square.

Once inside, Augie hauled me toward my rooms on the second floor. He deposited me none too gently on the sofa in my sitting room before walking into my bedchamber and returning with a basin, a pitcher, and a linen cloth. He brought everything over to the low table in front of me where he sat, facing me.

"Give me your hand," he said evenly. I'd always been impressed by Augie's ability to appear unruffled. The most expressive I'd ever seen him was when he'd caught Mary and me in the cupboard at Laurel Park. I nearly smiled at the memory before my amusement fell away.

Augie took the cloth and tore a section off, using the wider portion to dampen and clean off the blood on my knuckles. I hissed at the pressure and jerked away from his touch. Something was definitely wrong with my hand.

Augie flashed me an irritated look and grabbed my hand again, albeit gently. "You are an idiot."

Then he used the thinner strip of linen to carefully wrap my hand. My fingers were straightened and secured with only the tips sticking out of the white fabric. The wrapping continued over my knuckles down to where my thumb extended.

"See a doctor tomorrow," he said, tucking the end of the fabric firmly in place. "It's swelling up and probably broken."

I ignored his mothering and stared at the unlit fireplace.

Augie gathered up the supplies and returned them to my bedchamber, disappearing through the doorway momentarily before returning and removing his jacket. He sat heavily on the adjacent armchair and let out a sigh.

"We're getting too old for this, Silas."

I huffed a laugh. "You have never gotten into a brawl in your life —even when you were younger."

"Perhaps not a brawl," he allowed, "but I know what it's like to be angry enough to go after someone."

Finally, I turned to meet Augie's bright blue gaze.

He didn't elaborate but instead asked, "Do you want to tell me what possessed you to attack those men?"

"You heard them. You heard what they said about Mary."

"Before that," Augie clarified. "You'd been glaring a hole through them all night."

I could feel the severity of my frown digging grooves into my face, pulling the skin tight. "Genevieve told me what they said about Mary last season. How they whispered it behind her back, loud enough to hear. How they spread the name across ballrooms while she laughed away the discomfort and the mocking. Did you know?" The accusation was out before I could call it back, sharp and angry.

Augie watched me calmly. "Did I know Glenfellow was a piece of shit? Yes, of course. Did he and Brannigan deserve an unholy beating? Most definitely. But did I think I needed to defend Mary's honor and start a public brawl on her behalf? Not really, Silas, no. You understand how gossip works, do you not?" A lazy glare was my only response. "The more fuel you provide the fire, the harder it is to put out. Mary managed that snide horse-faced moniker just fine on her own. She gave it no weight, and soon Glenfellow and Brannigan and Hartley and whoever else lost interest. Their amusement died a quick death because she snuffed it out handily. Thank God they simply thought you mad and drunk and have no idea why you attacked them tonight or you might as well have lit a brand-new match. You would not have done her any favors."

I looked away, feeling shamed by Augie's words. I was angry and stubborn, but he was right.

"I just felt so helpless," I admitted. "To know that they'd . . . hurt her, when she is typically so untouchable." I swallowed against the pain of being too little, too late, and not enough for her in the first place. "And then I saw them sitting there so smug and pompous. Heard them laughing again at her expense, right before my eyes. I let my anger fill me up. And then . . ." I used my good hand to mime an explosion.

Augie nodded from the corner of my vision. "I know I said I didn't see anything or know anything"—he hesitated—"but obviously something happened with you and Mary. And then that something ended. You haven't been yourself since, Silas." Augie waited a moment, but when I offered nothing, he went on, "Do you perhaps want to, um, talk about it?"

His discomfort at the prospect of discussing my feelings nearly made me laugh out loud. God, Augie was repressed. I loved him, though. He was a good brother-in-law. My closest friend, truth be told.

"We were together—in secret—for months. It started over the Christmas house party at Laurel Park and then continued back in London. She made the rules, and I followed them. Until I couldn't any longer. I grew resentful, I suppose. I got tired, Augie, of feeling like someone's dirty little secret. She had no problem leading two lives while I was falling in love with her. I could hardly get her to talk to me about her day—her life, anything. And when I brought up the idea of calling on her or courting, she quashed it. Every time. I couldn't even convince her to stay the night, how could I get her to admit that we had a future, or, hell, get her to marry me someday. I wasn't going to beg, and I wasn't going to force her hand or compromise her or ruin her. I was ready to settle down."

I met Augie's gaze and admitted, "Seeing you and Em and your family. Miles and Patty and Franny. And now Gen and Julian. I realized how far behind I am. So many things are missing in my life. I'm tired of having no responsibilities, and no one to answer to. Father treats me like a child, like I'm incapable. I'm just the rascally Bartholomew sibling who never takes anything seriously. All I had was a woman too embarrassed to acknowledge me in public. So I decided to grow up. I acquired a home and a staff."

I took a deep breath and confessed where it all went to hell, "And I thought I should try to find a wife. Make myself respectable. Someone worthy."

"Silas," Augie sighed, running a hand down his face. "Did you tell Mary all this?"

"I didn't get the chance. Emery announced Mother's grand match-making plans—I'm not blaming Emery. It was my fault. I realize now that I mucked everything up. I should have been honest about what I wanted and how I was feeling. We had an agreement. She never wanted more."

Augie ran an exhausted hand through his dark curls. "Silas, no one thinks that about you. All those things you said. We don't believe you are irresponsible or without accomplishment. You're not behind in life. Of course we all want you to be happy. But I sure as hell don't think marrying Lady Sophia will make you content. Marriage to a woman you hardly tolerate won't fix your life the way you think it should. It might get you closer to having a family, if that is your wish."

"It is my wish," I interjected. "I adore Reeve and Beckett and Franny. I want children of my own. I will be an excellent father."

Augie allowed a small smile. "You will be." His smile faded as he asked pointedly, "But don't you want love? Isn't that part of what you want when you look at your sisters and their marriages? The reason you feel like you're missing out on something?"

I considered Augie's words. I supposed he could be onto something. All of my sisters had married for love and seemed happier for it. Would marrying Lady Sophia bring me even a fraction of that joy? Would I be right back in the same position of feeling envious of my family?

"When was the last time you were happy, Silas? Perhaps you should consider that. Because it is all we can hope for in this life. To live it with someone who makes every moment better simply by sharing it."

I thought about the last time I was happy—the last time I felt like myself. And I knew the answer. Of course, I did.

Soft, porcelain skin. Wild red hair. Sparring in public and loving in private. A flash of heat. An image of our hands clasped together, sinking down into the bedding. The slow unfurl of her smile and the way I could never seem to get close enough.

I prodded at my hand, wrapped tightly, and winced. I'd attacked two men tonight for what they'd said about Mary. I could blame it on liquor and compulsive decision-making, but that wasn't the truth. They'd hurt someone I cared about, and I'd wanted them to suffer—even after the fact. Even if she never found out about it.

God, I hoped she never found out about it.

With reluctance, I could admit it to myself. I missed Mary, and I was happier when we were living our double lives. Could I go back to being her secret—begging for another chance?

Or was there an alternative to hiding the truth of our relationship?

I finally lifted my gaze to Augie who waited patiently in the armchair. "How do you admit you were wrong? How do you ask for forgiveness when you hurt someone so horribly?"

Augie took a breath. "You have to set aside your pride. You have to be honest. And you have to be willing to burn it all down if it means you have a chance at something better."

Thirteen

MARY

"All right, Little Duck. We're going to have some tea and then give this toast our best effort."

Patting my stomach for reassurance, I picked up the saucer and teacup from the tray service in my sitting room. I took a tentative sip of tea and held my breath.

In the fortnight since the Ascot Races, I'd followed Emery's advice for consuming acidic food to varied levels of success. It seemed that today, I might be in luck.

I slathered the toast with marmalade and nibbled one corner. Then I took a healthy swallow of lemony tea for good measure.

The pregnancy vomiting had mostly ceased, but the nausea was still prevalent when I was faced with consuming food. If my parents found it strange that I'd requested the majority of my meals to be taken in my rooms, they hadn't commented on it. Or more likely, they hadn't cared. In fact, I'd seen very little of my family in the past month. The house had been quiet. And with fewer events to close out the season, I'd mostly been resting. It

191

seemed that being with child was exhausting. I found I could sleep nearly any time of day.

When I wasn't resting, I was spending time with Emery at Kendrick Manor. She and Augie were planning to retreat to Hampshire next week and join the rest of their family. But Augie had a few meetings with influential Parliament members before they were ready to depart.

Emery and I had been playing with the children amid all my questions about pregnancy and childbirth. The middle Bartholomew daughter was frightfully open and honest—perhaps that was why we got on so well. But I'd learned a great deal about what to expect. And according to Emery, I had several months yet before my waistline expanded and keeping the baby a secret would become more difficult.

She'd offered to send me several of her favored dresses from her pregnancies. I could not imagine asking my mother to visit the modiste in order to purchase button-front wrappers to be worn at home. But Emery promised to include a short corset with additional laces to accommodate a woman who was increasing.

With my summer plans still very much undecided, Emery was having Gansey transport the aforementioned items discreetly this afternoon. Gansey was Emery's friend and member of her household. She would not ask questions nor would she spread gossip about the articles of clothing being delivered.

Just as I'd managed to consume two pieces of toast between three cups of tea, our maid, Blythe, bustled in with an armful of laundered items. Blythe was my mother's maid and tended to me when my hair needed to be managed or I required extensive dressing for a ball or other event. She had been with my mother for many years and was quite handy with a needle and thread.

"Good afternoon, Lady Mary," Blythe said softly, attempting to curtsy with her armload of fabric.

"Oh, hello, Blythe."

She lingered, eyeing my empty dishes. "If you're finished up there, I'll return your tray to the kitchen."

"Thank you."

The woman nodded and turned to my bedchamber, crossing the threshold of the open doorway and making for my wardrobe, presumably to put away the washing.

I finished the last bit of cooling tea before Blythe returned and gathered up the china, going on her way.

The afternoon sun was shining warm in my bedchamber, so I opened the windows and moved to enjoy the fine day.

With another grateful pat to my stomach, I murmured, "What do you say, Little Duck, time for a nap?"

Then I removed the pins from my hair that prodded insistently along my nape before making myself comfortable and sleeping soundly for the next several hours.

It wasn't until three days later that everything went to hell.

My nausea had returned, and I was abed when my mother burst into my sitting room as she called out my name.

I was so surprised that I lurched forward into an upright position and had to clutch my protesting stomach as a result. "Mama! I'm here. What is the matter?"

My mother appeared wild-eyed in the doorway to my bedchamber. "Mary, tell me you are not with child."

I could feel the blood leaving my face, and whether the uncomfortable hollowing of my stomach was from shock or pregnancy, I could not distinguish. "I—I what do you mean?"

Her dark brown eyes, so much like my own, searched my face. Then her insistent gaze landed on my rumpled bed linens. She seemed to note that I was abed in the middle of the afternoon. "I mean," she replied pointedly, "that this morning's edition of the *Ton Tattler* made a wild claim that you were with child."

"What?" I breathed. "They accused me by name?"

She held the newsprint aloft. "No, not by name. Just the ridiculous abbreviations they typically use, but, Mary, there was no denying the implication." She brought the paper before her and scanned before reading from the gossip rag. "This publication received a notable report from a reliable source. An unexpected tale about a surprising Lady M. whose red hair is as wild as the aforementioned news. Our source confirms that this unmarried lady is currently spending her days removed from visitors in preparation for her early confinement. As this is a subject unfit for the eyes and ears of impressionable young ladies, that is all that we are at liberty to report."

I tried to swallow, but my mouth was too dry. "Mama . . ." I didn't know what to say. I was very certainly the only Lady M. with red hair. And the *Tattler* was one of the most popular weekly gossip papers. It circulated with regularity and frequency among the aristocracy. Everyone in London would know of my secret.

"Is it true?" she hissed, approaching my bedside.

How had the paper found out? My friends were the only ones who knew about the baby, and they would never betray my trust. This did not make any sense.

I didn't think I could stand as panicked tears welled in my eyes. With a desperate sob, I met my mother's shocked expression and nodded.

"Oh, Mary!" she wailed, collapsing onto the armchair at my bedside. The newsprint fluttered to the ground, and I couldn't look away from the neat lines of ink upon the page. "What have you done? And who is the father? He will marry you straight-away. Or your father will—"

"No," I interrupted, finally finding my voice and meeting her gaze. "The father has no part in this. We won't be married."

"But you'll be ruined! You won't be welcome anywhere. You cannot keep this child and expect to carry on with your life."

"I know that," I admitted quietly, begging the tears to abandon me when I needed to be strong. "Everything will change. I will go to the country, and I will remain there with my child, if I must."

My mother shook her head in confusion. "To Northumberland? You'll remain there and disappear from London? What will we tell everyone?"

Of course that was her concern. Society and perception. It was why she suffered a miserable marriage that made a fine connection for her family. It was why she smiled happily in public and lived in misery in private.

"Tell them I am unwell. Tell them I need the country air to convalesce. That the *Tattler* was mistaken. It doesn't matter. I'm not giving up this baby for any reason. And I'm not marrying someone to save my reputation."

"There is no saving your reputation anyhow. The truth is already in every drawing room and at every dining table in Mayfair." My mother threw herself back in the chair and covered her eyes with her hand, unable to look at me any longer.

I carefully swung my legs to the side of the bed and made to stand.

My mother's head snapped up. "Where are you going? You cannot leave this house."

"I'm going to pack," I replied, walking to retrieve my trunk and open my wardrobe.

"We must talk to your father. Right now. He must be told, and we must form a plan so that you do not destroy the future of this family with your selfishness. Perhaps you're right, and we can spread the rumor that you are unwell. That will give us enough time to acquire you a husband."

I ignored my mother's hurtful words and began sorting through the dresses hanging neatly in my wardrobe. Frowning, I ran a hand across patterns I didn't recognize. There were several wrappers with buttons running all the way down the front. These weren't mine, so what were they doing among my things? I continued pushing the fabric aside when I came to a corset. It had extra laces and was shortened and very clearly for a woman who was increasing with child.

My mother's voice was very far away—still going on about planting a story of an imagined illness and a wedding that would never be—but I was frozen, staring at Emery's dresses hanging in my wardrobe. She'd promised to send Gansey with them.

I turned to face the doorway and my sitting room beyond, remembering Blythe bustling in with heaps of fabric days ago. My mother's maid must have intercepted Gansey and put the garments away herself. She'd seen the evidence of my condition. And she must have been the one to spread my news far and wide.

Before I could let my anger fill me up, Mama appeared suddenly at my side. She grasped my hands firmly. "Mary, are you listening to me?"

I shook my head, too furious at Blythe's deception to respond.

"We're going right now to speak to your father."

And then my mother dragged me from the room.

The conversation went as well as could be expected.

My father's anger simmered below the surface before bubbling over in a magnificent eruption—right around the time that I refused to divulge the name of the baby's father.

He agreed with my mother's plan, surprisingly enough. They would tell everyone that I was unwell and send me off to Northumberland with Blythe to accompany me as soon as my things could be gathered. I had no intention of going anywhere with that woman. If two of us entered a carriage, only one would be coming out.

And so I listened to my parents speak. I nodded when appropriate and kept my eyes dry. And then I made plans of my own.

My mother had taken to her rooms, telling the servants she was not to be disturbed for any reason. My father had stormed out of the house following his mandates.

I was currently in the kitchens packing a hamper, careful to select foods that wouldn't cause me further illness on my journey, when I heard a guest arrive. Following the news from the *Tattler*, I thought it might be Emery coming to check on me. But it wasn't.

It was Silas. I heard his voice as he spoke to our butler, but something about it was off.

Oh, God. Had he read the rumors as well? Had he figured everything out and come to confront me? What could I possibly say to him?

My hands trembled as I gathered my skirts and moved toward the formal receiving room. "I will see to my guest," I told our butler, dismissing him with a nod.

When I turned to face Silas, I nearly jolted from the shock of it. He looked awful—like he hadn't slept. And if he had, it was in the gutter. His hair was disheveled, and his eyes were red and bloodshot. And most troubling of all, he stood in my home, hat in hand, wearing the most uneasy expression I'd ever seen on his face.

He must know the truth. That if I was with child, it must be his. He was panicking. There was no other conclusion to be reached.

I made an impulsive decision and grabbed his right hand, doing some panicking of my own.

He looked at me in surprise as I said quietly, "Come. I don't want to have this conversation here."

Silas didn't argue. He simply followed me up the stairs to my rooms.

Thankfully, my parents were not about, and we did not encounter any other members of the staff.

The march to my quarters didn't take nearly long enough. I had no idea what I was going to say to him by the time we arrived, and I discreetly closed my door, shutting us in with enough unease that I felt strangled by it.

"What's all this?" Silas asked, distracted by the open trunks and clothing spread all around the room.

I swallowed around the painful lump in my throat. "I'm packing. I leave for the country today."

He frowned. "How long will you be away?"

Glancing up sharply, I met his stare, unsure what he was playing at. My confinement would last months. Surely he knew that.

"I don't know exactly," I answered honestly. If my family had their way, I would remain there indefinitely . . . unless I produced the father of my child or found some other gentleman to marry me in his stead.

"Oh," was Silas's only reply.

Was he not going to say it? Was he waiting for me to bring up the *Tattler's* claims?

Frustrated by his silence and his sudden appearance in my home, I blurted, "Why are you here, Silas?"

His troubled gaze met mine, and he awkwardly crossed his arms, wincing at the contact and then uncrossed them all over again.

"What's the matter with your hand?"

He'd placed his left hand gingerly at his side. It was wrapped in linen. "Just a bit of an accident. Playing cards last night." I opened my mouth to question him further, but he indicated the sofa. "Can we sit a moment and talk?"

He wanted to speak after so many weeks apart? I'd briefly seen him in the grandstands of the Ascot Races before I'd been forced to flee. And we hadn't spoken since that disastrous croquet match back in May, nearly six weeks ago. So much had changed since then. I resisted the urge to touch my stomach, seeking comfort from the tiny life growing within—the life that this man had helped me create.

Instead of arguing or demanding to know his intentions, I walked to the small patterned sofa and pushed my traveling dress aside. I took a seat, and then Silas settled himself in the adjacent armchair.

"Mary, I wanted to—well, I needed to tell you how sorry I am about how things ended between us. I was idiotic to think I could create a future out of thin air, one that could never make me happy anyhow. I thought I was doing what was right. What was expected of me."

I stared at Silas, unsure what to make of this speech and frankly uninterested in hearing, once again, how he needed an acceptable wife.

I'd never been the model of a genteel young lady. I hadn't quite managed it. My looks and my personality hadn't lent themselves to all the things men sought in women. Silas wanted what every other gentleman wanted. More than ever, I knew that couldn't be me.

He shifted in his seat, obviously uncomfortable. "I'm not saying this right. Someone asked me recently to think of the last time I was happy—truly happy." Silas's gaze dropped to his left hand, unmoving and stiff atop his thigh. "And I'm fairly certain the last time I was happy was when I was with you."

He looked up then. His eyes, so striking in their color and directness, pierced me. "I was happy being with you, and I think that was part of the problem. You wanted everything to be secret. You wanted to keep *me* a secret. And I didn't want to be something shameful. I wanted to dance with you in public and escort you on my arm. Whenever I brought up the idea of calling on you, you reminded me of your rules. You were adamant that our families could never see us together. That no one could ever know." He sighed. "I felt like you were giving me bits and pieces of you and then asking me to return them when you were done. All the while, I was handing you parts of my heart that I never got back."

My hands were trembling, so I forced myself to smooth the fabric of my pale skirts. Why was he saying this? We'd both agreed. Our relationship—whatever it was—had to be hidden. His sisters could not know. I was an unmarried woman and therefore the world must remain ignorant of my misdeeds.

"What would you have me do, Silas? Announce my ruination. Take out an advertisement in the *Post*?"

He looked pained by my questions. "I wanted not to be the only one falling in love."

Shock had my grip tightening, clutching the muslin beneath my fingers. "You cannot mean that." He'd cast me aside and sought out other women while I'd been blindsided and lost, wallowing in the sudden realization that I cared for Silas Bartholomew far more than I ever intended.

"I recognized that I wanted more from you than you were ever willing to give. I couldn't even get you to stay the night. I was desperate for your time and your attention. But I also wanted a future—a wife, a family. But the woman in my bed had made it painfully clear that I was only good for one thing."

"What about the ideal you seek?" I said in challenge, suddenly angry with his accusation. "It was quite clear that you wanted someone young and beautiful to be your marchioness someday. Not me."

He frowned. "When did I ever say that?"

"The afternoon at Cawthorn Hall, the day it ended. You said you wanted someone appropriate—someone you could have a future with."

"Yes," he admitted, "a future. Not hidden in a cupboard or begging for scraps. You were unwilling to acknowledge what was happening between us, to ever allow it to grow. Our families would have understood. They would have been happy for us, Mary. We could still be happy."

It was increasingly clear by the turn the conversation had taken, that Silas was not here to talk about rumors that I was with child. He didn't know. He couldn't.

I could feel my brows wrinkling in confusion. "What are you saying?"

Silas leaned toward me, bracing his forearms on his thighs and taking my left hand in his uninjured one. For once, Silas wasn't wearing a smile. He looked earnest and determined. "I'm saying I want a future with you, if you'll have me. A real one. Where we court openly and I escort you to the opera or to promenade in the park. We dance at balls and argue and bicker because it's what we like to do. We go back to being happy together . . . but for all the world to see."

The press of his hand was the only thing I could focus on. That and the frightening pace of my heart. A part of me—the one who'd realized far too late what those nights in Silas's bed had meant—wanted to weep with relief. Then there was the realistic woman who knew that there were consequences for happiness. The proof of it was growing in my womb.

Silas and I had cultivated expectations for the better part of a decade. We'd never gotten along in public. Our antagonistic banter was legendary and common knowledge among our set. No one would ever believe that Silas Bartholomew had fallen in love with me. I hardly believed it, and he'd as much as admitted it in this very room. We didn't have time for courting or the opera or dancing at balls. I was carrying a child, and the world already knew it.

My mother's friends and my father's associates would allow the tale of my mystery illness with a wink and a nod. They'd whisper behind their backs, and everyone would know the true nature of my banishment.

"And then one day," Silas said, smiling gently, "we marry. And continue being happy for the rest of our lives."

Marriage.

If I went along with what Silas proposed, the *ton* would think him a cuckold, a laughingstock. He'd never be the respected heir he sought to be. And he'd be unable to shed the image of himself that he so despised. Silas would be gossiped about for the rest of our lives. They'd say he was a fool, tricked into a union with a horse-faced woman who no one wanted. Or more likely, that he associated himself with me to salvage my reputation. They would assume he was helping a Bartholomew close family friend out of a terrible situation, preventing my ruination and public shaming. The whispers would follow our child throughout their life as well.

A future for us would be tainted. I couldn't live with myself if I was the reason Silas never reached the potential he saw for himself. If he was never respected the way he wanted so desperately to be, the way he'd admitted to craving as his siblings matured.

But I didn't know how to say all that or admit any part of the truth. Silas would never rest if he thought this child was his. And, as a result, he'd never achieve his goals.

I would be an anchor about his neck, dragging him into an ocean of resentment and regret.

Shackled.

We'd be just like my parents, putting on smiles in public before returning to a loveless and joyless home—to a child who could only look on in confusion and hurt. The thought of turning Silas and myself into the reality I'd lived with my entire life had panic surging, coating every part of me. I couldn't let that happen. No matter the cost.

Warm pressure had my attention emerging from the turmoil within. Silas's hand gave me another squeeze, needing to hold on tighter, as if he could tell I was already slipping through his fingers. "Things can change, Mary. Just because our relationship started with secrets and lies, doesn't mean it can't change. *We* can change."

Emotion was gathering behind my eyes, but I couldn't do this if I started weeping all over him. My stomach was churning with unease and all the things I wanted so desperately to say, the things I already regretted.

Instead, I looked the man I loved dead in the eye and said coldly, "I've already changed. I don't want any of that with you. Not anymore."

Whiskey-brown eyes searched my face. I thought of the winter air in Hampshire when I'd been stranded on the roadside. How cold I'd felt, all the way to my bones. It was nothing compared to this moment now. My heart was a desolate landscape, chilling me from the inside out.

But I'd spoken nothing but the truth. I was changed. I would be a mother. And I needed to start thinking of my child. My path would lead me away from the possibility of happiness with Silas.

"Ashby, then?" Silas uttering that name so unexpectedly had my gaze snapping to his. *What was he—* "That's who you've moved on with?"

He thought—*oh God*. My stomach hollowed at the implication. When I'd been referring to my journey to motherhood, Silas had assumed I'd chosen someone else.

I blinked and directed my focus over his shoulder. I knew what I had to do.

So I said nothing at all. I didn't rush to correct Silas's assumption. I neither confirmed nor denied an association. This would force Silas to move on—to find the happiness he sought with someone else. Someone without so many complications. Someone who wouldn't ruin his life. Someone who wouldn't take his happiness and contort it into something unrecognizable.

Silas must have believed me because his hand loosened suddenly from the desperate grip he'd maintained throughout his speech. Then he stood without a word.

I kept my gaze fixed out the open window, but I saw nothing. Not the golden glow of the setting sun painting the tops of the trees. Nor the wind rustling the leaves on its journey toward nightfall.

My face crumpled as Silas's footsteps retreated down the hallway. I counted to twenty-five before I allowed myself a ragged inhale that turned into a hiccuping sob.

I buried my face in my hands, thinking our relationship would always be secrets and lies. He just wouldn't know it.

Later that night, I saw myself off to the country without Blythe or any farewell from my family. Marshall, my kind-hearted coachman, loaded the carriage with my belongings and helped me gently into the compartment. His gaze jumped nervously, occasionally alighting on my still flat stomach. Of course the staff would have heard the gossip before a single word had been printed.

"Is there anything I can do, m'lady?"

"I am fine," I assured him around a watery smile.

Marshall took in my red-rimmed eyes and my skin gone splotchy from crying, but he didn't call out my dishonesty, and for that, I was grateful. Right now, a liar was all I was.

"It's a long ride to Northumberland. Are you certain you would not prefer to start our journey in the morning?"

"We're not going on the Great North Road, Marshall. We're going to Hampshire. To the Duchess of Cawthorn. And we're leaving tonight."

Fourteen

SILAS

July

"Are you up for a visit to Langham's?"

Daly's question drew my attention away from the glass I was holding.

Unconsciously, I flexed my left hand and winced when my fingers extended.

Daly caught the movement. "Is that hand still giving you trouble? You're lucky Glenfellow and Brannigan ran off to the country before they could cause you more concern." He eyed my hand with a frown. "I'm surprised it's not healed by now. It's been at least a month since you lost your mind at the club."

Six weeks, truth be told. I was concerned it hadn't healed right. That was fine. It could match the rest of me.

"It's still tender," I admitted. "I don't think I'll be up for sparring at Langham's."

We typically visited the boxing club for a bit of exercise and sport at least once per month. Julian and Miles joined us in some combination when they were in London. But they weren't in town now. It was nearing the end of July, and Emery and Augie were well settled in Hampshire and had been for almost a month. I was the lone holdout.

Daly didn't care for life in the country and neither did his wife. They stayed in London nearly year-round, only occasionally attending house parties or celebrations beyond the city borders.

"Perhaps you should retreat to Laurel Park to convalesce," Daly said around a challenging smirk and a healthy swig from his glass. He'd joined me for supper and drinks afterward while his wife had rehearsal at the theater on Saint James's.

Daly knew I was avoiding Hampshire and my family, but he didn't know why. And I didn't particularly wish to discuss it. I wasn't sure how to admit that I'd swallowed my pride and begged Mary for a chance at a future and then been soundly rejected.

Then to find out later that very same day that Mary was rumored to be with child and had apparently run away to the country. Her family was spreading a story of illness that required recuperation up north. But the whispers of her situation were still fierce despite the summer months and the absence of many members of the *ton*.

My mood had vacillated wildly. Today, I seemed to be distracted and maudlin, which was a vast improvement to last week's anger or the prior month's utter despair.

There had been a moment when I'd heard the gossip surrounding Mary and thought perhaps I could have been the father to her rumored unborn child. But then I recalled all her time spent with Ashby after things ended between us—the dances and the bloody croquet. Mary constantly on his arm and whispering together in ballrooms. Her cold refusal had made so much sense. And, of course, the stone-faced confirmation I received in her study. She'd moved on, indeed.

I supposed I should be grateful that she didn't accept, making a cuckold and a fool out of me.

But what had happened with Ashby? Had he denied his responsibilities? Had the bastard refused to marry her?

I pushed the intrusive, meaningless thoughts away and cleared my throat. "I'm not ready to return to Hampshire. I'll be bored there."

Daly made a rude, disbelieving sound, but he allowed the untruth if not the reason behind it.

I couldn't imagine my family seeing me this way, wrecked and floundering after Mary's refusal and the truth of her situation. I wondered if my sisters had been in contact with her. Despite the gossip, I could not imagine they had abandoned their friend during such a tumultuous time. Everything was complicated. My family had been intertwined with Mary for a decade.

Shifting in my seat, I nearly shook my head at myself. Why should I care what happened to Mary or if her family had banished her to the country or if she had support? She'd taken my heart and handed it back to me with no emotion whatsoever on her face.

"I don't want any of that with you. Not anymore."

I forced myself to make a painful fist with my left hand. Perhaps I could visit Langham Boxing Club with Daly today after all. I could use a distraction, and drinking myself to sleep was losing its appeal when I woke up in the mornings with a pounding head and in a worse temperament than when I started.

"Don't even think about it," Daly scolded, noting the way I tested my hand. "It's not a fair fight with you one-handed."

I rolled my eyes. "You'll beat the piss out of me anyhow. No matter how many hands I have."

The duke grinned. "True. But I like it to be a fair fight."

I managed an easy smile in return as we fell silent, the lamps burning low in my study. The windows opened to allow a night-time breeze to cool the house.

Perhaps I hadn't been as successful with that smile as I'd hoped because, after a moment, Daly asked quietly, "What is really going on with you, Silas? I can't help but think you're avoiding something. Not that I mind the company." He raised a gloved hand in supplication. "But you haven't been yourself for a while now."

"Why does everyone keep telling me that? Perhaps I am a changed man, and this is who I am now?"

My friend appeared unconvinced. "A moody, sullen pain in the arse?"

I gave him a flat look and nothing else.

Daly chuckled.

"I . . ." My voice trailed off, hesitant and unsure. In the past, Daly had been made miserable by a woman—his longtime mistress—before he'd found his wife. I didn't want to bring up bad memories from a painful time in his life. "There was a woman."

The duke's fair blond brows rose. "Ah. Now we are getting somewhere."

"Not especially. There is nowhere to get to. It was all over before it really began," I admitted around the sudden tightness gripping my chest. The bitter ache of Mary's rejection blended seamlessly with the angry helplessness I felt now at her uncertain future.

Daly waited patiently.

"She didn't want anything real or lasting with me. We were together—in secret—for a time, and then I messed it all up by wanting more."

He nodded, expression knowing. "I'm familiar with that." In a swift motion, Daly had finished his whiskey and placed the glass gently upon the table. "You can't make someone love you, Silas. Believe me. I spent years trying. Making excuses and lying to myself. If your plans do not align, then perhaps it is time to figure out a different future for yourself. Expectations often keep us locked into our decisions. We're too afraid of the unknown to deviate from the path we've been following. Leave yourself open to the possibilities around you." He smiled. "That is the advice you did not ask for."

I laughed, genuinely this time. And after a moment, I asked, "Are you happier now?" I left the rest unsaid, but Daly still knew what I meant. *Than before? Are you glad your mistress refused you? Did it all work out in the end? Did you stop hurting?*

"I am. Truly. I am exactly where I'm supposed to be."

I nodded, relieved that he'd reached this point. Hopeful that someday, I, too, might be exactly where I was meant to be. "Good. Then perhaps I won't be a—what was it?—a moody, sullen pain in the arse forever."

Daly's big, booming laughter rumbled forth. "Thank Christ. I still think you should go to Hampshire. See your family. They love your moody arse, and you're much happier when you're with them. Besides, I've seen more of your ugly face lately than my own."

"All right," I agreed, chuckling, the sound rusty to my own ears. "I'll go home."

My family did love me. And I loved them. I'd stayed away for complicated reasons, stubbornness simply being one of them. My sisters and their husbands knew me too well. They wouldn't tolerate my foul mood—sullen or otherwise. I wasn't ready to have someone call me on my shit, but since Daly had already done that, I couldn't exactly argue.

Perhaps I could just work on putting the fallout with Mary behind me and come to terms with the fact that my sisters had lives and families. I could have those things, too.

This wasn't a race no matter how far behind I always seemed to be.

August

Summer in Hampshire was a rather glorious affair. The sun shone often, and the temperature was moderate—warm without being miserable. There was something about the country air in the summer months. It seemed somehow fresher and more hopeful.

I was trying to remain positive, and if anything could improve my mood, it was a visit to Laurel Park.

Jamie had decided to remain behind in London. He didn't feel comfortable leaving his mother and sisters for such a long period of time. He'd also argued about accepting payment while I was away to hold his position, so he'd promised to look in on the house in Belgrave Square and assist with anything that needed doing by a "big, strong lad." I'd rolled my eyes but told him he was welcome, though it was not necessary. The boy assured me he'd continue his literacy practice and argued that he'd need to frequent my library at the very least to acquire new reading material.

I'd spent the past two days since my arrival visiting with Mother and Father. I planned to venture toward Patty's nearby home today and check on the Owensby Farm operation to see how things were coming along. Perhaps Franny would be interested in a ride over to the stables with her favorite uncle.

"Good day, Dashwood," I said in early afternoon as Patty's butler opened the door to Pineview and allowed me entry.

He was unfazed by my arrival even unplanned as it was—probably used to it over the years.

"Good day, Mr. Bartholomew," the older man returned, accepting my hat and my jacket. "I'm afraid the lord and lady of the house are away currently. They've accompanied Miss Francesca for a horseback ride to the village."

I frowned. "Well, I suppose it serves me right for showing up unexpectedly."

"You are, of course, welcome to wait, sir. Lady Mary is in the garden out back enjoying a picnic. I am happy to send some refreshment for you as well should you care to join her."

My entire body—save my rapidly beating heart—froze at the casual mention of Mary. Here, in my sister's home.

I worked very hard to keep the surprise from my features. She was supposed to be in Northumberland, in her family's home. What was she doing here at Pineview?

Perhaps part of me had held out hope that the scandal sheets had gotten it wrong. While I didn't want her to be ill, as her mother had indicated all over town, convalescing quietly in the country seemed somehow preferable to carrying the child of another man.

With a subtlety I didn't quite manage, I asked, "Oh. Is Lady Mary planning to stay very long?"

Dashwood's gaze narrowed slightly. "Lady Mary is our honored guest for the foreseeable future." A pause. "Perhaps you'd be more comfortable returning when the duchess is available."

At my questioning, my sister's helpful butler seemed to realize he'd divulged a bit too much information—knowledge that was confidential.

Of course Patty would have offered assistance to Mary in such a situation—in any situation. They were like sisters, and Patty's fierce loyalty knew no bounds. An unplanned pregnancy wouldn't change that. Mary's reputation being dragged through the mud would only embolden my sister.

I wondered briefly if the Earl and Countess of Thisby even knew of their daughter's whereabouts. They were certainly aware of her situation as they were trying to mitigate the fallout.

Relying heavily on muscle memory, I smiled widely. "No trouble at all, my good man. I'll take luncheon out in the garden along-side Lady Mary. I'd be happy to. Thank you for the generous offer."

Dashwood opened his mouth, but I was already turning and heading for the hallway, my eager, curious feet carrying me toward the terrace and down the stone steps to the garden. I didn't spy wild red hair on any of the benches lining the patio nor between the beds of bright summer blooms. I continued my search along the carefully trimmed hedges lining the garden. The sun was bright overhead, and I imagined I knew where Mary might be.

Sure enough, I turned the corner and saw her beneath the shade of the large oak tree in the rear of the property. It had been a favored spot over the years. There was a swing attached to the solid branches, one that Franny had spent hours in as a little girl. I could remember her smiling gap-toothed grin and earning her affection by obeying her constant demands to go higher and higher.

I smiled at the memory and ignored the ache in my chest at seeing Mary sitting on that same wooden swing with a careful hand on her belly. She carefully cradled the slight swell. Her lips were moving, broken only by a soft smile—one I'd never seen before on her face. It spoke of love and tenderness, and the sight had me pressing a hand to my chest.

The toe of one shoe pushed her the barest amount, the swing hardly in motion. Nearby, I could see a blanket with the remnants of her meal laid neatly on the grass.

A sudden bout of nerves had me questioning my presence here. Surely, she did not wish to see me after our disastrous encounter weeks ago. The one where I'd confessed my feelings and made a fool of myself. Did I want to see her? After everything?

I hadn't even considered not seeking her out when Dashwood revealed her presence here. Would I always crave Mary's attention and presence in my life? I couldn't imagine this early meeting would help me get over my hurt and bitterness. It would probably be best to avoid her.

She'd rejected my advances, and I needed to accept that. Becoming a pathetic hanger-on would not endear me to anyone. Daly had been right. You couldn't force a person into loving you. Who wanted to gain someone's affection by wearing them down, anyhow?

I sighed. Returning to the country for the summer just became a whole lot more complicated.

I'd talked myself out of approaching and had taken a single step in retreat when Mary's eyes, made soft and sweet in this unguarded moment, lifted and met mine unexpectedly. She startled visibly before standing, removing her hand from her stomach and straightening her skirts hurriedly. As if she could conceal the truth. As if I could unsee how much she loved this child already.

I swallowed uneasily, unsure if it was too late to return to the house.

A range of emotions passed over Mary's face before she settled on a tentative smile, one that hardly reached her eyes. "Hello," she called. It nearly sounded like a question.

I raised a hand, uncertain if I could speak just yet.

She looked so uncomfortable to be caught in this garden with me. We'd never been this way before. Even back when we'd argued and taunted, we could find comfort and ease in each other's presence—a familiarity, honesty. We'd had an understanding. We'd been on equal footing then. But now I realized, loving someone doesn't give you the advantage. It makes you weak. I felt vulnerable and that just wouldn't do.

Yet I couldn't stop staring at her. With the cut of her dress and her position, Mary's emerging figure was hidden away. You'd never know that she was with child.

But I'd seen her on the swing moments before. Even more than the hand on her small belly, I'd seen that soft smile—witnessed her secret happiness. She didn't look like she was ill in Northumberland or recovering in some drafty country home in the north. Nor did she appear concerned over her ruined reputation. She didn't look like someone whose life was over. Or like she was trying to figure it all out.

Mary was hiding here in Hampshire with the support of my sister. She was carrying Ashby's child. And I needed to remember that.

She'd moved on from me long before I'd realized it. While I'd been pining after her and not acting like myself—as I'd heard so many times from family and friends—she'd taken up with Ashby. The lips that I'd kissed, the skin that I'd touched, given over to another man. The thought of her long limbs tangled up with the baron had something sour twisting in my stomach. Something irrational and undeserved, but there it was, consuming my thoughts.

My jaw went tight and hard as I commanded my body into motion. Anger, swift and hot, banished every idiotic romantic thought I'd had about this woman. She wasn't mine any longer. Hell, she'd never been mine. I'd been a convenient passing fancy until she'd landed someone from her bleeding list.

Well, it looked like she'd gotten more than she'd bargained for on that end.

I entered her space and stopped, crossing my arms behind my back in a picture of nonchalance. My hands fisted and I managed to control my wince as my left protested the movement.

Mary fidgeted with the fabric at her side and opened her mouth to speak, but I cut her off.

My voice emerged, sounding foreign to my own ears, sharp as a blade and twice as wicked. "I see the rumors are true, then."

Fifteen

MARY

The statement and the tone it was delivered in had me wincing. I could feel myself shying away from Silas for the first time in our long history.

But then I found my backbone and remembered that I did not owe this man anything, least of all confirmation for his venom-soaked accusation.

"I find that rumors rarely encompass the full weight of the story," I said pointedly.

When I'd first seen Silas standing in the garden in his shirtsleeves and sage-green waistcoat, I'd felt alarm. Had he seen me touching and talking to my stomach? Did he have confirmation of the truth?

But the hardness of his expression was something else entirely.

I had no doubt in my mind that if Silas thought he was the father of my child, he would have sought me out as soon as he'd heard the news. His bossy temperament would have demanded to see me, and he would have already acquired a special license for a speedy wedding, the sooner to protect my reputation and alleviate the gossip swirling about. He would have been domineering and insistent, but he would not be whatever this was standing in front of me just now.

Clearly he'd taken my silence on Ashby's position in my life as confirmation.

The Silas-shaped approximation scoffed a disbelieving laugh. "Is that so? How about another bit of gossip? One that says you are currently recovering from an unfortunate illness in the wilds of Northumberland. Have you heard that one?"

"Clearly, I am not in Northumberland. You've done nothing but prove me right. Rumors shouldn't be taken as truth."

His gaze dropped to my middle. Silas's meaning was clear. I resisted the urge to smooth the fabric, to ensure my newly developing body was hidden from this angle.

While the staff and household undoubtedly knew why I was the Duchess of Cawthorn's guest, they did not have confirmation. We hadn't yet explained things to Franny, who I spent time with daily. But the time was fast approaching when I would no longer be able to keep my condition a secret. The visits to the Marquess and Marchioness of Northcutt at nearby Laurel Park would need to be suspended until I could figure out how to tell them about the baby. Patty had said she would handle it and not to worry, but I'd long been acquainted with her parents, and I wanted to tell them myself. I hoped they would respect my decision. They'd always been so supportive of their children and the unconventional paths they'd taken. A tiny part of me worried they'd shun me for my decision to raise this baby on my own. And they'd be as lost to me as my own parents.

Despite sending Marshall back to London with our family carriage and a letter detailing my whereabouts, I'd yet to receive word from them. If Silas's accusations were accurate—and I suspected they were—my mother and father were still peddling the rumor of my illness.

My appetite had improved greatly after the pregnancy vomiting had ceased over a month ago. I felt much improved—exceedingly healthy, all told. Patty had insisted a local doctor examine me and all seemed to be progressing nicely. Emery had insisted on her midwife as well. My body was growing to accommodate the tiny life within. Miles was adamant that I not ride on horseback. And Emery and Augie had been catering to my every need since I'd arrived in Hampshire weeks ago.

But things were changing rapidly. My secret would be more than scandal sheet gossip, more than unsubstantiated rumor. It would be unavoidable. A woman bold and brazen enough to make decisions for herself. *Reckless* and *careless* would likely be bandied about as well.

Well, at least I was consistent.

"Are you denying it? That you are with child?" Silas's hard voice pulled me from my thoughts and worry over the near future.

My face heated. This was the moment I'd been dreading, coming far earlier than I'd anticipated. The truth, hidden away behind a locked door with no regard for privacy. Thus far, this baby had been entirely mine. Something secret and special that brought forth a patient tenderness I'd never possessed. But it could not remain solely mine forever.

Silas was not some meaningless acquaintance eager for gossip. He was part of Patty's family, and I imagined that due to our history, he felt he was more deserving of an explanation. In any case, Silas was not someone I'd ever be able to avoid, not with my future so uncertain and my reliance on the kindness and acceptance of my friends.

Refusing to be cowed, I kept my gaze steady on his, and admitted evenly, "It's the truth."

His frown shimmered on his face for a moment, like the surface of a lake disturbed by a tiny ripple. But then his whiskey eyes hardened and his glare solidified. "Well, I think what you're doing is madness."

"I don't particularly care what you think, Silas."

But he ignored me and kept right on talking. "As if you weren't irresponsible enough, now you're hiding out here and what? Relying on my sister to deliver you from this situation? Ashby should do his duty, dammit."

"Ashby," I breathed. So I was right. He *did* believe what I'd implied back in London. Silas thought I'd picked up with Ashby. Allowed the baron's touch to replace his own. He truly believed that I'd shared intimacies with someone else.

Silas was clearly angry enough to abandon his hopes for a future for us—one that would destroy everything he hoped to build. I'd gotten what I wanted. So, why did I feel like my chest was caving in on itself?

"If he was reputable," Silas went on, "he would have already married you. If he had an ounce of decency."

"You have no idea what you're talking about."

"I'm talking about a man taking some responsibility for his actions."

I had to force my jaw to unlock so I could continue speaking through my emotions. "I don't need anyone to assume responsibility for me. I am not a burden, nor am I some—some obligation."

"Even if it means your child is born a bastard and has nothing."

Angry tears threatened but I beat them back. Damn Silas for exposing every argument I'd had with myself, every fear and insecurity. "My child won't have nothing. They will have me."

He shook his head, incredulous. His expression fairly shouting what a poor consolation that would be, knowing I couldn't possibly be enough.

I felt the blood drain from my face, struck by how little he thought of me. This man with whom I'd shared my body. Whom I'd fallen far deeper with than I'd ever intended. I couldn't speak —couldn't respond—but it didn't matter. Silas wasn't done. He'd yet to strike his final blow. "And I suppose I should congratulate you as well. For landing number one on your list after all."

"Mary! Mary!" Patty's frantic cries sounded very far away, and I blinked bleary eyes open. It was nearly dusk and the gardens looked dull. The skin of my arms had long grown cold.

But suddenly Patty was there, collapsed on the blanket beside me, gently touching my forehead. Her eyes took me in from my undoubtedly tear-swollen face down my body, curled protectively on its side, searching for a wound she'd never find. "What's happened? Is it the baby? Should I call the doctor?"

I shook my head, pushing myself up to drape my head across her lap. "No," I croaked.

"What is it?" she begged, pushing the hair back from my temples as fresh moisture leaked onto her skirts.

"Silas was here. We quarreled." I didn't think I could do this anymore. I needed my friend more than I required her ignorance.

Patty's fingers stilled in my hair. "Silas?"

"He confronted me about the baby. He'd read the scandal sheets and seemed surprised to find me here. He said"—I hiccuped a little—"that I was ruining my life and the baby's life by running away and letting you take care of me. That I should marry Ashby —" My words cut off. I couldn't get the rest out.

Patty was quiet in the dimming light, but her thoughts were loud. Finally, she said very gently, "Mary, is Silas the baby's father?"

I gripped her skirts in a tight fist, fearful that what came next would drive her away and out of my life forever. "I'm sorry, Patty. I still don't understand how it happened. I never meant to keep it from you. I never meant for it to happen at all. One day, we were arguing—like we always do—and it was like we were overcome. After that, we were together, in secret, for a time. I'm sorry, Patty. I'm so sorry," I sobbed.

"Shhh, darling. It's all right," she soothed, smoothing my hair back once more. Her touch was cool and reassuring. "You're getting too upset. It's not good for your Little Duck."

I sat up suddenly, clutching her hands. "Please don't tell him. He thinks the baby is Ashby's. He accused me—he doesn't know. He can't know."

Clear blue eyes regarded me sadly. "Why would you keep this from him?"

"Because he would insist on marrying me, and I am not what he wants."

Frowning, Patty asked, "What does Silas want?"

I sniffed before giving up and wiping a hand under my nose. "He wants a wife. Someone young and beautiful to be marchioness someday. A perfect society wife. It was why he broke things off. He asked your mother to help. He was ready to settle down."

"Did he ask you to settle down?"

I fought a laugh at that. "I wasn't even in the running."

Patty seemed to consider something. "That day at Cawthorn Hall. The garden party. You left after Emery announced that Mama was helping Silas find a wife."

"That was when it all ended."

"Oh, Mary." My friend sighed. "Emery and her big mouth."

I looked down at the blanket. "She didn't know. He hadn't meant for me to find out that way, but I was still angry. I told myself I was being silly. We'd agreed to keep our arrangement secret. Nothing was to ever come of it anyhow. I feel foolish for allowing my emotions to get the better of me."

"And that's why you disappeared from our lives. Turned down invitations and waved at me from across ballrooms before hurrying away. I thought I'd done something, Mary. I thought I'd ruined our friendship somehow."

"No," I said emphatically. "It was never you. I'm so sorry I made you feel that way. I just—I just couldn't be near him or anywhere he might be. I couldn't go back to bickering for sport, pretending nothing had changed between us. Not when I'd somehow managed to break my own heart. I wasn't strong enough to stand by and watch when he was actively trying to find a wife. Dancing with Lady Sophia or entertaining with Annabelle Crawford."

"I see," Patty replied.

"I realized far too late how much I'd grown to care for him. Our arrangement was supposed to be simple, but my feelings became decidedly complicated. And if I told him the truth now, he'd insist on marrying me. Society would laugh at him. Everyone would assume I was using him to save my reputation. He would never be the respected heir he hopes to be. I could never do that to him."

My friend watched me carefully. "I've never known you to be concerned with what society thinks."

I sighed. "It's different when it's someone I care about, Patty. They can call me horse-faced or a spinster or whatever they please. But I cannot abide being the reason Silas is mocked and gossiped about, the reason he'll hate me." An image of my parents flashed in my mind. Silent meals around the dining table. Retreating to separate chambers. My lonely, bewildering double life with a family who hardly tolerated me. "And I must think of the baby as well. You know that rumors would follow them for a long time. Silas would only resent me when all was said and done. And I'm fairly certain that is not the sort of future he longs for."

"I don't know how to make this better," Patty admitted, her features strained.

"Just—just promise me you will not tell him about the baby yet. If he wants to hate me and think the child is Ashby's, then so be it. But I am not prepared for him to know the truth. Perhaps some-day, after he marries and achieves the life he wants. However, right now, it would ruin everything. Promise me, Patty."

I knew what I was asking of my friend. I was a scoundrel and it wasn't fair to make her choose between me and her brother. I was being terribly unfair, but I needed to do this my way. And I needed Patty to understand and respect that.

She regarded me for a long moment before nodding.

Tears threatened as I choked out, "Thank you."

We sat in silence for long minutes while the garden turned from day to night. The evening sounds of insects and the gentle breeze had me rubbing warmth into my bare arms.

Finally, Patty climbed to her feet and helped me to stand. "Come. You need to eat and then rest. It's been a trying day. Miles and Franny will be wondering where we are."

I took her hand and let her lead me back inside, unsure if I was asking for too much from my closest friend. Fearful that I was ruining more than my own life with foolish stubbornness.

Sixteen

SILAS

Staring into the strange golden eyes of Julian's house cat while it kneaded the fabric of my cravat, I could hardly hear my sisters speaking over the rumbling purr emitted by the beast.

"What are you sulking about anyway, Silas?" Emery eventually asked from her position across from me.

Tilting my head, I leaned to see around the animal as my middle sister dunked a biscuit into her tea. "I'm not sulking," I argued, sounding petulant to my own ears.

Returning to my slouched position on the sofa, I ignored Emery as she and Genevieve shared a look rife with meaning.

"You should have joined the men if you're just going to sit there and scowl all afternoon," Emery said brightly.

I didn't even bother trying to see around the blasted cat this time.

Genevieve's husband, Julian, had joined Augie and Miles over at Patty's estate. I hadn't wanted to run into Mary at Pineview again, so I was taking tea with my younger sisters at Genevieve and

Julian's newly built home a short horseback ride from Laurel Park.

"Why aren't either of you at Patty's as well?"

I brief pause before Genevieve replied quietly, "Patty thought it best if we gave Mary a bit of space. She hasn't been feeling well."

Sudden worry had me sitting up straight, dumping the cat off my chest. Undeterred, the orange beast simply settled itself on my lap instead. "What's the matter? Is it the baby?"

Genevieve and Emery shared another meaningful look.

"Oh, come now. Am I supposed to pretend I don't know that she is with child and hiding in the country as a result?"

"I didn't realize you knew," Gen replied carefully. "You haven't mentioned it."

"It was all over London, sister. Of course I was aware of the gossip."

Emery glared. "Well, it's not anyone's business. Her damnable maid is the one who sold the story to the *Tattler* after she ambushed Gansey and refused to allow her to see Mary when she was delivering items for her pregnancy from me."

My eyes narrowed on Emery. "How long have you known about Mary's condition?"

Her brown eyes—a near replica of my own—narrowed right back. "That's not anyone's business either."

That meant she'd known well before the scandal sheets had gotten wind of the rumor. Perhaps as long as Mary herself had been aware.

"Please be careful what you say, Silas. And to whom you say it." Genevieve's soft urging distracted me from my glaring match with Emery. "Patty hasn't explained Mary's situation to Franny yet or Mama and Papa. Mary wants to tell them herself."

My scoff was incredulous. "She wants to tell them herself, does she? Does everyone in the bleeding family get an explanation except for me?"

Gen frowned in confusion. "Did you . . . want an explanation?"

Before I could answer in an emphatic affirmative and give myself away entirely, Emery's accusation met my ears, "What did you do, Silas?"

"What do you mean?"

"You're over here pouting when you clearly want to be with Augie and the others. Are you avoiding Mary? Did you do something or say something to her about her situation?" Her face transformed to angry realization. "Are you the reason Mary was overwrought and needed rest?"

I looked away, feeling heat and guilt climb up my neck that had nothing to do with the summer weather. *Was I the reason Mary was feeling unwell? Had the venom I'd spewed in anger and pride caused her to retreat?*

"We spoke," I admitted. "Last week. A few days after I arrived in Hampshire. I was surprised to find her in Patty's home. I assumed she was in Northumberland since that is the story her family is spreading around."

"And what happened when you spoke?" Genevieve's calmly asked question was somehow worse than Emery's angry finger-pointing.

I finally met my sister's gaze and confessed. "We quarreled. I questioned her sanity for what she was doing. Told her she should marry so that she wouldn't be ruined." I swallowed uneasily, recalling my high-handed remarks, knowing they'd been hurtful. "I accused her of hiding in the country under Patty's protection."

Genevieve sighed. "Oh, Silas."

A glance at Emery showed that she shared in sisterly disappointment.

I tossed my hands up in frustration, startling the cat onto the floor. "I was completely caught off guard seeing her there. And you must know that I'm right about the state of things. If she has any hope of saving her reputation and protecting her child, she must marry."

"And you think guilting her into such an important decision when she is vulnerable is the way to go about it?" Emery said blandly as she reached for another biscuit.

"I don't know," I replied in annoyance. It was hard enough to think about Mary bedding someone else. The idea of her marrying some idiot who didn't deserve her made me want to punch Ashby in his affable face. It made me want to punch my own face for acting like I knew better than she. I couldn't imagine being in Mary's position—scared and uncertain, and painfully alone.

"Perhaps Mary wants to make decisions for herself, Silas." Gen's blue eyes were patient. "What she needs is support and friendship from the people who love her. She won't find that with her family—you know what a disaster her parents are. So she is here, in Hampshire, at our urging. For you to attack her in the only safe place she has remaining was not well done, brother." She eyed me for a moment. "But I don't think I need to tell you that."

I looked down at my lap—covered in orange cat hair—and felt nothing but shame. I'd allowed my own fragile masculine ego to guide my missteps and overrun my mouth. I should not have judged someone whom I cared so much about. And I should never have tried to punish Mary as a result of my own hurt and rejection.

Something struck me from my sister's speech. "What do you mean about the earl and countess?"

Genevieve looked momentarily unsure, as if she'd said too much. But Emery had no such qualms regarding gossip. "It's not a secret. Mary would tell you—if she were speaking to you, that is. They present a pleasant front for all to see in society, but behind closed doors, they're monsters. On a good day, they simply avoid each other and go their separate ways. But generally, they're quarrelsome and resentful and sling insults with unfailing regularity. Usually just her father. But I've heard Mary's mother breaking things in dramatic displays while I've visited Mary. And they don't just take out there resentment and unhappy marriage on each other. They don't deserve to have Mary as a daughter," Emery finished with a snarl.

I frowned in utter shock and confusion. Mary had grown up with a family like that?

Something tightened painfully about my chest. I was lucky. I knew that. My family was unusual among our set, but I'd been raised by loving and indulgent parents. I'd had a wonderful childhood. My father may not trust me with official duties or responsibilities, but he and my mother have always made me feel loved and cherished—frankly more than I deserved. And that comfort and acceptance extended beyond to my siblings as well. We're a rowdy lot, but we're loyal and steadfast. I would do anything for my sisters.

Mary's life looked nothing like mine.

It was with a sharp, shameful ache that I admitted quietly, "I never knew that."

"Mary has always wanted a family," Emery said.

I met my sister's gaze. "She has?"

She nodded. "She has always longed for children. A way to create a loving family of her own. Something she's lacked all her life. And now she finally has the opportunity. It's unconventional, and it will change the course of her life. But shaming her for something that has brought her so much unexpected happiness is the last thing she needs, Silas. We Bartholomews are all a bit unusual and scandalous. Of course we would support our friend when she needed it most."

The news of Mary's desire for children had my mind instantly flashing back to our conversation in the snowy carriage—before that first kiss. I'd asked about the list I'd found. If she was planning to marry one of those men. Her reply had been swift and angry, but also tinged with self-conscious hurt.

"There is no need to list potential suitors when one is firmly on the shelf . . ."

And then the list itself. She'd claimed it was for a liaison. Had she truly risked her reputation and future for meaningless encounters with someone from that collection of names? Had a child been her goal all along?

She'd always been adamant that I withdraw from her body to prevent pregnancy. It had been one of her bloody rules. Clearly, she hadn't been so circumspect with Ashby. Was it just my child that she hadn't wanted?

Accidental pregnancy was a fairly common outcome when gentlemen took mistresses. Typically, those mistresses were not unwed daughters of earls however. And if an arrangement did result in an indiscretion, those women were ruined in a variety of ways.

Mary was handling the consequences on her own, with the help of my family. I didn't know her situation with Ashby, but I realized it was not my place to ask. And it had not been my place to judge either.

I swallowed with some difficulty. "I shall apologize for my behavior. It was unacceptable." And it had been. It was no excuse, but I'd been hurt and angry. As a result, I'd been cruel and unjust. It was not Mary's job to manage my feelings or to placate me like a child. And it was wrong of me to punish her for not loving me back, for moving on.

"Good," Emery said before biting into her biscuit.

Genevieve met my gaze and offered a small smile.

A rather sad excuse for a meow erupted in the sitting room, and we all looked toward Percy. The big orange cat sat at my feet and seemed to stare into my very soul. He offered one more croak of approval before sauntering away.

Looking toward my baby sister, I wrinkled my nose. "Your cat is so strange, Gen."

She smiled. "He fits right in around here."

∼

September

· · ·

Three days later, I was sneaking into Patty's garden at a quarter to two in the afternoon with a speech I'd written out and rehearsed on the way over. I wanted to make sure that when I apologized, I didn't forget anything. I feared I had much to atone for.

Franny had joined us at Laurel Park for supper last night and mentioned that Mary was very strict about her schedule. When the weather permitted, she took a walk to the stables every day at two o'clock before returning to Pineview and having tea with Franny.

Now, I stood out in the very warm early September sun and waited for Mary to emerge for her daily exercise. Tired eyes kept watch. My guilt weighed heavily and sleep had been difficult in the past several days, as I'd worked out the words I needed to say and the apology I so desperately needed to make.

At exactly three past the hour, the woman herself exited from the kitchens onto the stone path. I watched as she donned her straw bonnet and tied it beneath her chin. Her morning dress fit high on her waist and was patterned with yellow flowers all over. She'd foregone a shawl and carried only a small beige reticule about her wrist.

I waited out in the open on the gravel path that led beyond the hedges. It was not my intention to startle her and eventually Mary looked up from her half boots and met my gaze. Her features hardened and her steps slowed, but she still approached.

"Did you come back to offer more of your opinions?" Her tone was frosty, and I deserved it.

I shook my head. "No. I came to apologize. Mary, I never should have spoken to you in such a manner. I was unnecessarily cruel and judgmental. There is no excuse for the things I said. I beg your forgiveness and vow to never impose my opinions upon you again unless you expressly ask for them."

Mary watched me carefully. I could see her weighing my apology, determining its worth right alongside my own.

I wanted to be better than the man I'd proven to be thus far.

In all our time together—first as antagonistic rivals with our public bouts of bickering and then later when we'd been secretly passionate and consumed with one another—we'd never managed to be true friends. And in Mary's current situation, with so much fear and uncertainty, I thought what she needed the most might be the support of a good friend. She had my sisters and their husbands, of course. But perhaps it wouldn't hurt to have one more person on her side.

"You won't tell me how to live my life?" she ventured finally.

"I swear it," I answered earnestly.

"And you won't drive a wedge between me and your family?"

I shook my head. "My sisters are very much their own women. I would never do anything to damage your relationships." I swallowed before admitting, "I would very much like to be included among your friends, Mary."

I thought of how loyal Mary was to my family. She would do anything for my sisters. She was kind and patient with my nieces and nephew. And she was intelligent and clever, always with a ready quip. If we allowed ourselves, I imagined we could get along quite well.

However, she still looked unsure.

I knew that Mary always found my jovial attitude a bit off-putting. She'd told me before that it never seemed genuine. At the time, I'd been irritated that she found so much of my character disagreeable, but, looking back, I could see that she'd perhaps been more interested in the person I was in private when I wasn't performing for society. Being the good heir, the friendly gentleman, the polite guest. I thought of her parents suddenly and what I knew now to be true. How they playacted for their peers, rearranging themselves to fit into something agreeable. Mary had probably had enough false pretenses and fake smiles to last a lifetime.

Wasn't friendship the desire to know someone beyond their polished surface?

So I withheld my smile and strove for sincerity when I said, "I have always thought you were bold and admirable. Funny and kind. Fiercely loyal. But you're more than that, Mary. You might be the bravest person I've ever met. You're made of courage." Her eyes went bright and liquid as I spoke. "That is the sort of person I would be happy to count as a friend."

She sniffed and blinked several times.

I gave a slight bow of my head and spoke to the pebbles beneath my feet. "I do hope you'll accept my apology, but if you wish me to return to London and not bother you here, I shall do—"

"No." She interrupted. I glanced up. "I accept your apology. You needn't avoid me. We are both adults. I would not steal your family from you, Silas."

I straightened. "I know that. But if my presence here makes you uncomfortable . . ."

"It doesn't."

I offered a small smile, less intent on charming and more focused on gratitude. "Thank you, Mary. I know I don't deserve your forgiveness."

She shook her head, her eyes welling again. "We all make mistakes, you know."

And I had no idea what she meant by that. The bastard in me wanted to pretend she meant Ashby, but I knew she would not consider the child she carried—the child she already loved—to be a mistake. But I forced away that thought and passed her my handkerchief.

She laughed a little. "It's these damn . . . feelings. Ever since— well, ever since, I'm a watering pot over the silliest things. Miles had the last helping of game pie last night, and I thought I might sob openly at the table."

I grinned. "That must have been some game pie."

"Oh, it was." She made a frustrated sound. "I'm getting sad just thinking about it."

"Well, we can't have that," I said, shaking my head in amuse- ment. "Might I join you on your walk, and we can go to Owensby and see the horses?"

"Yes, of course," Mary replied, holding up her reticule. "I have sugar cubes for my favorites."

I had an idea. "Will you wait for me to retrieve some sugar cubes of my own and put my jacket inside? I'll be just a moment."

"All right," she agreed with some skepticism.

I hurried to the kitchen entrance, deposited my jacket on a chair, and made my request with Patty's cook before hurrying back to Mary in the garden. I half expected her to have left me.

But when I returned, she was there on the path, waiting. "No sugar?"

Damn, I'd forgotten in my haste. "Afraid not. Perhaps we should ask for apples to bring tomorrow."

Mary raised a brow at my presumption, but I simply smiled innocently and started walking toward the tall grasses beyond the hedge row.

She eventually followed and fell into step beside me.

I kept my hands and my thoughts to myself for the duration. I didn't feel the need to fill our time together with idle chatter. And for a great deal of the afternoon, we simply existed in the same space.

After we'd visited six horses in their stalls and watched Charlie—the head groom—work in the round pen with a brown stallion, Mary turned us back toward Pineview.

"How is young Jamie doing?"

"Jamie is back in London, but he is doing quite well. I've received several letters since my arrival." I grinned. "And he will be thrilled to know you asked after him."

Mary laughed. "You hang on to him. He's a good one."

I nodded. Jamie was a good lad. He worked so very hard for his family and had dedicated his young life to caring for them. I thought of his sacrifice and what he'd overcome. And then I thought of his enthusiastic correspondence and the careful words written by his beginner hand.

"You've become more involved with the Watford House over the years, is that right?"

Mary looked briefly surprised but tilted her chin down in acknowledgment. "Yes. I act as Patty's proxy at times. I meet monthly with the headmistress to discuss everything from budgeting of expenses to donors and admissions. And, of course, I visit with the children regularly." Her words had grown soft by the time she'd finished speaking, a frown marring her features.

Perhaps she had not yet considered how the uncertainty in her future affected her work with the orphanage.

I turned to look at her as we walked. "You'll be able to visit them again. Patty would not prevent you from your charity work there. And you'll return to London. I know it might seem unmanageable right now, but some things will not change."

"Thank you, Silas. My work at the Watford House is important to me." She hesitated before facing forward again.

"What do you like best about it?" I enjoyed hearing her speak about a subject she was interested in, and we'd rarely discussed her involvement with the orphanage in Bethnal Green. I knew of it, in a vague sort of way, because of our acquaintance and Patty's occasional updates. But I was eager to learn more from Mary herself.

I could hear the smile in her voice when she answered. "Well, the children are my favorite part, of course. They are often so unpredictable. You never know what one might say. And they are honest in a way that is humbling and so pure."

"Yes," I agreed. "Reeve has often commented on my two-colored hair."

I passed a hand along the gray at my temples, making Mary laugh further at my little niece's teasing.

After a moment, she added, "And I also like knowing I am making a difference. Helping the children there, giving them a chance at a future, and showing them affection and care—it satisfies an ache within me that I've had for a very long time."

I considered what I'd learned from my sisters. Mary's long-held maternal desire for a child. The family she sought and the one she'd been forced to endure. My own goals of marrying and starting a family in order to catch up to my siblings felt arbitrary and incredibly narcissistic. How easy it had been for me to simply decide I was ready for that future. The marriage mart had flocked to me and welcomed me with open arms. I'd relied on my standing and privilege—allowed it to inform all my decisions.

Mary'd had no such luxury. Perhaps her list had been outlandish and reckless. But society hardly concerned itself with the desires of women. Sometimes extreme measures had to be taken to enact change.

Mary's voice floated to me on the summer breeze. "In fact, I was meant to speak to the headmistress this month about an influx of funding for expansion. Several of the wives of Miles and Julian's new buyers apparently became interested in Patty's efforts at Watford House. We're discussing ways we can best use the income whether by adding more dormitories or additional staff in order to accommodate more children."

That was very interesting, indeed. I'd been toying with the idea of seeking Patty's advice. After working with Jamie in his efforts to better educate himself, I was curious about how one might bring instruction and literacy to more impoverished areas. Perhaps there was a way for the Watford House to educate the community as well as the children it served.

"But I suppose I could write Mrs. Watford a letter to propose new options since I cannot be in London for the foreseeable future." Mary's tone had gone quiet again as we walked.

"I'm sure that would be acceptable," I replied. "And I'm sure Patty would be obliged to resume some of her duties upon her return to London in a few weeks."

"That's true." She sighed. "There will be time to discuss it, I suppose."

We remained quiet as the gardens and the house came into view, but as I entered the kitchen to retrieve my coat, Mary asked, "Would you like to stay for tea? I take it with Franny in the library most days."

I forced away the smile I wanted to unearth at the invitation and nodded instead. The idea of appearing victorious did not sit well. I hadn't earned anything yet. "I would be amenable to that."

Mary's eyes cut to mine as if looking for signs of teasing. Her lips twitched at the corners, but she didn't comment. Briefly, her gaze strayed to my mouth, and I felt the newfound easiness between us tighten into an ache of longing.

However, when we reached the staircase, Mary stopped abruptly and put a hand on my arm. I ignored the heat of her touch and searched her face for signs of distress.

"What is it? Are you unwell? Is it the baby?" I whispered.

"No," Mary replied, glancing about us. "But I wanted to tell you that Franny doesn't know about—about my condition yet. Please don't say anything."

"I won't," I rushed to say. "I wouldn't."

"All right. Thank you."

Then she released her hold on my arm and continued up the stairs toward the second floor.

We found young Franny waiting for us in the library with tea service and several serving trays. She greeted me in surprise. "Uncle Silas! I didn't know you'd be joining us."

I shared a brief smile with Mary before moving to sit beside my niece. "I didn't either, my dear. But I encountered Mary upon her walk and invited myself to tea. Besides, you know I am nearly always stricken by hunger."

Franny laughed. "Well, you picked a good day to intrude. Cook decided to send up game pies! Who's ever heard of having game pies for tea?"

Mary's quizzical gaze quickly located the silver tray bearing small game pies and then her bewildered brown eyes found mine. "Silas." My name more shocked breath than sound.

My smile was small and pleased. Patty's cook had been just as puzzled by my hasty request to warm any remaining game pies as Franny was now, staring between a suddenly emotional Mary and myself.

I clapped my hands together and looked to my niece. "Well, then it is a good thing I arrived when I did."

With care, I placed a game pie on a small round plate and passed it to Mary as Franny dutifully poured for all of us.

"Thank you," she murmured, seeming at a loss.

I nodded once before accepting the dish of tea from Franny.

I hoped today would be a new beginning for Mary and myself— one where I made her friendship a priority and kept my heart to myself.

Seventeen

SILAS

The next few weeks slid by in the lazy way of summertime. The weather had yet to turn. Mornings were chilly with fog clinging to the rolling hills of the English countryside, but by midday, the sun was bright and warm overhead.

As the weather was still agreeable, I joined Mary almost daily for her afternoon walk. I'd meet her in the gardens behind Pineview with a sack of apples for the horses. Somedays we'd talk. Other times we'd remain quiet and nearby to one another. We were learning how to be . . . together. Finding our footing after so much had happened between us.

Most days I'd stay on for tea and visit with Franny as well. Occasionally, I would remain until suppertime, reading through the warm afternoons in the library with Mary stretched out on a chaise nearby, the windows open and the summer breeze drifting in. Her hand would sometimes rest gently on her stomach, seemingly without thought and without her awareness. She was lovely. The subtle shape her body was taking suited her as did her happiness as a result.

For much of our time together, I could forget that she carried another man's child. But in those quiet moments with her fingers moving unconsciously over her midsection, it was a reminder that things were changing—that they'd already changed.

It was on one such afternoon that Mary made a strange sound that drew my attention. Her face seemed frozen in a state of alarm as she slowly closed her book and placed it at her side.

"What is it? What's wrong?"

Her wide eyes flew to mine. "I don't—I think I . . . felt the baby move."

My gaze dropped to her stomach, still mostly hidden by the fabric of her morning dress. "Is that normal?"

Mary seemed to be concentrating, her expression focused. She eventually murmured, "Yes, it's normal. Emery told me she experienced what felt like a tiny thump on her belly—but from the inside. And that is exactly what it feels like." A smile suddenly bloomed over her features, a rare wide grin that showed her even white teeth. "I think it happened a bit yesterday, too, but I wasn't sure what it was. The feeling had dissipated so quickly. But now though . . ."

She looked at me then, turning the full force of her joy my way. And then slowly the expression slipped from her face as if she remembered that I'd once scolded her about her pregnancy and her choices. I didn't want to dim what was obviously a special moment for her as a woman on this frightening journey to motherhood.

So I returned the fading phantom of her grin and said, "Tell me the next time it happens. I want to know."

Mary nodded despite looking a bit uncertain and went back to reading, but her hand remained on her stomach for the rest of the afternoon.

Two days later, all of my siblings and their spouses were in attendance for supper at Emery and Augie's nearby home, Kensworth Hall. Mary rounded out our party of eight and was seated across from me at the well-appointed dining table. She wore a gown in shimmering green that seemed to make her fiery-red hair glow.

I felt a boot collide with my ankle and snapped my attention toward Augie.

He narrowed his blue eyes before pointedly glancing in Mary's direction.

Oh.

Perhaps I'd been staring too long.

Reaching for my goblet, I took a healthy swallow before focusing back on the conversation at hand. Something about Patty and their plans to return to London soon.

I reached for a nearby pitcher to refill my glass but the movement of my fingers grasping the handle had my left hand protesting. I shifted and completed the action with my right hand instead.

"Is your hand still bothering you, Silas? Didn't you see a doctor after you injured it?"

Emery's sudden notice of my infirmity had me quickly glancing at Augie and then Mary. I had no idea if the gossip of my altercation with Glenfellow and Brannigan had gotten out. At the time, I hadn't noticed. I'd been too tangled up in Mary's rejection and then, shortly thereafter, the rumors of her pregnancy.

Clearly, my sister knew what had happened.

In the time it took me to worry over Mary finding out about the brawl, I'd failed to respond to my sister, so now the table was quiet, and everyone stared at me.

I cleared my throat uneasily and moved my traitorous hand to my lap. "It's fine," was my well-thought-out reply.

Emery rolled her eyes. "I don't know why men are so stubborn."

Luckily, that had everyone at the table scoffing at Emery's hypocrisy. The dinner guests then took turns reminding my middle sister of her obstinate nature while she glared and fended off the familial attack.

But Mary remained quiet throughout. Her thoughtful, considering gaze strayed my way several times for the remainder of the night.

I pretended I didn't notice. I ignored the way it felt to have her attention and her focus because I knew she was thinking about my hand and why I'd dodged Emery's questions. I was embarrassed by my behavior and what I'd done. I didn't want Mary to know the truth of my injury.

To be clear, I didn't regret attacking those bastards. They'd deserved it. But Augie had been right that night. I could have done much more damage by reopening an old wound. Mary would not be happy to discover that I'd acted in her honor and on her behalf. She would have abhorred such an idiotic, masculine display.

I hoped she would disregard what she'd heard during dinner. But watching the curiosity bloom in her narrowed gaze, I wasn't so sure.

On a Tuesday afternoon in mid-September, it was still unseasonably warm. And quite unbearable. I hadn't bothered with a jacket or a cravat and my sleeves were rolled up past my elbows.

Mary fluttered a fan with increasing vigor as we traipsed under the oppressive midday sun following our visit to the Owensby stables. We'd walked in the shade of the tree line for as long as possible before turning in the direction of Pineview.

"Why is it so bloody hot today?" She blew out an irritated breath.

I squinted up at the cloudless sky. "It has been an odd summer."

We typically skirted the very edge of a large pond on the property. Some days, we'd look for ducks or other fowl on the water, but this area wasn't frequented for the most part. Perhaps when Reeve and Beckett were older, I could bring them along to go fishing. Yes, that was a wonderful idea. I wasn't sure how Mary felt about fishing, but surely she would—my thoughts and my legs abruptly halted.

"What are you doing?" I called urgently as Mary walked determinedly in the direction of the pond.

"It's hot!" she yelled over her shoulder and then ripped her straw bonnet from her head, tossing it, along with her fan, into the long grass at the water's edge. She bent over and pulled off one half boot and then the other before wading directly into the pond.

"Mary!" I took off after her. Should a woman in her condition even be swimming?

I could see her pale dress beneath the surface of the water as she swam out away from the safety of the shallows.

As quickly as I could, I pulled off my boots and removed my waistcoat before splashing in after her.

Mary lay on her back, floating lazily in the cool water, arms moving rhythmically at her sides. "That is much better."

When I stood a few feet away from her, with the water at chest level, I said, "You can't just jump in the water. You shouldn't even—"

"Ah, ah, ah." She waved a finger in my direction. "I distinctly remember you telling me that you would not, under any circumstance, tell me what I should do with my life." I closed my mouth. "And that includes going for a refreshing swim to escape this damn heat."

"Yes, but—"

"No buts."

"I really think," I attempted.

"That your thoughts should remain inside your head at all times," she said, but she was smiling as she reclined in the water with her eyes closed and her face pointed to the sun. "Doesn't this feel amazing?" She peeked an eye open at me when I didn't answer. "Silas. Admit it. Tell me I'm right."

"Oh, am I allowed to speak now?"

She grinned. "You are if you're agreeing with me." And then the minx splashed water in my face.

I sputtered and wiped the moisture from my eyes, smoothing my hair back in the process. "Is that how it's going to be, then?"

She squealed impressively when I sent a wave of pond water in her direction. She flipped over and made to swim away, but I reached out a hand and snagged a delicate ankle beneath the surface of the water. Mary swung around laughing as we continued splashing each other and grappling to maintain the upper hand. I eventually lost my hold on her ankle as she tried, unsuccessfully, to drag me underwater by my arms.

Our laughter and taunting eventually faded away, and somehow, she ended up pressed to my chest, her hands gripping my shoulders and her legs wrapped around my waist.

Her dark lashes sparkled with the remnants of our battle, and a grin lingered on her upturned lips. "Truce," she murmured, her gaze drifting to my mouth.

I felt the pull of her. That mysterious attraction we'd succumbed to repeatedly in the past—in a carriage, in a cupboard, in my bed. I wanted to keep her close and be closer still. I ached to run my hands over the sheer, wet fabric clinging to her body. My lips longed to taste her again.

But that wasn't what Mary needed from me.

As my arms loosened and I opened my mouth to apologize, Mary tightened her hold and surged forward. Her mouth met mine in an urgent display. I steadied myself on the muddy lake bottom so I wouldn't topple us both underwater after Mary shifted unexpectedly. I placed my hands beneath her backside to keep her stable, and that was when she moaned into my mouth.

The sound was so unexpected yet so welcome. I'd savored her sounds when we'd been intimate in the past. It had felt like a reward—a tiny admission of pleasure. Mary was so rare with her approval and her affection that provoking a response often seemed like the greatest victory.

Despite the suddenness of her actions and my surprise, my lips were moving against hers before I could further question the wisdom of my behavior. She felt so good in my arms. The wet heat of her mouth and the cool water surrounding us had me desperate for her.

Mary's legs tightened around me as she started moving against me.

I sucked in a breath at the warmth of her center against my thickening cock.

"Please," she breathed against my lips. "I want—I want . . ."

"What do you want?" I asked, afraid to open my eyes. Afraid to lose her all over again. Terrified she'd come to her senses or, worse, that I would have to be the one strong enough to pull away.

"I want all the time," she admitted in a desperate rush. "I feel aching and empty, and no matter how I touch myself, it is never quite enough."

I groaned at the imagery her words provoked.

"Will you? Please, Silas. I need—I need—"

"You need my touch?" I asked, squeezing a handful of her ass.

"Yes," she moaned.

"You need my lips on your skin?"

I could feel her vibrating with impatience. "Yes."

"Do you need my cock, Mary darling?"

"Y-yes." It was a broken plea.

And she had to know that I would have given her any part of me that she wanted.

I kissed her long and deep and started walking toward the edge of the pond. Tightening my hold and keeping her safe in my arms, we kissed until I set her feet down gently on the grass. Removing my shirt, I spread it on the ground and helped her to sit carefully atop it. Then she held out her arms and welcomed me into her embrace.

My hands traced over puckered nipples that were visible through the wet fabric of her dress. Her body was changing as her pregnancy progressed, and her breasts filled my hands in a way they never had before. She was lush and feminine, and I ached to explore every part of her.

I kissed my way down the column of her throat as her fingers traced over my shoulders and back—needy and wanting. Eventually her eager heels dug into my ass, urging me along. I smiled against the soft, wet skin of her collarbone.

"Please," she whispered.

So I didn't tease or drag out the seduction as I would have normally done. I wanted to put my lips all over her. Make love slowly in the warm sunshine until we were spent. But instead, I answered her plea.

Reaching down, I unfastened my sodden trousers and maneuvered them over my hips. Mary was already gathering her wet skirts in one hand and baring herself to me. And with the other, she guided me to her entrance before wrapping her legs back around my hips.

We both sighed as I sank deep.

It was everything I remembered about being together before, yet completely different. In our months apart, I'd thought of this— dreamed of this. But being here now, feeling Mary move against me, whispering my name, I couldn't fight the fear and the desperation to hang on to this moment with both fists.

Because I had no idea how long it would last.

Her crisis struck and the pulsing of her inner muscles had me dropping from my outstretched arms down to my elbows. Mary held me close as I continued to thrust inside her. The familiar tingle of my orgasm ignited at the base of my spine.

"Stay," she begged, not loosening her hold to allow me to with-draw. "Stay with me."

And so I did. I stayed in the welcome heat of her body for the first time as pleasure consumed me.

Eventually, I shifted to the side, and Mary snuggled under my arm to rest her head on my chest. "Thank you," she said softly before turning to kiss the underside of my jaw.

I didn't know how to respond, so I stayed quiet. The sweetness of her affection, the gratitude in her voice. We balanced carefully on the edge of unknown territory.

The sun eventually dried our skin as I held Mary in the field beside the pond. After a time, we stood and brushed ourselves off. Mary picked some grass from my hair, and I helped her re-pin her mess of damp curls.

We didn't discuss what had happened. We made our way back to the house in companionable silence, Mary sneaking amused glances while I grinned back.

We needn't analyze our joining anyway.

Hadn't I vowed to be there for Mary in all the ways she required? I'd promised to devote myself to our friendship and supporting her.

She might have needed the relief I could provide. But she never once said she needed my love.

And as long as I remembered that, I would be fine.

Eighteen

SILAS

It rained for the next three days. A chilling, lashing rain that kept me inside Laurel Park and away from Pineview and, subsequently, Mary Lovelace.

Perhaps God had answered our prayers for relief from the unusual late summer heat. Or mayhap it was the universe's way of providing distance between Mary and myself before we made any more rash decisions.

I paused in the letter I was writing to Jamie and stared out the window. The raindrops sounded aggressive against the glass—a warning to remain indoors and out of trouble.

That was when trouble quite literally walked through the door to my father's study.

Mary's hem was soaked through, and the hair that had fallen from her coiffure was in tight spirals.

I dropped my pen and stood. Everything I wanted to say fell under the disallowed category of questioning her decisions.

Why are you here?

It is dangerous to be out in weather such as this.

You could become ill as a result.

So I simply said, "Hello," and stood there staring like an idiot.

She still lingered just inside the entryway. "Dalton said you were in here."

"Excellent butler, that Dalton."

"I wanted to . . ." She took a step nearer. We were separated by about fifteen feet, two pieces of furniture, and an unhealthy amount of tension.

"You wanted to?" I prompted.

Mary's fingers were digging into the patterned fabric of her dress. I couldn't recall ever seeing her nervous. She didn't answer me. Instead, she blurted, "Are you angry with me?"

I opened my mouth in confusion but nothing emerged.

"Is that why you've stayed away? Because of what happened at the pond? Because of what I asked of you?"

I watched the concern on her features bleed into mortification as heat flooded her pale cheeks.

Stepping out from behind my father's desk, I moved closer. "No, Mary. I have only stayed away out of necessity."

She winced.

"The weather," I clarified. "I thought it prudent to remain indoors while the conditions were so foul. I was not avoiding you." Another slow step in her direction. "I do not regret what happened, if that was your concern."

"I don't regret it either, but, Silas, I do not want to hurt you. I realized belatedly that I may have initiated more between us when that was not my intent."

Obviously, Mary's affections had been surprising at the pond. I had not expected her to kiss me, let alone suggest spontaneous outdoor sex. But I was not quite so dim as to expect more from her. She'd been quite clear all those months ago. A future was not something she wanted from me. *More* was not on the table.

I didn't know what had happened with Ashby. Why they weren't married now. Why he'd abandoned her and their relationship had come to an end. But the fact remained: I was here and Ashby was not. I was the one prioritizing her well-being. Yes, the thought of the baron was a painful reminder for our time apart, but it would be hypocritical of me to resent Mary for her past relationships. I'd had my own share of bedmates prior to my first encounter with Mary last year. We all had a past. And if I'd learned anything, it wasn't my place to punish Mary for hers.

However, with these recent physical developments, I didn't exactly know what she wanted from me.

But I'd never been particularly meek before. With Mary dripping on the carpets and awaiting my reply, now seemed like as good a time as any to figure out what our unexpected interlude *did* mean.

"And what *was* your intent?"

She searched the room for an answer, her brown eyes confounded and a touch embarrassed. "I don't understand what is happening to me." She lowered her voice and stepped around the armchair and within touching distance.

I slid my hands into the pockets of my trousers to be safe.

She pressed her lips together in obvious reluctance before admitting quietly, "I feel overcome with sexual awareness and . . . insistent desire."

My eyebrows must have gone up to nearly my hairline. Then I managed, "Like survival madness?"

Mary smiled as if remembering something fondly. "No, not exactly survival madness. But I do feel arousal most urgently."

"Arousal?"

"Yes." Her cheeks were the color of ripe tomatoes. "You probably do not want to hear this, but Emery confirmed that it was normal for women who are with child to feel a sense of insistence and need for release. It can be part of pregnancy."

"No," I said, holding up a hand. "No more marital wisdom from my sister, please. Jesus."

Mary looked as if she wanted to laugh momentarily. "I'm sorry. I didn't know how else to explain it. And I didn't know myself, at first."

"So, let me see if I have this right—you felt overcome when we were at the pond?"

"Yes," she confirmed. "You were being playful, and we were laughing and touching. Your shirt was practically transparent. And then I was in your arms and instinct took over. I acted rashly and out of character."

"Not entirely out of character," I murmured.

She gave me a flat look.

"It was all about circumstance, then? I could have been anyone?" The thought caused an unwelcome twinge.

But Mary was already shaking her head. "No. You are not *just* anyone."

I ignored the way that made me feel and sought to clarify, "What if you'd fallen in the pond with Miles?"

"I can control myself. I'm not an animal."

"Oh, so your arousal recognizes a happily married man? That's good."

Mary pressed her lips together, resisting her amusement.

I kept going, now that I knew it was me, and me alone that she desired in her time of need. "Should I go check on Dalton to make sure you didn't accost him on your way in? Perhaps you found him irresistible with his large gray mustache." I wanted her amusement, her joy to push aside her embarrassment and her hurt. Anything to wipe away the vulnerable uncertainty I'd seen when she'd entered the room.

"Stop." She finally laughed, lunging forward and placing her gloved hand over my lips. "You know that is not the case."

I smiled around the press of her delicate fingers.

Mary slowly removed her hand, her amusement fading into something serious—something brave. "It was you, Silas. I knew I wanted *you* in that moment. I knew how good it would be. How good it always was. But also, that I would be safe and cared for. Protected. And I was desperate to feel that way again."

A pleasant warmth settled in my chest. Mary had needed me. And she'd known I would take care of her. Hadn't that been my goal when setting our course for friendship this summer? I hadn't wanted to pressure her or make her uncomfortable after my earlier actions. Supporting her had been my main objective, and it seemed, in a way, I was doing that for her despite my past behavior.

I nodded. "Then I am glad I could be of assistance at the pond." Curiosity got the better of me. "Do you still feel . . . overcome? How long does this last for women in your condition?"

Her eyes shifted around the room and she replied cagily, "I—I don't know exactly how long it lasts."

I smirked and waited.

Finally, her brown gaze made its way back to me. She huffed a laugh. "Oh, do shut up."

"What?" I asked, feigning innocence. "I was just curious if you'd require my services again in the future. I am indeed amenable." She rolled her eyes, but a smile fought for freedom. "Or if I should keep Dalton away from your advances."

Mary shook her head, grinning at me. "Enough. Dalton is safe."

Raising my brows, I said with more sincerity than I'd intended, "And me? Am I safe?"

Something about my tone or words must have drawn the full force of her attention because her grin fell away, and her eyes focused on mine. "I don't know."

I would have kissed her then. I would have happily cupped her rosy cheeks and slid my fingers into her mess of damp hair. But I'd vowed to let her lead.

Love wasn't forcing someone to bend until they broke. It also wasn't wearing them down like a smooth pebble in a riverbed. Love was a choice, as was affection and intimacy. I wouldn't be wishing and hoping this go-round. I'd be patient. I'd be exactly who Mary needed me to be.

She watched me a moment longer before shaking herself and taking a small step back. "I apologize for interrupting your afternoon."

"Oh, you didn't interrupt much. I was writing to Jamie, back in London. He's been practicing."

"Practicing what?"

I realized I'd spoken without thought. And then I noticed Mary shifting on her feet.

"I'm sorry. Please, have a seat." I indicated the armchair behind her.

She settled herself, so I moved to resume my seat behind my father's desk.

"What was he practicing?" Mary repeated.

"Well," I started, nervously shuffling papers on the wooden surface before me, "Jamie has been learning to read since he began his employment. He sends correspondence to work on his penmanship and vocabulary."

Mary smiled. "That's wonderful. Is there a school that he attends?"

I swallowed. Why was this so difficult to discuss? "No. Actually, there is no school nearby for him and his sisters in White Chapel."

"Oh. Then how has he been learning?"

I cleared my throat before tugging on the fabric of my cravat. "I have been instructing him."

Mary's dark auburn brows lifted in surprise. I imagined it was difficult to picture me in the role of instructor. Silly, more like.

"You have been teaching your valet to read since he began working for you?"

Forcing a laugh, I admitted to the polished surface of the desktop, "I know it's unconventional, and I am in no way qualified to influence anyone in—"

"Silas, no," she interrupted, drawing my attention. "That is not what I meant. I know you are fond of the boy. And it is unconventional, but your efforts are commendable. You already provided employment to Jamie when he was not qualified and had only ever known hard, manual labor, even as a small child. What you're doing for him is admirable. I was not judging you."

"That is kind of you to say, but I'm afraid I'm not at all capable. He would learn so much more with proper instruction. He's bright and a fast learner. What he needs is schooling and an experienced instructor. I was actually hoping to speak with you and with Patty. Your involvement and experience with Watford House is invaluable and . . ." I was unsure how to broach the topic.

"You want to start a school!"

My gaze snapped up at Mary's exclamation.

"Silas, that is a brilliant idea. I told you we've had a flood of charitable donations as a result of Owensby's growing notoriety. We've been searching for a way to grow and expand Watford House to best serve the orphanage. More instructors and governesses to lead instruction beyond the children in residence would be such a benefit for the community."

"Do you think so?"

Her eyes were bright with excitement. "I do. We should talk to Patty before she leaves for London. She can set things in motion. I'm convinced she will support your idea."

"Your idea," I clarified.

"No, Silas," she insisted with a small smile. "Your idea. You just didn't know how to ask for it."

I still didn't think I was the right person to lead this sort of endeavor. Patty had much more experience and influence over her realm. But, perhaps, if I could even be a small part of bringing something like this about, it would be enough to help children like Jamie and his sisters. They might be considered for employment above their station. They could lead better lives than what they'd been born into.

"I want to jot a few things down. Pass me your pen," Mary said, already gathering a blank page from my stack on the desktop.

I made the mistake of reaching out with my left hand to grip the writing instrument. A sharp pang and responding tightness restricted the movement. I quickly scooped up the pen with my right hand and passed it to a waiting Mary, who watched me with a frown.

"What happened to your hand, Silas?"

I sighed, wondering how much I could say without admitting the truth. "I was being an idiot. It was most likely broken, and I didn't see to it. It's difficult for me to grasp objects and it aches a bit in the soggy weather."

Her eyes followed the unconscious way I massaged the soreness in my hand. "But how did you break it? Initially."

"I threw a punch that was probably unwise," I admitted, hoping she'd leave it at that.

Of course, she narrowed her gaze and sought clarification. "At Langham's?"

I could have lied. She knew I frequented the boxing club. It was a fine enough explanation. But it was also a falsehood she could easily uncover on her own if she really tried. And I didn't want to be dishonest and lie to her face.

"No, not at Langham's. I got in a bit of a scruff up at the club."

"That day in my sitting room. You looked like you'd been up all night, and you were favoring your left hand."

I nodded, ignoring the far greater pain that resulted from that meeting. "I'd hurt it the night before."

"Who did you quarrel with?"

I swallowed uneasily before confessing, "Glenfellow and Brannigan."

She blinked, not having been expecting that answer. "Why?"

Sighing, I leaned back in my chair and rubbed my face. "It was the first time I'd encountered them since the Ascot Races, and I couldn't bear the sight of them." I didn't want to bring up Ashby and hurt her more, so I only admitted part of what happened that night. "Genevieve told me what they said about you last season. She thought I already knew and mentioned Brannigan and Glenfellow in passing. I was so angry. I know it was unwise and that you don't need anyone—much less me—defending you. I didn't mention you at the club. I just started punching. I doubt *they* even know why. They're such bastards that they probably don't question it when someone has the desire to pummel them. So I don't believe I roused any gossip with my actions."

I paused to gauge Mary's reaction, but she just regarded me thoughtfully. "I know I was idiotic and impulsive, but I just couldn't sit by after knowing they'd hurt you."

Mary remained quiet before she nodded once, expression unreadable.

"You're not going to scold me for my actions?"

"No," she replied evenly. "Well, you should have had a doctor look at that hand."

I remained in a state of confusion even as Mary stood and brushed out her skirts. "Will you escort me back to Pineview? We can speak with Patty about your idea for a school at Watford House."

"Yes, of course." I stood on instinct, but I was still waiting for her anger or her censure to make itself known.

Then her face took on an impish expression as she lowered her voice. "And then perhaps you can stay for supper and then join me in my chambers for a nightcap."

I hid my surprise as well as I could, but her invitation was still so unexpected. Recovering quickly, I replied with a grin, "Do you have need of my services?"

"I believe I do."

"Shall I be your royal consort, Lady Mary?" I teased.

Her laughter was so free and happy that I joined in as well.

I survived the remainder of the afternoon: the productive conversation with my sister and the endless meal with the current residents of Pineview.

After a quick drink following supper, I figured it was time to plant the seeds of my exit from the property.

Around a very impolite yawn, I said to those assembled, "Well, thank you for a lovely evening, but I am quite ready for my bed."

I felt Mary pinch me on the back of the arm.

Perhaps I'd overdone my performance.

Mary said casually, "I'll walk you out, Mr. Bartholomew. I can provide my notes from our discussion this afternoon."

I looked at Mary and mouthed, "Mr. Bartholomew?"

She rolled her eyes and turned toward the door. "Come on, then."

As I directed my attention to my family, I noted Patty's worried gaze following Mary from the room, but it was over in a moment. I bid my sister and Miles and Franny all a good night and took my leave.

Mary waited for me in the corridor. She took my arm and whispered in my ear, "Go around to the garden entrance and I'll let you in through the kitchens. We can take the servants' staircase up to the guest wing."

"Yes, Your Majesty."

Another pinch to my arm had me laughing. "Fine. Fine. I will do as instructed."

"Wait five minutes," she said and then opened the front door and deposited me on the top step.

I waited *three* minutes and then hastened across the soggy ground, through the frigid rain to the rear entrance of Pineview.

Mary stood with the door open. I entered the warm, empty kitchen quickly and took her outstretched hand.

She placed a single gloved finger against my lips to indicate quiet, and I gave her a quick nip that made her smile and shake her head.

Then we were off, winding our way up the stairs and peeking around corners before finally entering her very well-appointed guest suite. It looked as if the sitting room had been arranged specifically for Mary in mind. The space was open and inviting with elegant draperies and enchanting artwork on the walls. Another doorway led to her own washroom. A gleaming copper hip bath sat within.

She still held my hand, so I followed on lush patterned carpets into the bedchamber. The fire was lit, and golden flickering light bathed the room.

We'd done this before. Mary and I were no strangers to stolen glances and sneaking around corridors. We were well-versed in garden entrances and hiding every aspect of who we were together. It was a bittersweet ache to recall that time. But something about this felt different.

I was nervous, I realized. And she was quiet.

Everything that had happened at the pond had been so spontaneous. There was nothing in this room except expectation. It was filled with it.

I waited for Mary to take the lead but could feel her hesitation. So I brought myself closer. I gave her a means to ask for what she needed without saying the words.

My hands slipped easily around her waist, still slight as it was. Her hands settled on my chest, and she breathed out a sigh of relief that I felt in my soul.

Closing my arms around her, I simply held on. The embrace seemed endless with Mary's cheek resting on my shoulder. Finally, I reached up with my good hand and started pulling pins from her hair. Once the strands were free and curling down her back, I massaged her scalp, eliciting another quiet sound of satisfaction.

I continued my ministrations before lowering my lips to the shell of her ear. "What does my lady require?"

I felt her smile stretch, the soft skin of her cheek pressing into my stubble. "Your mouth, if you please."

"As you wish."

It was not a hardship to divest her of her layers, to spread her out on top of the coverlet, and to feast on her. She came against my tongue, clutching my hair and murmuring broken pleas of *yes* and *God* and *just like that*.

And before she'd even caught her breath, she was up and removing my clothing, pulling my naked form atop her—within her.

The relief of joining was the same as it had been by the pond. The sense that we'd been given a second chance. The satisfaction of grasping something that had previously been just beyond my reach.

We moved together as experienced lovers—touching skillfully in the ways we knew the other liked. Because we'd been here. We'd loved like this before.

Yet everything had changed.

It was difficult to remember the history and the complications and the hurt with Mary's soft lips pressed against my neck, with her nails scoring across my back. It was easy to get lost in the illusion of intimacy when I felt her clenching around me as I lost myself in pleasure.

But as we recovered, Mary splayed out across my chest, the true nature of our relationship—here and now—began to intrude. Reality encroached, and I recalled that I was here in friendship to slake her needs. I made her feel safe and cared for. She could ask this of me because I wanted only her happiness. She trusted me, and that in and of itself was a gift.

As I stared at the canopy overhead, Mary's breathing evened, and her body loosened on the edge of sleep. I gave myself two inhales and two exhales to consider a future where we were married, and this child was mine. Where we loved openly and were happy.

And as her breath ghosted out on that second breath, I shut down all of those wayward thoughts. They would lead to nothing but heartbreak.

Mary had a complicated future that she was figuring out all on her own. She didn't need the added pressure of my presumptuous heart.

I would be the man she needed me to be—the one who made things easier for her and not more difficult. It was *still* not her job to manage my feelings. If heartache was on the horizon, it would be my own. And I would weather it.

Nineteen

MARY

Late September

"And you're certain you'll be all right at Pineview on your own? You could always stay with Julian and Genevieve. They won't be returning to town for another month at least."

I smiled at my friend. Patty would be off to London today along with her husband and daughter. She was worried I'd be lonely in her country home without anyone else in residence. And while I appreciated her concern, I knew I wouldn't trouble Gen and Julian with my presence.

"Goodness, no. I don't think I'll inconvenience the newlyweds with my skulking about," I replied teasingly. "I will be fine, Patty. Not to worry. I mostly read and walk. And with the weather so soggy, I'll be spending most of my days tucked up in the library until your family returns for Yuletide."

Her blue eyes were still troubled. "And you'll alert the staff if there is anything you need to be more comfortable?"

Nodding, I said, "I've gotten quite demanding since residing at Pineview. I won't hesitate to order the servants to fluff my pillows and bring me all manner of treats, day or night."

Patty gave me a flat look.

I smiled widely. "I will be fine, Patty! Don't worry so. And, anyway, I have Silas to keep me company."

If anything, my statement seemed to intensify Patty's look of unease.

Silas had been spending most of his days at Pineview since he'd joined me in my bedchamber just over a week ago. He hadn't returned to my bed since, but we spent rare dry moments walking the gardens and the rest of the time in the library, reading or discussing the plans for Watford's new school.

That was the reason for Patty's early return to London. The season would be underway in a few weeks, but my friend had been eager to meet with the headmistress of the orphanage and begin the planning stages for the addition of the new school elements. The building itself had the available space, but new governesses and instructors would need to be hired as well as consultation with current schooling locations for basic guidance in establishing our own institution.

Patty, Silas, and I had put together an extensive plan to develop this new school in Bethnal Green. I felt a great deal of guilt that I could not be in London to assist with all the work required, but Patty assured me that the initial stages would mostly be adminis-trative tasks and dealing with her solicitor as well as coordinating with Mrs. Watford, the headmistress entrusted with overseeing day-to-day operations at the Watford Home for Children.

My friend promised to write to me with any news and developments as to her progress. And I looked forward to hearing from her and providing any counsel that may be required. Furthermore, I knew Silas was eager to be involved as well. Despite his typical confidence, he'd seemed rather hesitant to voice his ideas and opinions. His self-assured nature had somehow abandoned him in all of this. He kept qualifying every opinion by saying he was no expert or didn't have the first idea about providing what children needed. But he'd cared enough about his young valet to dedicate his own time and attention to helping him learn to read.

I thought, in this one area, Silas hadn't given himself nearly enough credit.

There were more differences I'd noticed during these weeks in Hampshire. He'd seemed to really take his apology to heart. He hadn't shied away from discussing the baby, which was equal parts encouraging and devastating. Silas still believed that the child I carried was the Baron of Ashby's, though he hadn't brought the man up again. Guilt nearly consumed me whenever the subject of the baby arose. A hopeful part of me ached to tell him the truth—that he was the father of my child. But another part of me could envision a future in which Silas knew the truth. One in which he'd marry me out of obligation and then resent me and our child for the rest of his life. The fear of that murky future kept my mouth firmly shut, even when he asked after me or wondered if I'd felt the baby move lately.

"I'm worried about you and Silas." Patty's quiet words drew my attention and jolted me out of my ruminations.

She continued, "You are spending a great deal of time together. I'm concerned that you will be hurt, Mary."

I shook my head quickly in an attempt to reassure. "We've decided on friendship. You should be proud of us. We've never quite managed it before."

In truth, it was too late for me to worry about being hurt. He'd taken my heart for himself back in London, months ago, and I'd realized it too late. I would accept this time with Silas—for however long it lasted—and enjoy it. He would have the life he was meant to lead. In all likelihood, he would find a wife this season and settle into the future he'd envisioned for himself. His involvement with Watford no doubt aided in his sense of accomplishment. I knew that Silas longed for a purpose beyond his life of means. Things were coming together for him, and I wouldn't derail that now.

I would raise our child away from the disapproving eyes of society and be grateful for the small part of him I'd always have.

My main concern was keeping Silas's heart safe. At one time, before he'd known of my pregnancy, Silas had claimed to want more—a relationship in truth. Pouncing on him at the pond had not been my intent, but I could not bring myself to regret it. Yet I didn't wish to hurt Silas by asking too much of him. I knew what it was to have your romantic expectations grow beyond the bounds of reality. And out of concern for Silas, I had not asked him to return to my bed. My fear of ruining our delicate new friendship held me back.

"Well, if you are such good friends now, perhaps you should consider telling him the truth. Mayhap he will not react as you believe."

I snapped my attention to Patty and lowered my voice. "I know exactly how he'll react. He would marry me."

Her expression was pleading. "Would that be so terrible?"

"Yes," I hissed in exasperation. "I refuse to be a duty or a source of resentment. He has his own plans for the future. And none of those involve an unsuitable wife and an unexpected child."

Patty sighed.

"Please, Patty. Please do not tell him yet. Not until I figure things out. Not until Silas has the life he wants."

My friend frowned but nodded. "I should go."

I hugged her. "Thank you for everything," I whispered, my voice breaking on the final word. Patty had done so much—risked so much for me. I'd never be able to repay her for her support.

"Be safe. I'll see you in a few months."

And with that, Patty whirled about in her crimson wool traveling gown and was gone.

It wasn't until later that afternoon that I noticed a commotion at the front of the house. I'd been in the kitchens attempting to retrieve a bit of shortbread for a snack when I'd heard Silas's voice.

Making my way through the corridors to the main entrance, I saw a footman enter with a large trunk. Silas held a traveling bag, and Dashwood looked on impassively.

"Your usual suite, sir?" the butler inquired.

"Thank you, Dashwood. Good man," Silas said jovially, patting the older man on the shoulder as he continued on into the foyer.

When he spotted me, his grin widened. "Mary, good afternoon! How do you fare? Are you feeling well?"

I frowned in confusion and ignored his greeting. "What are you doing?"

He slipped his hand through my arm and urged me along toward the grand staircase. In a low voice, he replied as we walked, "With Patty and Miles and Franny off to London, I didn't want you to be alone." I opened my mouth to protest, but he continued undeterred, "I know you're capable and absolutely fine on your own. But I would feel better if I were nearby. And I know Patty would be relieved if you had some companionship."

I fought a wince. Somehow, I didn't think Patty would be comforted by Silas's presence in this instance.

"And what will your mother and father assume by your absence?" I asked.

"Nothing whatsoever. I regularly visit my siblings and their homes." And then Silas tugged me gently to a stop before saying pointedly, "And there is no expectation while I'm under this roof. I am not here to seduce you."

"Oh," I murmured, not having come to that conclusion yet and still very much conflicted about asking Silas for anything beyond friendship.

His brown eyes fairly sparkled. "However, I am at your service should my lady require it."

"I see."

"Come," he said, guiding me onto the first step. "What were you doing before I interrupted with my grand entrance?"

"Nothing really. Just being a nuisance in the kitchens, trying to retrieve sweets before tea is served."

Silas paused. "Now that, I am well-versed in. Top-notch nuisance at your service, as you well know."

I bit my lip to contain my grin, but his eyes tracked the movement. His features shifted and I could see his smug sense of accomplishment at having amused me.

Silas took my hand and placed it on his arm as he led me off the staircase and back in the direction of the kitchen. "Let's see what we can pilfer, shall we?"

I nodded and set off with him, knowing he'd retrieve shortbread or game pies or anything else I wanted. All I needed to do was ask.

The day was overcast and chilly, but the threat of rain had abandoned us momentarily.

Silas had been in residence for nearly a week. I hadn't asked when he planned on returning to London. In truth, I hadn't wanted to know. Life at Pineview had been . . . fun since his arrival. I had laughed more during my time in Hampshire this summer than I ever had in my own unstable home. Silas and I played card games and games of chance. He dined with me and we took tea together. We read often, and spent time in the garden as much as we were able.

True to his word, he hadn't suggested I visit his chambers after dark, and he hadn't invaded my personal space once.

I still felt aggressively attracted to him, and my body still craved physical connection, but we seemed to truly be on the path to friendship. I didn't want to ruin that.

Since the weather was as fine as one could expect for autumn in Hampshire, I'd suggested a walk beyond the gardens and over to the Owensby stables for the first time in weeks. Silas had retrieved some treats for the horses and we'd set off.

My body continued changing, my stomach a bit more noticeable. However, with the high waist of my gowns and the pregnancy stays that Emery had provided, I was able to move about undetected and without curious stares from the Owensby grooms and stable hands for the most part. But an insecure part of me wondered what Silas thought of the changes to my body.

"What's happening there?" Silas's words drew my attention as he indicated three observers standing in front of a stall in the large main aisle of the stable.

While it wasn't unusual to encounter Julian or Charlie during our visits to Owensby Stud, they were usually busy elsewhere with training or other farm work. To see them standing in the middle of the aisle with another groom on a Wednesday afternoon was a bit odd.

"I don't know," I murmured as we walked closer.

Charlie, the head groom, noticed our approach first. He raised a hand in greeting, offering a gap-toothed grin. "Good afternoon, Lady Mary. Mr. Bartholomew. You picked a grand time for a visit."

The boy had grown quite a bit since becoming acquainted with Julian and the other Bartholomews. Being well-fed and well-cared for had that effect. At seventeen, he'd been a stable boy for his horrible stepmother at her inn in London before coming to work at the Cawthorn stables as a result of his growing friendship with Julian. And a year later, when Owensby Stud Farm came about, Miles and Julian knew right away that Charlie would be the perfect addition.

I smiled at Charlie as Julian gave me a quiet nod of greeting. "Why is that?"

Silas and I approached the doorway of the stall to see what everyone was staring at.

"Because our Matilda here is foaling at long last."

I looked on in horror as a gray mare lay on her side in the center of the stall. Her chest heaved with effort and her coat was dark with sweat.

"The water bag just ruptured," Charlie said happily with his arms crossed. "The foal should be here soon, if all goes well."

I could hear Silas swallow audibly at my side. "Perhaps we should . . ."

His voice trailed off as we watched the poor horse tense in pain. Various fluids covered the straw on the floor, and I could feel my stomach heave a little at the sight before me.

This was childbirth. Well, horse birth. But surely there would be similarities. I knew I would be required to expel this baby from my body at some point, but it had been a vague sort of awareness, lingering in the back of my mind. And Emery had done it. Twice! Surely, I would be able to—

My thoughts broke off abruptly as something emerged from the hindquarters of the horse. It looked like a pale sack. And then suddenly there were legs. I heard myself gasp.

"You're doing great, Tillie girl." Charlie encouraged the mare.

Next, a head, dark as pitch, pushed its way out onto the straw as the rest of the foal seemed to slide from its mother. I fought the urge to gag.

I looked to Silas, who had one hand covering his mouth. He was as horrified by the afternoon's events as I felt.

I leaned in to his side and voiced my sudden dismay. "Silas, do you think it will be like—like that when my baby is born?"

Silas didn't look my way as he nodded slowly. Finally, he removed his hand from his face and replied, "While I am no expert, I imagine it will be very similar." A beat passed. "Fewer legs, though."

I turned my incredulous gaze to his deadpan expression before whacking him on the arm and startling myself into laughter.

Then Silas broke next, pressing a kiss into my hair and shaking against me in amusement.

"You are ridiculous," I said, refusing to look toward the stall again.

He leaned down and said quietly, for my ears alone, "And you are the strongest person I know. You will be fine. And the baby will be healthy and well."

I nodded, feeling emotion threaten.

Silas straightened away and met my eyes. His smile was smaller now. He regarded me with fondness that did nothing to dispel the tears gathering. After a quick glance to the side and into the stall, he returned his gaze to mine. "But we are never watching a foaling again. Just to be on the safe side."

We did stay, however, to welcome the new tiny life into the world

—a filly Charlie decided to name Lovelace. I'd been immensely pleased at that.

Silas and I made the return trip to Pineview a short while later.

"I cannot believe that mare was already standing after what she just endured," I said into the chilly breeze. "I plan to be abed for a fortnight."

Silas grinned. "I believe that is standard."

I realized suddenly that it had been weeks since I felt odd discussing the life growing inside me. At first, when Silas and I had been finding our footing following his apology, I hadn't wanted to discuss the baby or my pregnancy or anything related to either. I'd been fearful of awkwardness descending and Silas's continued disapproval making itself known. But slowly, as Silas consistently asked how I was feeling or if I'd felt the baby move, I'd lowered my guard. Now, it wasn't strange at all to watch a horse give birth and then discuss my own future laboring.

Silas never made me feel like he was judging me for my situation. He hadn't brought up Ashby or the consequences of my decision again.

"Thank you," I blurted abruptly, feeling warm and comfortable— supported beyond what I deserved by the very man I was lying to.

He frowned and came to a halt.

I stopped walking and turned to face him.

"For what?" Silas asked.

For caring for me so well.

For being my constant companion and raising my spirits.

For being exactly what I need when I'm not strong enough to ask for it.

Instead of any of those truths, I offered what I could without giving away another piece of my heart. "For coming to stay at Pineview. For spending your days with me. For what you said at the stable."

"It was the truth," he replied simply.

And how I longed to give him the truth in return.

Twenty

MARY

October

Life continued on at Pineview.

It seemed I was spending my confinement with Silas Bartholomew.

We took our meals together and spent most of our days in a similar fashion. We talked all the time about ridiculous things and serious things, about Silas's travels, about my family and his, and about the baby.

Mary from a year ago would never have believed that I could tolerate listening to Silas speak for hours on end. But here we were—practically in each other's pockets for the majority of the day.

It was odd to realize that Silas had somehow become my closest friend.

Yet despite our closeness and our proximity, our nights were still our own. I was too conflicted to seek Silas out for intimacies. My body craved his, but I didn't visit his rooms and he didn't visit mine. And at this point, it wasn't only his heart I was worried about protecting.

My love for Silas had started growing back in London. It had been such a tender thing, like a spring shoot that had just barely taken root. But now—after months in Hampshire—living together and growing closer in friendship, I didn't know what I'd do without him. That tiny sprout was gaining strength and growing more and more every day.

I'd been too fearful of asking after his plans for the season. I dreaded the day when he'd pack his things and be on his way to London.

"Just take your shoes off if they're bothering you."

Silas's voice startled me out of my musings. I'd been sitting across from him in the family's informal receiving room on the second floor. It was our favored spot aside from the library. The wide windows allowed adequate light for reading and the furniture was the most comfortable. I found the lovely blue shade on the walls quite soothing as well.

I set aside the knitting I'd been working on—a tiny hat for the baby—and focused on Silas. "What?"

"Your slippers." He pointed at my feet as if I didn't realize where shoes attached themselves to my body. "I can tell they're irritating you. Just take them off."

I sighed. My feet had started swelling recently. The midwife from the nearby village had been given strict instructions before Patty had left to see to me regularly. The old woman had assured me that all the things I was experiencing—burning in my chest after mealtimes, slight swelling of my feet and ankles, and odd food cravings—were all quite common for women in my condition.

"It wouldn't be appropriate," I mumbled. "And I am fine."

"Appropriate." Silas raised one dark brow. "It's just the two of us. The staff pays us no mind. We could run around in the nude and no one would say a word to us."

I could feel myself flush at his ridiculous statement. Would I very much like to take off all my clothes in this sitting room with Silas? Of course, I would. But he didn't need to know that.

"Here," he grumbled, leaning forward. Silas worked to remove his boots one by one before flexing his toes on the patterned rug. "Pineview shall be a shoe-free household. I'll alert Dashwood."

I finally allowed a small grin but still did not remove my footwear.

Silas grumbled something about pigheaded women under his breath and reached for me across the distance.

"What are you doing?" I shrilled in surprise.

Bent in half, he gently grasped my ankle. "I am easing your stubborn suffering. I can hear you shifting and trying to alleviate the pressure on your feet." His hand eased the slipper off one heel before he returned my stockinged foot carefully to the ground. "Now you can be more comfortable. In your silk stockings. No one cares, Mary."

I stared on incredulously as he maneuvered the other slipper off and set it neatly on the plush carpet.

Silas's thumb slid firmly down the arch of the foot he was still holding before he brought his other thumb up to dig gently into the ball of my foot.

A low moan escaped entirely against my will as he massaged me.

Silas looked up and smirked knowingly. "That feels better, does it not?"

"Perhaps I am ticklish and will accidentally kick you."

He shook his head slowly, grin still in place. "I'm quite familiar with all your sensitive spots."

It was difficult to think with his hands on me. I wanted his touch to trail up beneath my skirts, to tease along the edge of my stockings. I knew I could ask, and he would do it.

Thankfully, Silas chose that moment to flip his left hand over and cup my heel. He winced slightly at the movement.

I pulled my foot slowly from his grasp as the heat I'd felt was coolly extinguished by his obvious pain.

"Is your hand still bothering you?"

"I'm fine," he replied, not looking at me.

"Now who's the pigheaded one?"

Brown eyes lifted, amusement shining from within. "You, darling. Always you."

"I'm sorry you hurt your hand, especially on Glenfellow's worthless face."

Silas looked unsure of what to say, a rare and unexpected sight.

"I'm not angry that you brawled, Silas. Perhaps I should rant and rave and tell you that I can fight my own battles. But the fact of the matter is, I like that you defended me. It wasn't rational or wise, but anger rarely is. Besides, I'm unable to get away with pummeling him so neatly."

It was unbearable to admit, but Glenfellow's words *had* been difficult to endure. I'd been forced to feign disinterest—to ignore his mocking, hate-filled words about my appearance. To hear insults whispered and keep your head held high was no easy feat. There was nothing quite like pretending to be unbothered about something sensitive to your nature. It was not a knife slicing neatly. It was one twisting instead. Doing the most damage for nothing but the sake of cruelty.

When Silas had admitted the truth of his injury—that he'd been overcome by his anger and sought retribution on my behalf—perhaps I should have scolded him for his violence or pretended to be above such petty vindictiveness. But those men targeted a woman for their malice. They knew any sort of reaction would only paint me as a humorless bitch. Glenfellow—and Brannigan, too—got exactly what they deserved. Some bloodthirsty and grudge-holding part of me wished I'd been there to see it. I simply regretted that Silas had been hurt in the process.

"Their cruelty was unconscionable. I'm sorry that you had to endure it at the time," Silas said.

"Yes." I stared at the half-knitted cap on my lap. "It is more difficult to hear out loud the things you know people are thinking about you."

"Mary." His voice was low and urgent, drawing my attention. "It wasn't true—what they said about you."

I shook my head, reluctant to endure well-meaning platitudes from a man—especially one I'd been intimate with, one who knew the truth of my appearance.

"Tell me you don't think—"

"Thank you for being angry on my behalf," I interrupted quickly. Silas looked like he wanted to argue, so I continued on, "Thank you for caring that they'd hurt me. But next time, do be mindful of your hand."

"You needn't thank me for that," Silas finally replied after watching me resume my knitting and avoid his gaze. "Caring for you is quite out of my control."

That night, like nearly every night, we dined *en famille* with all the dishes readily available on the table and no set courses to speak of. It was informal and suited us perfectly. Neither one of us had worn footwear for the occasion either.

Following the meal, Silas escorted me to the guest wing. The corridors were quiet. The maids had already been through to lay the fires as we both would retire soon.

Silas stopped abruptly in front of the door to his own set of rooms. "I just wanted to say something. And you can be angry about it, but I want you to hear it. To really hear me."

Anxiety gripped me as I watched Silas be fairly overcome with urgency to speak. The stern line of his dark brows formed slashing lines of consternation as he turned his body to face mine.

"What is it?" I asked in concern.

"I know you don't want me to tell you you're lovely. The way you retreated earlier when we discussed Glenfellow and how you've never allowed me to compliment you or tell you that you're beautiful makes it plain to see. You have never once been comfortable with praise or discussions of your appearance. And it's fine if you don't find yourself beautiful—you know what? It's not fine," he amended, throwing his hands up in irritation. "But I can't change the way you see yourself. The same damn way you cannot change the way I see you. You do not get to influence my opinion of your beauty."

I could feel my surprise morph into heated unease. My cheeks were undoubtedly pink. I shifted uncomfortably, my insides squirming at having been seen so thoroughly by Silas.

He stepped forward, cupping my jaw. "I treasure your smile." His thumb brushed lightly over my lips. "It is so rare and genuine, lovely in its sincerity. I feel as if I have accomplished something monumental if I can persuade you into a grin. Like I earned it, and it's all mine. And I love your body. Every long, graceful line. From your neck"—he traced a finger along the pale column of my throat—"all the way to your legs wrapped round my hips."

I brought my hands up to grip his waistcoat and made an inarticulate squeak.

"And your hair . . ." Silas shifted the hand cradling my jaw into the mass of curls falling out of their pins. "The vibrant color. The scent of lavender it always carries. Nothing is more gorgeous than this hair—wild and fiery just like its owner. No sight more erotic than having it spread out across my pillow."

"Silas," I breathed, clutching him to me.

Whispering into the sensitive skin behind my ear, he said, "These are the things I find beautiful, if only you'd let me."

I didn't intend to kiss him. For there was no conscious thought behind it. One moment, I was listening to Silas praise every part of me, and the next, I gripped him in a desperate embrace. I couldn't get close enough. I wanted to live within his golden light —the one that shone on every diminished part of me. The places I never allowed myself to look at too long in the mirror. The ones that made me feel weak and unbearably small.

Perhaps I'd allowed Glenfellow's insults to take root because the soil had been ripe for planting. I'd criticized my appearance, hated pieces of myself with such fervent intensity that it made a cruel sort of sense for gentlemen of my acquaintance to demean me in the same way. The weakness hadn't been in allowing their mockery to circulate. It had been in agreeing with them.

Silas had given me a gift just now—not in calling me beautiful but in demanding I hear it. He was right. He could not change the way I saw myself. But I could not change the way he saw me either.

Our kisses carried us toward the doorway to Silas's rooms. I reached behind him to turn the knob, and we stumbled our way inside. Fires glowed warm in the sitting room and the bedchamber beyond.

I unbuttoned Silas's pewter waistcoat, pushing it from his shoulders onto the floor. With quick efficient tugs, I had his shirt out of his trousers and over his head.

Silas brought me to stand before the fire in the bedchamber. He began undoing the front closures of my dress before sliding it from my shoulders. He carefully removed my stays and underskirts until I stood warm before the fire in only my stockings and my shift.

There was a moment when I considered the changing curves and planes of my body, the unusual fullness of my breasts, and worried about what Silas saw when he looked at me. But following his passionate speech, I found it was quite easy to ignore the doubtful and cynical voice within.

With tenderness, Silas pressed kisses across my shoulder to my collarbone. His right hand gathered the sheer fabric I still wore as he pulled me closer to his body. Silas's eager mouth worked itself up my neck and along the edge of my jaw until I grew restless and turned his head to meet my lips.

From there, we turned frantic, and the remainder of our clothing was quickly dispensed with. Heat built in my center. The ache of being without him made me restless. Tonight, what had started as being overcome by emotion and love for this man, was boiling down to passionate longing. Weeks of innocent conversation and friendly touches hadn't been nearly enough. I needed more. And I thought he did as well.

I led Silas to his bed and urged him to lie back. Climbing over, I settled myself on his lap and the rigid length of his erection.

Never once shying away from the new shape of my body, Silas's hands went to my hips as I moved—circling and rising and falling, rocking and taking my time.

"Mary," he finally breathed when it became too much and not nearly enough.

Reaching between us, I gripped his hard length and lowered myself to take him in. The stretch and the feeling of fullness had me groaning quietly.

I leaned forward, eager to keep our connection and continue kissing and licking into Silas's mouth. My chest pressed flat to his, and I could feel the rapid beat of his heart. The urgency that brought us into his chambers slowly bled away, transforming into slow-simmering heat. I longed to touch every part of him and make this moment last forever.

I rolled my hips at a leisurely place as Silas's hands came to my backside. Deep, drugging kisses seduced, and I could feel every place where our skin touched.

When our measured pace could no longer be maintained, we chased our pleasure together. I laced my fingers through his and rose atop him, and Silas thrust from beneath. Through endless heat and gasping breaths, we lost ourselves. Almost as if an inevitable turn of events had led us right back to one another.

I didn't know how to quit Silas Bartholomew, especially not now when we were more than an arrangement, more than secrets and shadows. He'd become something else entirely: safe and sure and anchored deep within my heart.

And I had no idea how to keep him in my life when I was lying with every breath.

How could I ask him to court scandal and abandon the future he desired just so I could be happy?

I couldn't.

Silas had vowed to never again dictate how I lived my life. I owed him the same courtesy. Telling him I loved him and begging him to stay would only derail his plans. Admitting that this baby was his would only further change things and force his hand.

I had to do what was best for Silas. Even if it hurt.

As our breathing slowed and my thoughts churned in the quiet of his bedchamber, Silas pulled me into the unbearable comfort of his arms.

"Stay," he murmured to the skin of my neck.

And for the first time, I did.

"Have you seen my pillow?"

"Hmm?" Silas murmured, glancing up from the letter he was reading.

"My pillow. You know the one." I held my hands up to indicate the general size of the plain blue-striped cotton muslin pillow that I preferred above all others. "Do you know where it is?"

"Perhaps you left it in the bedchamber," Silas replied distractedly, having already returned to the correspondence in his hand.

The bedchamber in question was, in fact, Silas's. We'd spent every night together for the last fortnight. Some nights, we made love, and others, we simply slept. I sprawled and stole the bed linens. Silas woke me with sweet kisses on my shoulder and eager fingers beneath my night rail. We were happy, and I didn't know what to do about it. Just last night after he'd fallen asleep, there had been a moment when I'd simply watched him at rest. I thought about how happy we were in this little bubble we'd created. And I'd practiced the words I so desperately longed to say. I made my soundless confession to a sleeping man—one who deserved to know the truth.

Everything was changing so fast. When I'd grown brave enough to ask after his return to London, Silas had simply said he wasn't ready—that he'd prefer to remain in Hampshire for the time being. He just kept staying. A selfish and weak part of me was grateful. But the part who knew I could never truly make him happy was dying inside at the thought of keeping him from his future—the one he deserved.

My body was also changing. The baby moved all the time, and my stomach grew larger every day. Hence my need for the damned blue pillow. It was the only pillow in the whole of Pineview that was sufficient. It fit perfectly in the small of my back, and I carted it from room to room, wherever I went.

"I shall go and check the bedchamber," I finally replied to Silas's suggestion. Why couldn't I remember the last place I'd had it?

"Actually," Silas called when I'd just reached the doorway, "you had it after the morning meal. Perhaps you left it in the library when you took your nap."

"Oh, that is right." I returned to Silas and kissed him on the cheek. "Thank you. I'd forgotten about my nap."

Silas smiled up at me but ran a nervous finger over the paper he held.

I eyed the letter, easily recognizing the elegant script upon the page. "Is that from Patty? Is everything all right?"

He swallowed and glanced back at his sister's handwriting. "Everyone is well. They are all still planning to return to Hampshire for Christmas. But there have been some developments with the Watford School. She'd like my assistance . . . in London."

Patty had been corresponding regularly to check in but she'd also been happy to share the progress she'd made in establishing a school within the orphanage. More staff had been acquired, and everything was on track for community education to begin for young students in the new year.

"Is there a problem? Is that why she needs your help?"

Silas looked troubled. "She didn't say."

"When would you go?"

"Straightaway, I imagine."

"Oh."

He folded the letter and stood from the desk. "Go and find your pillow. I'll go make arrangements and see to gathering my things for a quick trip to London." He cupped my cheeks. "I won't be gone long."

I could feel the frown on my face and couldn't do a damn thing about it. Silas pressed his lips to mine, but before I could respond the way I wanted, he'd already pulled away.

I didn't find the pillow until later that night, right back in the study where I'd lost it in the first place. I swore that my mind was becoming more addled the longer this baby grew in my belly.

Silas was packed and ready to depart the following morning.

We made love that night—slow and impossibly sweet. My emotions were heightened with Silas's return to London looming. He didn't comment. Simply kissed the tears from my skin and held me to him until I fell asleep. I awoke with a start when the sun was still far from rising. Turning over, I shook Silas awake.

He sat up faster than I anticipated and said in a sleep-roughed tone, "Is it the baby?" He reached for me, his warm hand a comforting weight on the swell of my stomach. It was the first time he'd ever touched me there in such a manner. Suddenly, I felt awash with longing.

Silas seemed to realize what he'd done and stiffened. I watched his dark eyes flash to mine in the glow of the fireplace embers.

Before he could jerk away, I laid my hand atop his, stilling him and halting his retreat. "I am well. The baby is fine. I simply awoke, worried that you might leave in the morning without saying goodbye. Will you wake me before you go?"

"Of course," he said quietly. "I won't leave without—"

Silas's words cut off as the baby thumped hard against our joined hands.

I smiled into the cool night air as Silas's eyes jumped uncertainly between my stomach and my face, as if to read my expression.

The baby pressed against my ribs in what felt like a long stretch causing another jolt beneath our palms, extended this time.

I didn't think Silas was even breathing. Finally, he whispered as my Little Duck gave another helpful roll, "Is that—is that the baby, moving within you?"

"Yes." I nodded. "It happens very frequently."

"Is it all right for me—"

"Yes, you can feel." And then I urged Silas to lie back down. I settled my back to his chest and pulled his arm around me. I placed his hand where I noted the baby shifting within.

Silas didn't speak. I grew drowsy but could still feel Silas's hand —his fingers spreading wide and repositioning often, following the baby's movements. Eventually, he pressed his lips to my shoulder and that was when sleep finally claimed me.

True to his word, Silas woke me before he left for London. He was dressed and sitting next to me on top of the coverlet. My state of barely conscious grogginess was probably all that kept me from clinging to him and weeping openly.

He kissed me on the forehead and told me to go back to sleep— that he'd return as soon as possible.

When I finally awoke midmorning, Silas's absence was everywhere. His letters from Jamie were still on the desk in his sitting room. A jacket was thrown haphazardly over the back of an armchair. And it was unbearably quiet.

I eventually dragged myself out of Silas's bed and got dressed simply in one of Emery's borrowed wrappers. I padded down the stairs in my stockinged feet intent upon a bit of breakfast. Before I made it to the dining room, however, Dashwood informed me that several packages had arrived for me.

I stood in the receiving room surveying the approximately twenty-two wrapped parcels. They were all the same size and covered in brown paper and secured with twine. I lowered myself slowly to the nearest sofa and plucked one of the packages up to unwrap.

My breath caught as the rough brown paper gave way to blue-striped fabric.

I kept opening and opening, tears filling my eyes and laughter spilling from my lips. Finally, I reached the last parcel with a handwritten note attached.

Mary Darling,

You needn't take your favorite pillow from room to room any longer. I apologize for stealing it yesterday afternoon for a bit, but the seamstress in the village needed to measure to ensure each replica exactly matched the original.

I shall miss you while I am away. I'll return as quickly as I can. Take good care of your Little Duck.

All my love,

Silas

A tear landed on the corner of the paper, and I hastened to wipe it away. I took in all the wrappings and all the blue pillows lying around me as if they'd been shaken loose from an upholstery tree. I thought of how well Silas took care of me. How kind and thoughtful he'd been all summer. How he worried after me and the baby.

And I thought of the guilt eating me alive.

Silas deserved to know the baby was his. I'd been wrong to keep this information from him. I'd known that, of course. But I'd been too afraid. Silas was a good person with a loving heart. He'd proven it time and time again. He would be a tremendous father to our child. I'd been the one making everything complicated.

And it was time I simplified them.

I stood and grabbed one of the pillows and made my way to the study.

My heart was beating wildly in my chest. So many times I'd imagined a beautiful future in the past few months. Daydreamed of Silas holding a baby girl with his eyes, being a father in truth.

A future—one where everyone lived happily ever after. It was a fantasy that ravaged my heart. But what if it didn't end so happily? Dreams did not always come true, and oftentimes, people let you down.

Nevertheless, it was time to be brave—to wield that courage that Silas saw when he looked at me.

With a shaking hand, I put pen to paper. I wrote out the truth and begged for forgiveness.

Twenty-One

SILAS

November

I took in the scent of furniture polish and something baking in the kitchens. The tables and chairs were arranged in neat rows in this schoolroom and four others just like it. Slates and chalk sat on each student's desk, just waiting for possibility.

They wouldn't need to wait long—barely eight weeks. The Watford School was ready for instruction beginning in the new year. There were teachers for varying levels of education based upon the children's ages. There were governesses for comportment lessons. And after yesterday's community meeting, there would be students to fill those classrooms.

It had been difficult to be away from Mary and Pineview since my departure two days ago. But I was glad that Patty had summoned me here. I'd met and talked with distrustful mothers and fathers. I'd helped explain the purpose of the school and the benefits for their children. For once, my long-winded nature and tendency to be verbose had come in handy.

Jamie had attended the community meeting with his sisters and his mother as well. He'd been so brave and kind, talking about his experience and how beneficial it had been for him to learn to read. He had been our connection to the people here—a bridge. They'd looked at Patty and myself—even the staff at Watford— and had seen something other. But Jamie was one of them. His family could be their family. And his experience could represent so much more. So they'd listened when he spoke. We had him to thank for those who chose to enroll their children at Watford School.

"What do you think?" Patty asked from the doorway.

I let my gaze touch on every surface in the room before turning back to my sister. She looked proud and pleased. I couldn't articulate how grateful I was that she'd taken me seriously—that she hadn't laughed when I'd asked her what she thought of starting a school in Bethnal Green. "I think it will be a triumph," I said instead. "You have achieved something magnificent here, Patty."

"*We*, Silas. *We* have achieved something magnificent."

I shook my head. "You did all the planning and hard work."

She stepped into the room. "We did all the planning, back in Hampshire, along with Mary. This school"—she used a delicate gloved hand to encompass the room and more beyond—"would never exist without your idea. We would not have convinced all those mothers and fathers of the benefits of education without your kind heart and influence. The compassion you had for Jamie and your efforts in supporting his literacy are the reason for all of this."

I remained quiet, unwilling to accept her praise. All I'd done was see a boy who'd been thrust into an impossible situation—a boy bright and eager to learn. He was like so many others who never got a chance. I was not this leader or pioneer she seemed to think I was. I was simply privileged by chance, given a life of ease when most were not.

Patty meandered closer and continued her impassioned speech. "Young girls who can read will have comportment lessons with our governesses. Instead of being seamstresses, chambermaids, or serving girls in taverns, they will have the opportunity to be a companion or something more."

"Especially with a letter of reference from the Duchess of Cawthorn," I teased.

Patty eyed me knowingly, so I looked away.

Attempting to divert, I said, "I told Jamie he was free to attend and continue his schooling along with his sisters."

"I know. He told me. He also mentioned that your carriage would be transporting his sisters from White Chapel on school days."

Patty waited for some sort of reply, but I didn't manage it. She smiled. "You're giving Jamie the best life he could possibly lead. He'll have an employer who cares for him, will provide good wages, and is seeing to the success and well-being of his entire family. No one else in London would do such a thing."

I felt humbled by my sister's praise and a touch choked up, if I was honest.

Patty finally came to stand beside me. She tucked her hand through my arm as we surveyed the large schoolroom. "You are a good person, Silas. I'm proud that you are my brother. You care about people and you take care of them. I know you have some silly notion that you need to accomplish more, some golden ring you're reaching for, but you are good enough. Just as you are. We, as your family, only want you to be happy."

Happiness was such an elusive, ever-changing target. This year alone, I'd placed several ideals on a pedestal for perceived happiness.

My goals had transformed over the years from travel and self-serving pleasure to settling in one spot to concentrate my happiness. I'd wanted to spend time with my loved ones, all in one place. I'd wanted to watch my nieces and nephew grow and be a part of their lives as well.

As I'd witnessed my sisters find their own happiness and our family grow to encompass more and more love, I'd realized I wanted that sort of future for myself. Making an arbitrary decision to find a wife and settle down was supposed to bring me a sense of accomplishment. It was intended to be a signal to my father that I was ready—to ensure that the marquessate would be safe in the hands of a responsible family man.

But it hadn't resulted in the happiness I sought.

My happiness was back in Hampshire. My future was wild red hair and the babe growing in her belly. I just needed to convince her of that.

"I am happy, Patty. Or, at least, I will be."

Patty, Miles, and Franny left immediately following our school tour to return to Pineview. I knew my sister was worried about Mary being alone so close to the baby's expected arrival next month.

Augie and Emery were still in London as the duke had a few meetings left with members of the Lords. They would be bound for Hampshire soon for my mother's annual Yuletide house party and Christmas celebration thereafter. Genevieve and Julian were already back home in the country.

I would return to Pineview shortly. I felt the need to remain in London a few more days to see to the household I'd neglected for nearly three months.

"Sir, there's a letter that arrived for you," my housekeeper said, stopping me on my way out the door.

"Put it with the others on my desk, Mrs. Fullerton, if you please. I'll see to everything this week."

"Yes, sir," she said, tucking the letter into her apron pocket.

Tonight, I was joining Augie at the club for supper and a bit of socializing. I hadn't been in London since the summer, but for some reason the thought of cheerful back-slapping and inane conversation did not rouse me as it once had. I wanted to be back in Hampshire.

I wanted to be back with Mary—reading and talking and playing Écarté or piquet at the dining room table while she had a blue-striped pillow wedged behind her back. I wondered if she and the baby were well. If her feet were still swelling and if she was wearing her shoes indoors again. I was eager to know if the baby was moving at all hours of the night and if Mary was sleeping well enough. Was she still craving bacon in the evenings?

I desired nothing more than the life I'd been leading with her.

Was Mary happy to see me gone from the country? Had I been suffocating her with my presence? She'd spent every night in my bed for weeks. There had been no hasty re-dressing and abandoning me in the middle of the night. I was happy. *We* were happy, I knew that. But I didn't know how to broach the subject of making that happiness last.

Augie waited for me in the large entryway of the club. I gave him a nod of greeting and passed my outerwear to a waiting footman. Reluctant to even be here, I held on to the fabric a moment longer than I meant to before releasing it and allowing the staff member to proceed to the cloak room.

"Everything all right?" Augie asked quietly as we walked in the direction of the dining room.

"Perfect," I replied as the sounds of conversation and cutlery met my ears.

We discussed Watford School and the latest legislation in the Lords over our meal. I was noticeably subdued. I could feel Augie watching me carefully as a result of my uncharacteristic behavior. He was undoubtedly replaying the last time we were at the club when I'd been similarly off-kilter and had attacked two men instead of talking about my feelings.

"I'm fine," I said, apropos of nothing. Augie's dark brows lifted in surprise. "I'm not even drunk," I amended. "No brawling this evening. I don't care who walks into the room."

It was unfortunate timing that had James Letford, the Baron of Ashby, strolling into the dining room with a bright smile on his face. I was up before I could even think better of it.

Augie groaned quietly and stood to follow.

But I wasn't going to hit Ashby. I didn't need my fists to make him regret his actions.

He saw me coming and smiled, the clueless idiot. "Bartholomew! Good to see you! It has been quite a while indeed. Heard you were spending your days in the country."

I led him to an empty corner of the room and lowered my voice, ignoring all of his inane prattle. "You are a fool, Ashby. I just wanted you to know that. To abandon Mary in such a way. To force her into an unfair and impossible situation in which she must raise your child on her own. If you were any sort of decent person, you'd marry her. Not to save her reputation or do your basic duty to her. But you'd marry her because she's remarkable. You're a lucky bastard who doesn't deserve her or your child."

Ashby stared at me open-mouthed and uncomprehending.

I kept my voice low because it would not do to cause another scene and stir up more drama for Mary, but I could not censure the anger in my tone. I hated Ashby, not for his irritating personality or anything so trivial. I hated him on principle and circumstance. I hated that he was the father of Mary's child, and I was not. I loved her and wanted her—every part—and this man couldn't see or appreciate what was right in front of him. "It doesn't matter that you've left her to fend for herself. Because I am going to be there for her. And I will dedicate my life to her happiness and that of her child."

I was breathing hard by the time I'd finished speaking. Ashby still appeared to be in a state of shock at my words, so I started to turn, having already said all I'd meant to say and perhaps a bit more.

"Wait," the baron called, having finally found his voice. "Bartholomew, I don't know what you think happened with Lady Mary, but there has only ever been friendship between us. I would never dishonor her the way you have accused."

I frowned at his words. Augie's muffled curse came from behind me.

Ashby continued, "I am sorry to hear of Mary's situation. I had no idea. I understood from my mother that Mary was convalescing in

Northumberland. I've written to her several times but received no response." He glanced around the room and lowered his voice further. "It was not I who fathered her child, Bartholomew. It's not possible."

My mind was spinning faster with every word Ashby spoke. He truly seemed shocked by my accusations, and honestly, I didn't think the man capable of lying convincingly. I considered that day in Mary's chambers, when I'd begged for another chance. She'd confirmed her relationship with Ashby—how she'd moved on. Hadn't she?

"But you were so close and spent so much time together this spring," I accused, unable to comprehend this turn of events.

The baron's cheeks went pink before he admitted in a whisper, "Lady Mary was helping me. I was infatuated with Miss Louisa Gregory, but I couldn't buck up the courage to speak with her, or when I did, I'd stammer and sweat through my words. Mary assisted me. We practiced discussion topics, and then Mary would approach Miss Gregory and help lead me through our conversation. I eventually grew comfortable enough to speak on my own, without the crutch of Mary's support, but that was what instigated our time together—in addition to our friendship. Miss Gregory and I are betrothed now." Ashby smiled brightly. "We plan to marry in the spring."

"Congratulations," Augie said as he came to stand beside me.

My mind was collapsing in on itself. Scenarios ran over one another, and I could hardly hear the voices around me. Ashby and Mary dancing, promenading in the park, playing bloody croquet.

If the baron was not the father . . .

My mind went back to Mary's sitting room months ago. I'd questioned, "Ashby?" and she'd said—she'd said . . . nothing. She'd stared vacantly and stoically behind me. She'd allowed me to fill in the blanks and make assumptions, and she hadn't corrected me.

Every muscle in my body tensed with confusion and disquiet. I swallowed hard and interrupted the conversation happening between Augustus and Ashby, "I apologize, Ashby. For the accusations I made against you. I am sorry for the things I said."

Because I believed the baron. Everything he'd said made sense— from Mary's assistance to a betrothal that was easy enough to confirm. Naturally Mary would have helped Ashby gain his sweetheart's affections. She was loyal beyond measure.

But it was obvious that Ashby had not even known of Mary's condition. Despite the gossip and the rumors circulating, of course the man would believe what his mother had told him about a dear friend. He would never assume the worst.

Oh God.

"That's quite all right, Bartholomew," Ashby replied easily, far more congenially than I deserved. "You were understandably upset on Lady Mary's behalf. You confronted me as her friend. I, too, would like to know the identity of the blackguard who has left her in such a position. Disgraceful, the man is."

My mind similarly turned to the person who had fathered Mary's child. I thought of her list. Her desire for a child. And the secret arrangement we'd carried on for months. The way she'd insisted I withdraw from her body. I'd been blinded by her association with Ashby, so sure that the closeness I'd witnessed had to be more than simple friendship.

Augie was talking again, telling the baron that we needed to be going. My friend turned me in the direction of the exit and gathered our coats. My hands were shaking.

I thought of the idiotic way I'd ended things, believing I wanted some unknown future so I could compare myself to my siblings and impress my father. My breath sawed in and out of my lungs in white puffs as we waited for our carriage in the cold night air.

My mind raced through the months we were apart, the way she'd run from me at the Ascot Races. I'd come to her and asked for another chance. I'd wanted a relationship in truth, in the light of day and she'd turned me down. She's already been with child then. The scandal had broken that very day. My mind was spinning.

My anger and hurt. The cruelty I'd spoken in the gardens behind Pineview. I was going to be sick.

The apology and the months we'd had together in the country. Summer and autumn. Our friendship and closeness had grown over time and proximity.

And then the pond, the nights in my bed. Loving her and wanting her until I couldn't breathe from it. Feeling desperate to hold her but knowing if I clung too tightly, she'd push me away. My hand on her stomach, feeling the life within.

"Augie," I choked out, feeling pressure build in my chest. I needed to sit down.

"Come on," he replied, guiding me into the carriage.

I collapsed on the seat and put my head in my shaking hands.

I'd assumed it was Ashby all this time. I'd accused her, and she'd never let me think otherwise. Why? Why would she do such a thing?

You said you wanted someone appropriate—someone you could have a future with.

That was what she'd said when I sat in her rooms and begged her to try again. To tell our families, to court me openly, to marry me someday.

And the scandal sheets had printed the news of her condition that very day. Her privacy had been breached, and her name was whispered on the lips of every aristocrat in town.

Did she push me away because she thought I wouldn't want her? Did she decide for us both that the scandal was too much to bear?

"What are you going to do, Silas?" Augie's words were quiet, but I jolted just the same.

I couldn't spend my life hyperventilating in a carriage. "I'm going to Hampshire and getting some answers."

Twenty-Two

MARY

Signs of life had returned to Pineview.

It was no longer the quiet household it had been since Silas's unexpected departure earlier in the week. I awaited his response to my letter and felt a mix of nervous trepidation and an aching loneliness. I missed Silas desperately. Sleep had been difficult without his warm body next to mine.

But the estate was back to some semblance of a home.

The heavy footfalls of Miles on the staircase. Franny's happy laughter and her dog Daisy's responding bark. And Patty's watchful gaze following me wherever I went.

Perhaps I was reading too much into it, but I felt Patty's judgment and her worry like a tangible thing. Along with the general irritation of being uncomfortably pregnant, I allowed myself to be further aggravated by my friend's obvious concern.

Miles and Franny had gone on horseback over to Owensby's stables despite the threat of snow. So it was just Patty and I in front of the roaring fire in the blue sitting room on the second floor. She was embroidering while making note of my every pinched breath or change of position. It was difficult to get comfortable and doubly hard to remain so, even with all my pillows about. Everything felt squashed behind my ribs, and I longed to stretch out on this settee and beg a footman to rub my feet.

I shifted, crossing one satin-slippered foot over the other before disliking that immediately and reversing them. Perhaps I should just go to my bedchamber where I could lie down.

I felt guilty, however. Patty and her family had only just returned. It would be rude for me to take my leave now.

"You can relax, you know," Patty said without looking up from her embroidery. "You needn't keep your back straight for me."

"I know that," I snapped, pressing a hand to a sharp pain low on my side.

Patty registered the movement and ignored my tone. "Are you all right?"

I sighed. "Yes, everything is fine. I'm sorry I was short with you. The midwife was here two days ago and said everything was progressing nicely."

"Did she say how long?"

"No. She said it was difficult to tell, but she expected the baby to arrive before the new year."

Patty smiled. "You'll get to meet your Little Duck soon, then."

I attempted a smile in return, but I must not have managed it because my friend appeared concerned again. I didn't want to admit how afraid I was and how alone I felt. I no more had a plan established for the future than I did when I'd arrived here six months ago.

I had not heard one word from my parents. The idea that they'd written me off completely made me bitter and angry but also terribly sad. Our family had never been a priority for either of them. I'd felt like a burden most of my life, especially after my mother had been unable to conceive an heir. But having proof of their disappointment and very conditional tolerance was quietly devastating.

I didn't know what I would do when the baby arrived. Was I just going to remain at Pineview forever with no means? And with Silas's reaction on the horizon, I didn't know what to expect. I just knew I needed to talk to him before this baby arrived. What that meant for the future was something we would need to figure out together, as much as it terrified me.

Patty had returned from London with a trunk of baby things: tiny clothes and dolls and blankets and books and even a stuffed knitted duck. A beautiful crib had been delivered by footmen and placed in my rooms. Patty had thought of everything while I'd simply been hiding away, allowing life to happen to me.

I shifted again, deciding I would rather be standing than all scrunched up on the sofa. Rising slowly to my feet, I began pacing the sitting room.

"I'm sorry you are so uncomfortable, Mary. Would you like me to send for the midwife or the doctor?"

I pivoted when I reached the far bookcase and looked at Patty, releasing an annoyed breath. "No, I'm fine. You don't have to look at me as if I'm going to break."

She paused in her stitching and appeared momentarily as if she would respond, but went right back to sewing instead.

"That." I pointed in her direction. "Right there." I lowered my hand and placed it against the small of my back. "Before this baby, you would have argued back—stood your ground. You have things you are dying to say to me, but you won't allow it because you think me weak or incapable of hearing them."

My friend took a deep breath and then lowered her embroidery hoop to her lap. "Mary, I do not pretend to know what you are going through."

Shame swallowed me instantly. Patty and I had once shared the same dream of motherhood. She'd taken Franny in as a girl of nearly six. There had been no confinement for Patty. No swollen ankles or pregnancy vomiting and no intimacy of feeling your child growing inside you. Somehow, in my selfishness, I'd forgotten how difficult this might be for my friend to witness. She'd known to prepare and provide me all the loveliest things because those had likely been the very same things she'd longed for.

"Patty, I'm sorry."

She held up a hand. "The point is, I do not think you weak. I think you are going through a trial and you're alone and confused and I do not want to add to your troubles by making my opinion known. It is not good for you or the baby to have additional worries. Yes, I will ask you how you are feeling. You are my friend and I am concerned. I apologize if I have been smothering you."

I ignored the sharp ache low in my belly and went to Patty's side. I lowered myself gingerly to the sofa and met her earnest blue gaze. "I'm sorry. I have been selfish and horrible. I appreciate your unwavering support. I don't want to ever take that for granted. The truth is that I am terrified of what happens next."

Finally, she spoke, "The future needn't be so uncertain. I understand you are afraid of what happens when the baby arrives. But, Mary, you will always have a place here."

"Thank you," I replied, grateful beyond measure, but she needed to know. "I told Silas."

Her brows furrowed in confusion.

"I wrote to Silas to tell him about the baby. I knew as soon as he left for London that I needed to tell him. I should have done it sooner, you were right. I was just so very afraid of ruining his life."

Patty's lips pressed into a firm line.

"Say it," I urged. "Please tell me. Don't hold back. I need your friendship and the honesty that comes along with it."

"You aren't ruining anything. He loves you, Mary," she said fiercely. "I know my brother and I know that he would be overjoyed to have a life with you and your child."

My eyes welled, too frightened to hope.

"I don't know precisely what you're afraid of," Patty continued, "but sometimes the risk is worth the reward. Trust in the love you share with Silas. Let him be a part of a future you create together. He'll forgive you for keeping the truth from him."

"You don't know that," I spoke around the emotion choking me. "You don't know that he won't turn his back on me. I know what it's like to be cast aside by Silas. I don't want to ever feel that way again. I love him. But I know he deserves to have that choice."

My friend reached for my hands. "You need to tell him you love him. He deserves *that* truth just as much as he deserves to know about the baby."

"I'm terrified that I won't be enough. Silas wants a young, beautiful wife. And that's not ever going to be me—baby or no." I loosened one hand from her grasp to wipe away the tears on my cheeks.

Patty's blue eyes were bright with unshed emotion. "There was a time when I thought you might strangle each other at the dinner table." I smiled through my misery. "You never expected to be here, loving him so completely. Isn't there a chance that Silas's future happiness looks different from how he first envisioned it? Perhaps you've both changed."

She was right. So much had changed between Silas and myself. Through the months and the years and the seasons. We weren't the same people we'd been before. And in the past six months alone, we'd grown and changed together. There was a chance he might want a scandalous wife, after all, and a baby to shower with his unending love and affection. I owed it to him to give him the chance to accept us both.

I could not have predicted the path Silas and I were on. How we'd journeyed from near rivals to the very best of friends with several other steps along the way. Our relationship had changed many times over. I reflected on our arrangement back in London, all the secret liaisons and sneaking about. Silas had wanted honesty and light. I'd been the one who'd insisted on secrets and lies. He'd adhered to my own demands of pretending in public while I'd been falling apart under his hands in private. Bitterness and shame mixed with the sharp ache in my belly. Despite all my fears, I'd turned us into my parents after all.

The hand that still held mine squeezed gently, pulling me from my tumultuous thoughts. "No matter what happens, you are family to me, Mary. I need you to understand that. To Emery and Genevieve and all of us. You're a part of our lives, and we won't abandon you. No matter what happens with Silas. Whether you marry or raise this baby together or not."

I nodded, feeling so grateful and unworthy in that moment. This family that had done so much for me. And I risked driving a wedge between them.

Hope was a dangerous thing. It gave you leave to abandon your instincts. To ignore the warning signs and follow the whispers in your heart. Hope was a killer.

Yet . . .

"You might be the bravest person I've ever met. You're made of courage."

"All right," I said, breathing through a particularly sharp ache low in my back. "You're right. Silas deserves to know. I'll tell him I—"

"You'll tell me what exactly?"

I turned toward the doorway at the sound of his voice, so tight and angry. Silas stood there, still in his hat and black great coat. Snow stood out against the dark fabric as if he'd come here straight from the mews in a great hurry.

I stood on unsteady legs, placing a bracing hand on my back as the pain there intensified.

"Was it that Ashby is not the father of your child?" Silas removed one glove at a time as he spoke. "Is that the truth of which you speak? Or that you simply allowed that lie to perpetuate even though he was only ever your friend. A friend you helped become engaged to another woman."

"How—"

"How did I know about your plan to help the baron land Miss Louisa Gregory?" he replied with a stony expression. "I know because I confronted Ashby in London. Called him a fool for abandoning you and leaving you on your own. I told him it didn't matter if he refused to marry you, because I was going to be there in his place. I was going to support you and your child. And that he was an undeserving bastard."

"Silas." My mouth formed the words, but there was no sound. There was only pain. The pain of the truth. The pain of Silas's anger. And the pain of everything crashing down around me.

Twenty-Three

SILAS

The carriage ride to Hampshire had been cold and wet and miserable. I'd been trapped in a small space with nothing but my thoughts, vacillating wildly between anger and hope and disbelief.

I'd left London without packing, without telling my staff, without any preparation or forethought whatsoever.

And then, when only a handful of miles remained in my journey, the steady drizzle had turned into snow. And that felt more than fitting. Unexpected November snow to slow my desperate dash back to Pineview. Thankfully, I hadn't been stuck along the roadside as Mary had nearly a year ago. But the weather had slowed our progress. Christ, so much had changed in a year's time.

I'd stewed in my wounded indignation, playing both sides of an imagined argument.

It wasn't until I'd arrived at Pineview and marched straight toward the sound of Mary's voice that every prepared speech and line of questioning had abandoned me entirely.

But then I'd heard the end of her conversation with my sister—who'd apparently known the truth all along.

I watched Mary's lips trace my name as she stared on in horror at my approach. Or perhaps it was the knowledge that I'd confronted Ashby in London and then pieced everything together.

"Sister, dear. I should like to speak to Mary alone." I shrugged out of my snow-speckled overcoat and tossed it onto a nearby armchair. "We'll have a conversation at a later time about sibling loyalty."

Rising from the sofa, Patty opened her mouth to argue, but I tsked. "Not right now, if you please. I am not in the mood."

Patty glared at me but squeezed Mary's hand before quitting the room.

And then it was just me and the mother of my child.

"Explain it to me," I demanded. "That day in your sitting room, you refused me. You knew you carried my child, and I'd shown up completely by chance, intent on having a future together. Yet you sent me on my way rather than tell me the truth."

Mary gritted her teeth. "I didn't want to force you into something you didn't want."

I raised a brow in challenge. "But I did want it. I sat in that uncomfortable armchair with a broken hand and told you I wanted it—wanted you. To court you and tell our families and to marry you."

She looked visibly ill as she shifted on her feet. Her shoe-covered feet.

"Christ, you are stubborn." I stepped forward, intent on helping her sit and remove her damn slippers, but she sidestepped me. "I tell you I want you. You refuse to believe me. So, then you what? Ran away to the country? Do I have the order of events accurate?"

"I didn't want you to be attached to scandal, Silas! We'd fought for years. No one would have ever believed the baby was yours. Even if I'd told you the truth, even if we'd married straightaway, all of society would have thought you a cuckold and a fool."

"Who bloody well cares what society thinks? I would have been happy. I would have been married to you with the family I have always wanted."

Mary grimaced and turned away, a hand planted firmly on her lower back. "You cared, Silas. You told me before. You wanted an appropriate wife. You wanted to be taken seriously. The heir your father deserves. It's why you focused your attentions on Lady Sophia and the others. They were what you wanted to achieve your goals."

I marched over to her and forced her to look at me. "And things change, Mary. I was wrong. We have been over this before. Lady Sophia cannot make me happy. Nor can Annabelle Crawford. I'm sorry it took me time to figure that out. I made a horrible miscalculation. And I am sorry I hurt you. But you have to listen to me when I tell you what I want. Stop assuming you know."

I pressed my hand to the spot on her lower back that troubled her. I worked my fingers beneath her own and started massaging. "I want *you*. I love *you*. Even if this baby was Ashby's, I would want it as well. Because it is a part of you."

She sniffed loudly and fought off another grimace. "I wrote to you."

"What?"

"The morning you left for London. After I sat among twenty-two pillows and realized how well you care for me—care for us," she amended, placing another hand on her stomach. "You deserved to know what I had been trying to tell you for weeks. What I hadn't been brave enough to say out loud."

I thought of the stack of letters in my study, untouched since my arrival in London days ago. My plans to remain and handle everything. My mad escape from town to get back to Hampshire to seek the truth.

Mary's face twisted. "I'm sorry I didn't tell you sooner, Silas. There was no one else. This baby can only be yours."

"I know." I closed my arms around her and pulled her as close as was possible.

"I love you," she murmured wetly into my shoulder, and I rejoiced at her admission.

I smiled. "I know that, too."

Her annoyed huff met my ears, and she squeezed me tighter.

I pulled back to look at her face, using my free hand to wipe her tears. "I didn't come here to punish you or write you off, Mary. I came here to get some answers and to tell you that you are what makes me happy. I can also be exceedingly angry with you. It doesn't mean I don't love you."

She shifted her hand lower on her belly, and I moved to massage that point in turn.

"I missed out on so many things," I admitted.

Mary stared up at me in confusion, cheeks a bit flushed. "What?"

"If I had known the baby was mine from the beginning. Things like this," I replied, massaging tight circles where I felt her muscles going tense. "And rubbing your feet. And giving you gifts and making you more comfortable."

"You haven't missed out. You did all of those things. Literally, every single one," she said incredulously before taking a deep, bracing breath.

"Well, I always wanted to touch your stomach and feel the baby move. I would have done that more. Oh, and bring you all manner of odd foods, day and night," I argued.

She stared at me for a moment before doubling over and practically shouting, "Well, you can do it for the next one."

Alarmed, I brought my arm around her. "What's wrong?"

After several panted breaths, Mary managed to say, "This baby is coming."

My mind blanked of all intelligent thought.

I had no idea what needed doing. I could only watch helplessly as Mary grimaced in pain. And then abruptly I realized, we were having a baby.

I couldn't contain my grin as I leaned forward and scooped Mary into my arms. When I reached the corridor I shouted for someone —anyone, really—to go and fetch the midwife from the village, and the doctor too. When I'd reached the door to Mary's rooms, Patty hurried up behind me, out of breath. She opened the door, and moments later, Mary was settled on her bed, breathing through her obvious pain.

"What do we do?" I asked anxiously.

Patty was already moving about the room, retrieving linen towels and clearing away the items on the bedside tables. "The maids are bringing hot water and everything she'll need."

"It's too soon," Mary gritted out. "The midwife said it would be another month, at least."

Worry had me stepping closer. "What does that mean? Is the baby all right?"

Patty looked between both of us, her face the picture of calm reassurance. "Some babies arrive early. Some late. It is not an exact prediction. Everything will be fine."

I nodded dumbly as maids bustled in and around me.

"You're supposed to wait outside," Mary called as sweat beaded on her hairline.

"What? Why? I'm just supposed to leave you?"

"That's very sweet, darling." She paused briefly and closed her eyes. When she opened them, she said rather unfairly, "But think of the mare, Silas. Think of Matilda."

I frowned, but Mary's eyes were closed again as she did some complicated breathing through her nose.

Patty approached me and patted my shoulder. "I will stay throughout. I'll take good care of them."

I nodded as she turned me in the direction of the door but then thought better of it and made my way to Mary's bedside. I pressed a kiss to the crown of her head before meeting her eyes. "I love you. I'll be right outside that door. Mare or not, just call for me and I'll be here."

Pain had tightened the lines around her eyes and mouth, but she smiled at my words and said softly in return, "I love you, too. We'll see you soon."

Grinning at that, I allowed my sister to guide me from the room.

❦

Twenty-six hours later, I paced nervously in my sitting room.

Augie and Emery and the children had returned early to Hampshire following my revelation at the club. The duke, perceptive as he was, figured I could use the support depending on how my confrontation with Mary went. They'd arrived a few hours ago to news of Mary's laboring.

As a result, Augie, Miles, and Julian had all joined me in my quarters as we hoped the baby would arrive soon.

Emery and Genevieve had been in and out throughout. Patty had remained ever-vigilant at Mary's side.

Nothing was wrong, the midwife had said. A bit earlier than anticipated, but everything was progressing nicely. The local doctor brought in early this morning had agreed. The baby was positioned correctly. Mary was healthy and strong. But some babies took longer than others, they'd assured us.

Seeing as it had been over a day since Mary had first experienced labor pains, I thought some babies were rather stubborn like their mothers.

"She is in good hands," Miles reminded me for the twelfth time.

"Mrs. Cranston saw Emery through both deliveries," Augie added helpfully, reminding me why Mary had consulted the midwife in the first place.

I resumed my pacing as another scream rent the air. We could hear her clearly from all the way across the hall. I'd hardly slept, and I knew that Mary hadn't either. "She must be exhausted," I murmured. "And so frightened."

"Well, she's rather more cross than anything," Emery said as she strode in.

I rose and walked to my sister, who was bearing the latest update. "How is she? Any progress?" I felt weighed down with worry. Why hadn't the baby come yet? Was something wrong?

Emery winced. "Everything is about the same. Mary is just put out that it's taking so long. The doctor finally left. Tired of all the swearing, I'd imagine." My sister grinned, shaking my arm and rousing me from my maudlin imaginings. "She's all right." Another violent scream made its way through the wallpaper, causing Emery to wince. "First babies can take a while."

I covered my face with my hands.

"I've come to call you all down to dinner actually," Emery said. "Franny is waiting for us."

The men filed from the room, following my sister and making for the staircase.

Mary's agonized wail reached my ears again. And my feet carried me to her door. I didn't wait for someone to stop me. I didn't care. I needed to be with her.

With my gaze firmly on her face, I walked determinedly to her side. Kneeling beside the bed, I watched her, marveling at her strength. Mary's eyes were shut tight against the pain, her face twisted as her muscles tensed all over.

Patty looked over from Mary's other side and gave me a small smile. "Here," she said, passing me a cool cloth. "For her brow."

I concentrated and carefully dotted her forehead with the fabric.

Mary finally released a long breath and relaxed back into the bank of pillows at her back. Her features loosened, and she blinked bleary eyes open.

When her gaze focused on me at her side, I smiled. "How is my darling?"

To my utter horror and astonishment, Mary's eyes welled with tears. They immediately flowed over her cheeks. "I can't do this, Silas. I'm trying so hard, but—"

"Shhh," I said, rising to my feet and wrapping my arms around her thin shoulders.

She sobbed against my chest until another wave of pain struck. She clutched my arms in an iron grip and shook from the effort of holding herself together.

When the moment passed, I leaned away to look at her face. Her hair had been plaited back, but several strands had escaped their confines. I brushed them away and picked up the cool cloth to resume wiping her brow. "Do you remember what I told you that day in the stable?"

Mary's voice emerged watery. "No."

"I said that you were the strongest person I know." I tucked another wayward red lock behind her ear. "I know this feels impossible. But I also know that you can do it. I'm going to stay right here with you."

She nodded, looking miserable.

Before I could offer any more assurances, the midwife spoke from her place at the foot of the bed. "All right, Lady Mary. I believe we are ready to push. Your Grace, if you please."

Patty stood at the ready. "Silas, take her arm and help her to lean forward. She needs to bear down and push with all the strength she has left. Mary, the next time the pain comes, you push hard."

Mary was wide-eyed and panic-stricken. The sight was almost more than I could bear.

I gently stroked her cheek before taking her arm and positioning myself to mirror Patty. "This is it. Our Little Duck is coming."

Something solidified behind Mary's gaze. Her expression held determination as if viewing the finish line after a very long and grueling race.

More painful tensing and deep breaths followed over the next quarter hour. But finally, the midwife said the baby's head appeared. It didn't take long after that. Mary breathed and grunted through the worst of the pain. I murmured words of encouragement as she fought to bring our baby into the world.

"It's a wee little lass," Mrs. Cranston called happily. She held the tiny, squalling red-faced infant up with a grin. I felt the world go quiet and slow as I took in my daughter for the very first time.

Then my eyes went blurry and my surroundings rushed back into motion, I turned to Mary, eager to share this moment.

But that was when Mary's eyes fluttered closed and all hell broke loose.

Twenty-Four

MARY

It was Silas's voice I heard first.

Because of course it was.

Through a haze of bone-weary exhaustion, I managed to open my eyes. I blinked away the dry blurriness that seemed to envelop the room. But then I was able to focus on the warm glow from the nearby oil lamp. Without turning my head, an image of Silas came into view.

He held a tiny bundle, wrapped in a pale knitted blanket and my heart lurched. She was here.

The last thing I remembered was the midwife holding her aloft and pronouncing that I'd given birth to a baby girl.

". . . And when you are ready for one, you shall have a pony. I shall find you the loveliest pony in all the land. Your auntie Emery will not be in charge of your riding lessons no matter what she promises."

I nearly rolled my eyes at Silas's running commentary, but I worried the action would take me back under. And I was too happy to fall back to sleep right now. Despite the soreness and bone-deep weariness, I felt nothing but joy.

"But we have plenty of time to discuss all of that," he continued on for his captive audience. "It will be ages before you're grown enough to ride a pony. I know you've just arrived and after such a long wait, but I look forward to seeing the person you shall become. I can already tell that you will be stubborn like your mother. It looks as though you've inherited the Bartholomew chin. However, this red hair is courtesy of your mother as well. I hope you get as many traits from her as possible, little Matilda. Because she is strong and brave, fiercely loyal, and undeniably beautiful. And she will love you nearly as much as I do."

Ignoring the sweetness of Silas's words as he rocked our baby daughter at my bedside, I focused on one thing only when I cleared my throat. "Did you name our daughter after a horse?"

Silas's relieved gaze sprang to mine. He rose swiftly, cradling the baby gently before sitting on the bed by my hip. "How are you feeling?"

"Tired."

"Everything is all right. You've been asleep for a few hours. We called the doctor back in. Your bleeding was well under control, but your body was weakened, exhausted from laboring for so long."

Silas held the baby out to me. "Would you like to hold her?"

Nodding, I peeked at my daughter's sweet face. She was sleeping peacefully. Silas gently passed her over, supporting her head down into the crook of my arm.

She felt so small. With tears threatening, I asked without taking my eyes off her, "And she's healthy? She's safe?"

Silas's warm hand settled on my knee atop the covers, a comforting weight. "She's perfect. The midwife said she was a bit early—you were right—but everything is well. The doctor examined her as well. Tillie is just our petite little girl."

I nodded, shaking loose two substantial tears. Relief made me weak. Silas's hand squeezed.

My eyes traced the curve of her cheek, but I was too afraid to touch the soft skin there. Too terrified of something so perfect. She was everything I'd always wanted, finally—*finally*—in my arms. Joy, fear, doubt, and elation bombarded me simultaneously. *How could I do this? Be someone's mother?*

"You'll do it as you do everything else." I jolted at Silas's statement, not having realized I'd spoken aloud. "With unwavering love and fierce loyalty. With that brave heart."

My chin trembled and I didn't trust my voice.

I reached out, and touched the baby's tiny fist, tucked up neatly beneath her chin—her Bartholomew chin, apparently. Her fingers opened and closed reflexively around my finger and I marveled at the simple action. The strength and the trust of someone so precious.

This was my family—this little girl. And the man sitting next to me.

I glanced up to see Silas watching me, taking in this meeting between mother and daughter. "I was worried when we couldn't wake you. Terrified actually."

"I'm all right," I assured him.

"The thought of losing you when we'd wasted so much time was inconceivable." He leaned forward and cupped my cheeks, voice soft but pleading, "I don't want to waste any more."

"Nor do I," I admitted.

"I want to get married and be a family with you and Tillie."

"I want that too, more than anything," I said.

"Sooner, rather than later," Silas amended.

"Agreed," I supplied and then raised a brow. "But we do need to discuss this Tillie business."

Silas looked affronted. "Matilda is a fine name. It means 'of strength and bravery.'"

I huffed a disbelieving laugh. "You just made that up."

"I did. But it *could* mean that. I haven't had time to research it."

Shaking my head, I realized the name was fitting. "Matilda Bartholomew, then?"

He grinned. "Matilda Bartholomew."

Looking down at my daughter, I couldn't believe that she was finally in my arms. For so very long I'd prayed for a child, and then I'd been blessed with one in the most complicated way possible. But she was here now, and she would never want for love. She would have a father who had adored her since long before her birth. And a mother who would protect her from anything. And Matilda Bartholomew would have aunts and uncles and cousins and an unconventional family who knew what it meant to love.

I glanced at Silas who wore a smile I'd never seen before as he stared at our little Tillie. We had been through so much—Silas and I—and this wouldn't be the end of it. We'd become even more together. Parents, husband and wife, and who knew what else along the way.

Nothing about my life had been expected. I was sitting next to the very last person I ever thought could make me happy. Yet here I was, staring at the product of that unexpected love.

My future had gone from murky gray to bright, bold color.

There was no space in my life anymore for second-guessing. There was only room for love.

Epilogue

SILAS

June 1865

"I think you should name the baby Emily for a girl or Renley for a boy."

Genevieve put a hand on her stomach and made a face. "Emery, those names are terrible."

My middle sister made an affronted squawk. "Emily sounds a great deal like Emery, you know."

"I know," Gen replied, deadpan.

As the sunny afternoon devolved into insults slung between my sisters, I heard Tillie make a sound of unrest.

Our Little Duck liked to be on the move. It was rare for her to sit still on anyone's lap. She enjoyed being walked and bounced and paraded about.

I rose from the picnic blanket and held out my arms.

Mary smirked up at me before passing the baby over. "Going for a walk?"

I shook my head. "Just stretching our legs."

My family was gathered in Hampshire for the summer. We were enjoying the fine weather with a picnic at Laurel Park—the whole lot of us.

As Genevieve neared the end of her confinement, every meeting between family members became a competition to name her and Julian's first child.

As I bounced Tillie on my hip, I stayed within earshot.

"You know," Mary announced grandly, "I think we should make a list of baby names for Genevieve and Julian. They can rank them, and after the child is born, they can surprise us with a name from the list."

Murmurs of agreement came from those gathered.

I shot my wife a look. She was already grinning in my direction. "No more lists for you, Mary darling."

She laughed brightly, so open and happy that it was difficult to remember a time when she measured her smiles and guarded her heart.

"Actually"—Genevieve interrupted with a smile—"I think we've decided on a name—for a girl, that is. Julian and I would like to name her Mary and call her Marianne, to avoid confusion."

My wife's brows lowered in confusion. "Why would you want . . ."

Genevieve shared a knowing look with Julian before turning to

Mary. "It's actually quite common to name one's child after a sibling."

I saw Emery begin to comment, but Augie placed a hand over her mouth and laughed, burying his face in her hair.

Mary's confusion had not abated. She looked to Patty for assistance but my sister merely smiled and reached for Miles's hand at her side. Franny, in the way of all-knowing adolescents, said simply, "They want to name the baby after you, Aunt Mary. Won't that be sweet? A little Marianne."

"I—yes. That would be lovely," Mary finally managed, emotion making her voice tight. "Thank you, Gen. And Julian."

Tillie chose that moment to smack my cheek with a sticky fist. "I'm sorry, sweetheart. Was I ignoring you?"

The baby smiled, showing her two bottom teeth. A tuft of bright red hair gleamed from beneath her bonnet, and her mother's dark brown eyes stared back at me.

Chatter continued around our party. Franny eventually took off into the garden with little cousins, Beckett and Reeve, and Daisy the dog was fast on their heels. Miles and Patty looked on in amusement. My mother and father sat nearby, speaking quietly to Genevieve and Julian, both so delighted by the growth of our family. Emery and Augie shared whispered words on the picnic blanket.

I meandered around the grounds that Mary and I called home with our daughter in my arms. We'd made the move from Pineview to Laurel Park shortly after Tillie was born. With Mary's parents a painful absence in her life, my own mother and father were overjoyed to welcome Mary and Tillie to our family. We spent a happy, private Christmas together before marrying shortly into the new year. I was grateful that Mother and Father were so loving and accepting. They'd known Mary for years, after all. And the prospect of a new baby was a welcome addition. I knew that my wife still mourned the loss of her parents, as chaotic and unpredictable as they were. A part of me thought they'd come around—at least her mother—when we made our way back to London. Only time would tell.

We planned to return to town in the autumn despite the scandal of our hasty marriage and the birth of our child. We'd weather the gossip and the chin-wagging because it did not truly matter what anyone thought. We had our family and our happiness and the support of those who mattered.

Our lives existed in both the country and the city. We craved the comfort of Hampshire, where our friendship had grown and love had bloomed. But we also had responsibilities in London. We were both eager to visit the Watford School. And I knew that Mary desperately missed the children and her regular duties at the orphanage. We were looking forward to sharing my home in Belgrave Square.

I felt Mary's hand press warm between my shoulder blades as she peeked around my shoulder and made a silly face at the baby. Tillie squealed in delight.

"Marianne will be a fine name for a new little niece," I mused as I stepped behind the trunk of a large magnolia and into the dappled shade beneath.

My wife smiled widely. "Yes, it will."

For a moment we stood silent, grinning at each other and this life we'd created. And then I leaned in. Mary's lips parted on a sigh as I tilted my head and deepened the kiss. I was careful to keep space for the baby between us. Just before I thought it prudent to pull away, I heard footsteps on the nearby path and a muttered, "For God's sake," coming from behind us.

I pressed one more soft kiss to my wife's smiling mouth before looking back over my shoulder. Augie strode down the footpath, shaking his head.

"Apologies, Augustus!" I called as Mary dissolved into laughter. That had Tillie grinning happily at us both.

With amusement still clinging to her voice, my lovely wife said, "Look at us now. I never would have imagined I would end up right here."

I swung Tillie around to my other side, eliciting a sweet giggle. "Oh, but, darling, this is not the end. I imagine if we looked at any part of our future taken out of context, it would seem strange and unexpected. That is why a lifetime is built one step at a time leading grandly into the next."

Mary watched me with a soft expression.

"It might start with a friendly rivalry," I continued, "before flowing into a bewildering carriage encounter."

"And then perhaps . . . survival madness?" Mary offered.

"Exactly. The next step might come entirely unexpectedly." I pressed a kiss to Tillie's soft cheek. "Followed by friendship and love. But taken all together, it stacks up exactly how it's meant to be."

As the sounds of laughter and love filled my ears, I thought, finally, this was the future I'd wanted all along.

Happiness.

The here and now with the people I loved most in the world. Not some sense of accomplishment to compare to my siblings. And not arbitrary success to impress my father—who already loved me just as I was.

"You know," I whispered into the soft skin of my Mary's neck. "I'm thinking of adding a croquet lawn just beyond the hedgerows."

I felt her grin tug up the corners of her mouth. "That is an excellent idea. Perhaps that friendly rivalry portion of our history shall make a reappearance."

Under the summer sun, in the place that held my greatest memories, I pressed my smiling lips to my wife's.

My life with Mary and Tillie made me feel complete—whole. And I was right where I was supposed to be. It had all led up to this surreal happiness with the great loves of my life.

Second Epilogue

10 years later

The portrait hung at the top of the grand staircase at Laurel Park. It had been installed over a decade ago and should have long since been replaced with a newer, far more accurate image of the growing Bartholomew family.

However, there was nostalgia and meaning attached to the painting.

And it succeeded in infuriating Emery Ward to no end. So there was that.

The original image had been painted just before the wedding of Genevieve and Julian, as a gift to the Marchioness of Northcutt from her loving husband.

While the portraiture was not an entirely accurate portrayal of her children, their partners, and her grandchildren, with its elaborate costuming and grandiose style, the marchioness loved it regardless.

And after eleven years on the wall, it was a long-held family treasure that had been amended for much happiness over the years.

The portrait artist had been asked to return to record every subsequent child born to the Bartholomew siblings. The composition had changed with each addition but the border and the frame had been able to accommodate every new grandchild of the marchioness.

Of course, Francesca was no longer the adolescent girl positioned beside her father, Miles, within the constraints of the painting. Rather, she was a lovely young woman of three and twenty, happily married and embroiled in the daily activities at Owensby Stud Farm.

Reeve and Beckett Ward were now sixteen and thirteen years of age, respectively. And along with their mother, the source of the premature graying at Augie's temples.

Delicate brushstrokes painted the three children of Genevieve and Julian Moore: Marianne (currently age nine), Patrick (having just turned six), and little Emily (barely two years of age).

The painter had been summoned less than a year after completing the original portrait in order to add Mary and Tillie to the composition. And he'd been beckoned later as Silas and Mary had welcomed their son, Harry, in the spring of 1867.

For the past eleven years, the painting had been a source of great amusement for the Bartholomew siblings. Patty never missed an opportunity to point out Silas's aggressively smiling features. And there was that one time that Emery had been caught in the middle of the night at Laurel Park with a paint palette and a ladder at the top of the staircase.

Above all, the portrait exemplified the abundant, chaotic love these individuals shared. There was not another family quite like them. And the painting reflected that rather nicely.

Acknowledgments

To Blythe: thank you for bringing my characters to life with your amazing talent. And for being consistently wonderful to work with. I'm ruined for all future cover designers.

To Emily: thank you for seeing solutions when I'm determined to only see problems.

To my readers (I still can't believe I have readers): thank you for loving this wild and wonderful fictional family right along with me. The Bartholomews are the siblings of my heart. I'll be forever grateful that you've welcomed them into yours.

While this *is* the last title in the Bartholomew series, I won't say I'm closing the door on them forever. I have plans for Daly that involves a newsletter serial to catch you up on his life (so make sure you're subscribed). And there's a little something simmering in the back of my mind for my dear Franny as she makes her way in the world. I'll keep you posted.

Thank you, again, from the bottom of my heart for reading.

About the Author

Sign up for my newsletter: https://bit.ly/3SbXg2v

Laney Hatcher is a firm believer that there is a spreadsheet for every occasion and pie is always the answer. She is an author of stories both old and new where the HEAs are always guaranteed. Often too practical for her own good, Laney enjoys her life in the southern United States with her husband, children, and incredibly entitled cat.

Find Laney Hatcher online:
Facebook: https://bit.ly/3s6KnuY
Newsletter: https://bit.ly/3SbXg2v
Amazon: https://amzn.to/3IaOwU7
Instagram: https://bit.ly/3s4IRcS
Website: https://laneyhatcher.com/
Goodreads: https://bit.ly/3BD0Gme
TikTok: https://www.tiktok.com/@laneyhatcherauthor

Newsletter sign up

Also by Laney Hatcher

Bartholomew Series

First to Fall: A Friends to Lovers Historical Romance

Second Chance Dance: An Enemies to Lovers Historical Romance

Third Degree Yearn: A Second Chance Historical Romance

Last on the List: A Surprise Pregnancy Historical Romance

Kirby Falls Series

Take It or Leaf It

Smartypants Romance

London Ladies Embroidery Series

Neanderthal Seeks Duchess: A Smartypants Romance Out of this World Title

Well Acquainted: A Smartypants Romance Out of this World Title

Love Matched: A Smartypants Romance Out of this World Title

Find bonus content, reading order, and other news at my website: https://laneyhatcher.com/